Authored by: Rhae Aeden

Copy Edits by: Bridget L. Rose Books Inc.

Cover Design: Rhae Aeden

Second Cover: Rhae Aeden

Interior Designs: Rhae Aeden

Track designs: Cristina Scafidi

Dear Reader,

This book contains a wealth of triggering content; thus, I want to emphasize the importance of reading the trigger warnings before embarking on this emotional journey:

Blood

Child Abuse

Death

Gore

Gun Violence

Murder

Pedophilia

Physical Abuse

PTSD

Sexual abuse

Sexually Explicit Scenes

Transphobia

Racism

Violence

Rhae Aeden

For everyone who hid their true self.

Don't be scared, let the world see how bright you shine.

AUTHORS NOTE

It all began with a television series, Orange is the new black and a remarkable actress whose portrayal of a transgender character sparked a curiosity within me, in fact I was so in love with the Character of Sophia in the show, that I made it my life's mission to learn everything about Laverne Cox.

Imagine my face when I found out she herself is a trans woman!

Her journey opened my eyes to the struggles and triumphs of the trans community, and I went down a rabbit hole, my thirteen-year-old self-wanted to fix all the problems that this community had faced, but later I would discover life was a little bit more complicated than that. However, from that moment on, I made a commitment to educate myself and advocate for transgender visibility and rights.

Later in my life as I started reading more and more books (the romance ones we all love and cherished), I noticed a glaring absence: the lack of transgender protagonists. While LGBTQ+ characters were present as sidekicks or supporting roles, the main stage seemed devoid of transgender voices.

This realization fueled my determination to change the narrative. Enter Daniel, the protagonist of this book. His story unfolded in my mind with a clarity when I wrote my second book. And as soon as I was done with it, I was in a rush to write Daniel's story. Writing his journey has been heart breaking, but also an amazing experience that my thirteen-year-old self would be really proud of.

However, I want to acknowledge that, as a bisexual cisgender woman, I will never fully comprehend the complexities of being transgender. I will never know the depth of pain or the height of joy that accompanies such a journey. But what I can do, what I strive to do with every word, is to amplify transgender voices and experiences.

This book is my attempt to shine a light on a community that deserves to be seen and heard. It's a reminder that everyone, regardless of gender identity, is the protagonist of their own story.

You are not alone, and your narrative matters.

To all those who have supported me on this journey, thank you from the bottom of my heart. And to my transgender friends, readers, and allies: I hope this book serves as a beacon of hope and validation for you.

CHAPTER ONE

A sharp scream catches in my throat at the sight of a woman's body lying on the floor. Her skin is pale, almost grey, and her eyes are wide open, completely glassy and void of life. My sister closes the door of the wooden closet swiftly and then rushes to hold her hand over my mouth, suffocating me, forcing my lungs to burn from holding my breath to keep us safe.

"I am going to get us out of here, Daniela," Ximena whispers into my ear.

Cold drops of sweat start falling from my forehead, and a shiver runs down my spine. I know it's just a matter of time before the man who enjoys hitting women with the buckle on his belt comes back. He has killed seven women out of the three dozen that arrived with us two weeks ago.

Seven are already dead; some died on the way here, others were assaulted by the men keeping us. Twenty have been raped and pimped out in the worst streets of the continent.

My sister and I are part of the remaining nine. The youngest amongst us. They call us 'almas puras,' pure souls. But it's not our souls that make us pure to them.

It's our virginity.

"I am scared," I manage to whisper in the darkness.

"Shhh," Ximena tries to soothe me, but nothing helps.

The tremor cruising my body only gets worse when I hear one of the doors in the room shrieking, followed by the sound of a metal piece against the marble floor. Each one of his steps echoes in the room, forcing my heart to pump faster.

"Donde están, *meninas," he asks.*

Ximena takes a look through the thin slit between the closed closet doors and without taking her eyes off the room, she mutters, "At my signal, run."

I nod in the darkness.

The man's steps sound closer, the wooden floor screaming underneath his weight until, suddenly, it all stops. Time stays still for what feels like an eternity, and I can feel my older sister holding her breath next to me.

"RUN!" she screams, then opens the door, hitting the man right in his nose.

The impact is so hard that I can see him lifting his hand to his face right as he falls on his back.

"La puta madre!" he curses.

"Run, Daniela! Run!" my sister repeats.

I do as she says and run towards the door.

Then, I hear the gun.

Finally, I wake up.

My mind is no stranger to the nightmare that has been plaguing me since I made it out of that terrible place. It's always the same, the memory of the night my sister died and I escaped the organization that went by the name of The Red Horses plays in my mind every single night. I should be familiar with the feeling of pain it has on me after over a decade of dreaming the same dreams, but still, my body can't help but feel the same desperation I did when I was a child. My muscles still tremble in fear, and the tattoos covering my skin are bathed in a thin layer of cold sweat.

I take a deep breath, forcing my heart to stop beating so hard against my chest. It takes a while, but eventually, I am able to forget about the pain The Red Horses has caused me and the millions of women and kids they have kidnapped only to sell to the highest bidder. It takes a while, but the trembling finally stops, and my heartbeat slows.

Me and my sister were some of the unlucky victims of the organization. Little did the people who took us know that I would be the person to bring them to their knees almost a decade later.

I was in a dark and lonely place when I escaped and barely survived.

The only thing that kept me going was my revenge.

Daniela Conde died that night with her sister Ximena. Daniel Conte was the person who made it out of that grave. I took my pain and made it into a motivation to keep going no matter what. That motivation was what pushed me to find Sasha Valine while I was still in the early stages of my transition and drafting my plan for revenge.

I wanted to kill them all.

Sasha was just as thirsty for revenge as I was, and together, we were able to kill every single one of the men who had wronged us and bring down an entire organization of terror.

That was a year ago.

Things have changed now.

The world is a slightly safer place this year.

Nonetheless, a part of me still aches to right the wrongs of the past. Our decade-long plan came to an end by the time the 2024 Formula One season came to a close, when Sasha killed the last head of The Red Horses organization. However, for a year, I have felt restless and haven't been able to shake the feeling that something was escaping our hands.

My instincts were to look deeper into Cavaglio Nero. After all, that Formula One team had been used for money laundry purposes by that disgusting organization. They had put in place a complicated scheme involving ghost sponsors and more team staff taking part in it than we originally knew about. But Sasha had killed the big guys by the end of 2024, and I was ready to do the rest.

Since then, I have been looking at the team closely, making sure everyone from The Red Horses is really gone. I don't want them hurting any more people, or putting any more lives at risk. It's for that reason that I find myself getting ready for my meeting at the Cavaglio Nero Racing Team headquarters in London.

Most people working in Formula One last year know that something happened with the racing team last season, but nobody was brave enough to ask any questions. After all, they are the most prestigious team in the history of F1 and vital for the sport.

I have spent the past twelve months figuring out my next steps. Turns out I am good at some things, but I excel at making people pay for their sins.

Two hours after my nightmare woke me, I find myself in the Cavaglio Nero meeting room. Men with white hair sit around the oval table, all of them vibrating with their hate towards me. I am everything they stand against. I have no royal blood in the world of motorsports, I don't come from a rich European family, I have no background in finance or law, and most importantly, I am not a biological man.

My transition has not been a secret to the world, but I never made a public statement about it either. The people who need to know about it already do. The rest of the world found out last year after social media decided Sasha and I were the new "it" people of the paddock. Someone found out and streamed it to the world.

I didn't really care about it, after all, I am proud of who I am and who I am is a man. I just never felt the urge to tell anyone what sex I was born with. I identify as a man and present myself as such. I was never one for big public statements and displays of pride. I am proud of the person I have become, and that is what matters to me, not what a couple of people on the internet have to say. I applaud everyone who wears their colors and their identity on their sleeve, it just isn't me.

Not much has changed now that people know about my transition. Most of the time nobody really cares, other times, like now, surrounded by the white wigs of the board, I am not so lucky. Their judgmental looks and intimidation tactics are lost on me. They think they can scare me away from going through with my plans. Little do they know that I have been face to face with the devil, and I don't scare easily anymore. What happened last year was only the beginning of the end. The Red Horses have established such a long network through the years that it's impossible to know for certain how many of them we really brought to justice and how many are left unpunished.

Cavaglio Nero is the perfect example of that. The team is corrupt, and I am willing to finish what Sasha started. The blood of the heads of the organization is still warm in our hands. But my mission isn't over. I have spent a lifetime in the dark, planning the demise of my enemies, and now I am willing to step into the light and play a new game of chess.

"Mr. Conte." My lawyer's voice drags me out of my thoughts.

I stare at him in silence.

"You need to sign this paper here," he instructs.

I snatch the documents out of his hands, noticing the blank spot where my signature needs to go. I don't hesitate. In an instant, the ink of my pen is bleeding over the white sheet of paper forming my initials. I have seen and read this contract over and over for the past month. I know it by heart at this point and don't need to read it again.

"Don't you want to read what you are signing, Mr. Conte?" my lawyer asks.

I look up at him, ready to respond with a deadly comment. Instead, I control my temper and give him a coy smile.

"I trust you."

I don't. I don't trust anyone.

The lawyer takes the contract back, making sure that my signature is in place and then gives the people sitting in the room a loaded look. I know they think I have gone crazy, and perhaps, there is some truth to that. But the reality somewhat differs. They are clueless, know nothing about me, nothing about my past, future, or what I plan to do with this company.

"Is that all?" I ask, impatient.

The lawyer looks at one of the older men sitting in front of him. They exchange a look and then the older man nods in agreement.

"Daniel Conte, you are the new owner of the Cavaglio Nero Racing Team."

Game On.

CHAPTER TWO

I was supposed to be travelling the globe, chasing the adrenaline high and finishing my nights in a stranger's bed whose name I would forget as soon as the sun came up. My twenties should be celebrated.

Reality is far away from that.

Instead, I am staring at a dry piece of half-burned toast sitting on top of the office kitchen counter, thinking it's the most appealing thing I have seen all day long.

Strike that.

All week long.

To be fair I haven't seen anything else besides mugs of coffee and the odd protein bar from the vending machine downstairs. *Whatever helps to keep you going through the day, right?*

The clock on the fridge marks two in the morning when I open the door to grab some butter for my burned toast. Two years ago, I wouldn't have set foot in an office past six, and now, here I am, happy I'll get to go home before three in the morning.

This was never the plan; I was never supposed to be an accountant, tracking the money movements of a company. In 2023, my business peaked after a while of working as an accounting consultant in Monaco. The company was doing well, but I wasn't getting diamonds out of it.

During the 2024 Formula One season, shady things were happening with the Cavaglio Nero team. People were killed and lost documents found their way into the light. Selene, my best friend who was working in the marketing department, needed a trustworthy person to check the accounts after the head accountant of the team seemed to be involved in said *shady* things and ended up impaled against a wall. That is how I got my job as a senior accountant for the oldest team in F1 history.

I have not regretted my decision since joining the company, but recently, after so many late nights stuck here, trying to figure out what the hell is going on behind the curtains, I can't help but question my choices. At least I know I will feel incredible satisfaction once I determine where those big money movements come from.

Four billion dollars.

The entire company is worth that much, and I have a hunch Cavaglio Nero is being sold, but there have not been any rumors about it. Nobody knows anything, and something as big as that is difficult to hide for long.

A yawn escapes my lips while I spread the butter on top of the toast with the pathetic excuse of a knife that won't even cut the bread. I take a bite and stand in the darkness of the kitchen, with my gaze stuck on the streets of London. I was skeptical when I first moved, but a year later, and with my best friend living across the hall, I feel almost at home.

I am about to take another bite when I hear footsteps coming from the corridor. "Marcos?" I call out the name of the night guard.

I have watched enough murder mystery shows that my mind automatically conjures up the worst possible situations and images of the dangers the shadows hold. Panic spreads through me. I take a deep breath, trying to calm myself. I scan the space in front of me and snatch the butterknife without thinking, wrapping my fingers tightly around it. I duck behind the kitchen counter and wait, feeling like prey instead of the hunter. And, to be honest, after glancing at the weapon in my hand, it's more than obvious I am not going to leave this place alive.

So much for all those hours of training.

The footsteps grow louder. Time seems to move slower the closer the footsteps get. I move silently to the kitchen door, almost dragging myself across the floor, clutching the knife in my hands, ready to defend myself.

Suddenly, the footsteps cease.

I jump up, ready to strike, using the advantage of surprise right when shadow makes it through the kitchen door. It doesn't matter that my hands are shaking with fear. I still lift the knife, but the other person is faster, stronger, and they see me before I can even land the blow.

The man holds my wrist tightly, forcing me to drop the knife. His hands feel oddly soft over my skin, but the hold is so strong that I wouldn't be surprised if bruises appeared there tomorrow. His face is still in the shadows, but his smell reminds me of someone.

Someone that I have not seen in almost a year.

"Didn't your mother teach you that knives are dangerous?" His face is still in the darkness, but I know he is smiling, and it doesn't take me too long to figure out who that man is.

Daniel Conte's face emerges from the shadows, allowing me a glimpse at who I have grown to hate over the past year. His brown hair is longer than usual, flowing in silky waves behind his ears, while some wild strands frame over his face. His rich brown eyes are piercing into mine, an intensity in them. I don't want to break eye contact, but I'm weak and look at the tattoos coming out from under his shirt.

Daniel loosens the hold on my wrists a little, and then his brown eyes look down at the floor, right where the butterknife is lying.

"Interesting choice of weapon," he mocks.

"Didn't your mother tell you that it is impolite to scare young ladies in the night?" I snap at the same time I try to free my hand from his hold.

"She did, but you are no lady."

My jaw drops, but I don't let him see it.

Instead, I let fury ignite me. I know I have the power to break free. I shift my weight and pivot on my toes, then twist my arm outward in a fluid motion using the force of my entire body against Daniel's grip. His eyes widen when his back hits the wall and my forearm presses against his neck. He makes a small attempt at escaping me, but the weight of my body holds him in place.

With a heavy breath, I look up at him, noticing the smirk on his face, and the look of amusement he gives me. I hate him. I hate that he feels some sort of twisted excitement from this, while I thought I was about to lose my life.

"I don't think you would be able to recognize one," I snap.

With lightning speed, Daniel shifts his weight and drives me backward. Surprise crushes me when it's my back hitting the wall. His arm lands right over my head, caging me with his entire body. Daniel leans in, standing mere millimeters away from me, his forehead almost touching mine. We are so close that I can feel his breath on my skin, and flashes from a night long lost in my memories come back to me for the first in months.

"Is that the way to treat your new boss?" he whispers.

"Excuse me?" I mutter, feeling my heart racing.

"I just signed the contract that makes me the new owner of Cavaglio Nero Racing. That makes me your boss."

"You're lying," I say with disbelief. But the wheels in my head are already spinning, and things start clicking into place. Those big money movements finally make sense. Those four billion dollars weren't money laundering.

It was Daniel Conte.

Fucking Daniel Conte just bought Cavaglio Nero.

"Aren't you going to congratulate me for becoming the youngest F1 team owner?"

"Why?" I bark.

"Why not?"

He is so close that I can perfectly see his amused expression, and how his lips are slightly tilted upwards in a confident smirk, one that tells me he is hiding something from me.

"Let go of me," I command.

Daniel notices the shift in my voice and the desperation in it. He doesn't hesitate and takes a step back, giving me some space to breathe. A strand of his long brown hair falls down his forehead, and I can't help but fixate on it. I hate it. I hate everything about him.

"Should I be worried that my accountant was incapable of noticing the sale going through?"

"Are you calling me incompetent?"

"Should I?"

"Fuck off, Daniel!" I yell, feeling defensive. "You know that I am one of the best accountants at Cavaglio. Fuck it, I am one of the best accountants in F1. I was the one to track Mancini's money trails, and those of his partners too. So, don't you dare undermine my work."

"I would never dare, Miriam." He purrs my name.

"Don't say my name like that."

"I'll see you around."

I take a step back, feeling annoyed, while Daniel walks away with his signature swagger. I can't control myself, and my eyes trail his body, enjoying the firm muscles of his broad shoulders making an appearance through his blue shirt, and then my eyes wander further south. Such an irritating person can't possibly have that great of an ass.

I groan, frustrated at my own thoughts.

What is wrong with me?

CHAPTER THREE

Me: Cavaglio Nero has a new Owner

Blonde Dread: Philip bought the team?

Ginger Bestie: Ha. Ha.

Me: Don't act like you don't know, blondie.

Blonde Dread: I plead the fifth.

Me: We are not in America.

Ginger Bestie: Wait. Hold On! I just saw the news!

Ginger Bestie: Please tell me Daniel didn't do it?!

Blonde Dread: Enjoy the ride girls.

Ginger Bestie: You are a masochist.

Blonde Dread: Maybe ;)

...

Sundays are a blessing; it's the only day of the week when I indulge and stay in bed for as long as my body needs. Today would have been no different had Daniel Conte not given me the news of the century last Friday.

I walk through the streets of London until I make it to the cute coffee place where I was summoned to last night. I arrive there half an hour early, so I sit down, order a flat white, and start toying with my now long, thick, straightened hair, mourning the loss of my braids in silence.

I haven't styled my hair like that since I started working at the office, and it feels like a part of me has died with it. I used to express my mood through my hair, and now I am just destroying it with a hair straightener. I guess in a way I am still expressing myself.

I am burning out in this line of work.

I can't even remember the last time I braided my hair.

I huff at the lie. I know it perfectly well: plain thick black braids, adorned with golden hoops in the front pieces. That was the day I met Daniel in Monaco. How could I ever forget the day I met the most insufferable, aggravating man in the history of humankind?

"You are going to get wrinkles in your face if you continue to frown like that." A female voice distracts me.

"Elizabeth," I greet the woman.

Elizabeth is one of the youngest agents working at Interpol. She is a remarkable woman, and one whom I had worked with last year, while she was trailing a serial killer around the globe. She needed information about Mancini, his deals, and his partners, and what better way to find it than to track the money movements. So, when I started digging into the accounts, Elizabeth approached me, and I was willing to help, not as an undercover agent, but as a girl who wanted to make the world a better place.

Elizabeth and I have met a couple of times over the year and indulged in a less professional relationship. She stayed over at my place a couple of times, but it was never more than sex. Two friends enjoying each other's company.

But this is the first time in a year we're meeting for something Interpol-related. I started noticing the big money movements a couple of weeks ago, and all the alarm bells inside my head went off. I was afraid that the bad guys might come back, so I warned Elizabeth about it over a week ago, thinking that by now I would have found out what the hell was going on.

"Why did you want to see me?" she asks.

"I might simply want to enjoy your company," I joke.

Elizabeth raises a brow. "Then we would have met at your place or mine, but you no longer wanted to do that."

A nostalgic smile appears on my face. I can count on one hand how many times we have shared a bed, but there were no feelings involved. That's what made having sex with her great. There was no compromise or expectations between us. But you can only have sex so many times before you start to feel empty. My sexual life is as boring as the one of a nun at this point, but my mind is as filthy as the smut books on my shelve.

"I found something," I start, forcing my dirty thoughts out of my mind. "The money movements I was talking about a couple of weeks ago. They are not shady."

"Then what are they?" Elizabeth asks.

"Daniel Conte is the new owner of Cavaglio Nero."

Her dark eyes go wide for a second, right before she controls her facial expression again. "What is he up to?"

"It's Daniel Conte. Your guess is as good as mine."

Somewhere, between heaven and hell, souls exist that might not entirely be made of light, but neither are they of shadow.

Daniel is one of those.

As much as it pains me to admit it, his tainted soul does more good than bad. I might hate him for my own personal reasons, but I don't hate him enough to turn a blind eye to the good he has done for thousands of women around the globe.

"I want you to trail him," Elizabeth orders.

"Me?"

"Yes, you. I want to know all his plans, where he goes, when he eats, who he sees, and most importantly, what his goal is. I want to know everything."

"But I'm not an agent. How am I supposed to do any of that?" I ask.

"Get creative," Elizabeth says.

Then, I remember the butterknife and how useless my training was when I had to face Daniel Conte.

He is going to eat me alive.

CHAPTER FOUR

I swallow my vitamins and other pills with my morning coffee while scrolling through the emails. The acquisition of F1's oldest team has gone smoother than I thought it would, but what was to be expected after what happened last year?

Cavaglio Nero broke into a million pieces when we got rid of Mancini and his friends. Sasha and I made sure to put a story out there so we could give a name to the victims that didn't make it out the same way we did. Nobody in the Formula One industry dares to say his name, but everyone knows who the old team principal was and his part in one of the biggest organizations of human trafficking in the world.

I am pretty sure that everything in this team went rotten from the moment Mancini and his friends became part of the team. The legacy of it is in danger after everything they did. It's a miracle that we're still in business. A team like mine should be winning championships every year, but besides the one Philip Burton won in the 2023 season, there is not much they have accomplished on their own in the past decade. In fact, the only thing the team accomplished was to leave a trail of misery.

Someone knocks on the door of my new office, and I look up to see a petite figure who is responsible for the demise of empires. A smile makes it to my lips at the sight of the blonde woman.

"This is a step up from the commentator booth," Sasha jokes, looking impressed at the dimensions of my new office. I have to admit it will take me a while to adjust to the new life of luxury that my new job description brings.

I have always flown under the radar. Even when I was working as a commentator with Sasha and interviewing drivers for shows that would get broadcast to millions, I still managed to keep a low profile. I have never been interested in being an influencer broadcasting their lives to the public. But I guess things might change a little bit now that I am the owner of Cavaglio Nero.

"I wasn't expecting to see you here so soon."

"I wanted to be the first journalist to meet the new owner," my friend mocks. Sasha has known for a while of my intentions to buy the team. There is hardly a thought of mine, that Sasha doesn't know about. That is the nature of our relationship. We are a tandem, it's the way we work.

"Well then, what will your headline be?" I muse.

"No need to embellish things. The story speaks for itself," she starts. "From commentator to savior. How Daniel Conte went from journalist to owning a Formula One team." Her voice is magnetic, after all, it's her job to make uninteresting things seem relevant. "It won't be a challenge to make the readers like you, but it will be hard to answer how a commentator was able to afford this team."

"You are a smart girl, you will figure it out," I tease. "But you can always say that I made my fortune investing in something like Bitcoin. Who cares really?" It's not too far from the truth. I've made money from that and some other investments over the years. Being able to hack into any system has its benefits. There are people who are willing to pay good money for information.

"So, what is the real purpose of your visit?" I ask.

Sasha takes a seat in the chair in front of me, resting her arms on the table and looking at me with those pitch-black eyes of hers.

"I saw a familiar face on my way to your office..."

I don't need her to say the name out loud. I already know who she is referring to. Hers is a familiar face indeed. One that screams trouble, trouble that I can't take care of right now.

"Get to the point."

"How did she take the news?" Sasha asks, curious.

"She tried to stab me." A soft chuckle escapes me, but my friend isn't as amused, and I can see her body tensing underneath the oversized blazer.

"Excuse me?"

"With a butterknife," I clarify.

Sasha instantly relaxes.

She's one the few people who would kill for her friends, so I rather not give her a reason to take Miriam's life, even if that would solve some of my problems. I regret the thought as soon as I'm done conjuring it in my head. I shake the thoughts away, realizing the lie I just told myself.

Sure, in a way she might annoy me and make me want to crawl out of my skin. In another, I might want to know her whereabouts all the time and make sure she is always taken care of and doing all right. Miriam is like a drug that I have withdrawn from. If I come close to her again then I might fall into the temptation of her plump lips again, and that is something I cannot allow myself to do.

"Interesting choice of weapon," Sasha teases, now relaxed.

"Said the woman who uses daggers and plastic bags," I joke… kind of.

Murdering someone isn't something to joke about, but I don't necessarily feel bad about my comment, nor about the part I took in all those murders. After all, there are worse things in life, like assaulting minors and then selling them to whoever is willing to pay the most for their innocence.

"Don't joke about that," she reprimands. "What are you going to do about her?"

"I'm figuring it out."

"You have been doing that for over a year."

I give her a murderous look, but she doesn't back down.

"Maybe I should change the angle of my next article and talk about how the team's owner fell head over heels for his accountant."

"Sasha," I warn. "Don't start with that."

"You went there when I asked you not to a year ago," she reminds me. "And look at me and João now."

"That was different." I huff.

"No, it wasn't," she snarls at me. "Whatever happened in Monaco, you two need to sort it out and start having sex. That will solve most of your problems."

I know it's meant as a joke, but it hits harder than it should.

"We are never talking about that day."

That was the day I decided I *had to* hate Miriam Lefebvre.

CHAPTER FIVE

Sasha and I make a run for it right after the cameras stop recording. We have been in the studio for hours working on the pre-show for the Monaco GP. The combined smell of the Monegasque breeze and the gasoline of the Formula One cars fills my nostrils and the sound of the V6 engines roars in my ears.

When I was a child and still lived in Argentina, my dad and I used to watch the races together. He would wake me up in the middle of the night and we would watch the Grands Prix sitting on the couch, munching on whatever Mom had left us the night before. But our relationship took a turn the moment he noticed I was changing. When I started stealing my brothers' clothes, instead of wearing my usual dresses, and started expressing my true gender identity. He thought it was a phase, but once he realized I wasn't his little princess anymore, he no longer woke me up at night. Instead, he picked up one of my brothers and continued the tradition with him.

I could have picked up any other job to make The Red Horses pay for what they did to me, my sister, and so many other victims. But Formula One was a happy place for me. In a way, it always made me feel connected to my father, even after I left home and lost touch with them. For all they knew, I was dead. So, when the opportunity to land a job in Formula One appeared, I didn't need to think twice about it.

The memories start fading, and I focus my attention on Sasha as she walks next to me. As soon as we are out of earshot, I look at her, and give her a questioning look, and she does a wonderful job of ignoring it.

"I'm still waiting for the Silverstone gossip," I pry.

"There is nothing to tell," she says.

"Stop lying to me." I know about her escapade with the Brazilian driver, and I bet it was everything but uneventful. Those two are meant to be together.

"Ugh. I don't know, okay? I feel safe with him, and I'm trying to simply enjoy the moment without letting it get too personal."

Jealousy curses through me. I am the only person who has achieved that in the past decade. And now? What am I now that she has found a person who gives her that, and then some more? Sasha and I will always have a special bond – a trauma bond at that. She is like a little sister to me, the person that I know will always stand by me no matter what happens. We are parts of different puzzles that fit together. And even if I love her with all my heart and want to protect her with my own life, I know what she's feeling for João *is love, and she deserves to be happy.*

"You feel safe with him?" I ask.

"Dani," she mutters, noticing my sudden change of mood. "You are the brother I never had. Our friendship is unbreakable and nothing will ever come between us. João *makes me want to face the darkness inside of me, the one I have been avoiding for so long. He makes me want to be a slightly better person. But that doesn't mean I don't love you, or that I will ever forget you. You are Daniel. My Dani."*

"I know," I admit. "It fills my heart with so much joy to see you like this. There is a spark in you, something I haven't seen before, real happiness. I am just sad I couldn't give that to you. But I know now it's only because life had other plans. You needed to look darkness in the eye to be able to appreciate the light. We are flawed humans, more than the average, but I am glad you have met someone who makes you feel this way. Safe."

"You have given me everything." Her voice breaks and tears roll down her cheek. "I am here because of you, never doubt that."

"Sasha?" a voice calls out.

"Miriam," Sasha calls out, removing her tears before anyone can spot them. After all, she is the blonde dread for a reason.

"If it isn't the famous Sasha Valine. I missed you!"

"You saw me in Silverstone, Miriam. Love the new hair," I hear my friend commenting, but I am too star-struck to listen.

The girls engage in a conversation, and I don't make an effort to join them. Instead, I take the chance to look at the woman standing in front of me, effortlessly commanding my attention with her striking presence. Her black hair falls over her shoulders, perfectly braided and adorned with thick golden hoops. Her dark skin shines under the sunlight, and then I notice her hazel eyes. She catches me looking at her, wanting to know everything about her. Miriam blushes when she notices the way I'm studying her and taking in every single thing about her.

My mind is running, scanning her, enjoying the pitch of her voice, and I can even feel the hairs in my arms raising at the simple sight of her. I don't know what it is, but I am in a trance, one that I need to escape, because for the second time today, I feel my heart beating a little faster than it usually does.

Three decades on this earth and I have never seen someone shine the way Miriam does, her smile captivates every single part of me, and for the first time, a woman makes me feel something more than only lust and desire.

Never have I felt anything like what I feel right now, and I am fully aware of how ridiculous I sound, but an urge courses through my veins, the most primal side of me wanting to steal her away and keep her for myself.

But what kind of hypocrite would I be if I did that? Nonetheless, I want to know everything about the woman in front of me. Who are her parents? Where is she from? Who was her kindergarten boyfriend? What does she eat? Does she take cold or hot showers? Endless questions start filling my mind.

I bite my lip with a fierce intensity when I notice Miriam's eyes are scanning me, and the glint in her hazel ones tells me she feels something similar in a tamer dose.

"Daniel," I introduce myself, extending my hand towards her, and when they touch, I can't help but relish the soft sensation of her warm skin on mine. "Pleasure."

"The pleasure is mine," she whispers in an almost shy tone. I have always been great at reading people, and something tells me this is not her standard behavior. She doesn't strike me as a shy person. On the contrary, she seems like an outspoken woman, and I want to find out more about her.

Sasha clears her throat, forcing me back into reality. My little swan will have to wait a little bit longer until I figure her out.

"Did you come here with Selene?" my friend asks.

"Huh? Oh. Yeah, I am doing a project for Cavaglio," Miriam answers, appearing slightly rattled. "Just some accounting and consulting. I have an NDA, so not much I can tell," she explains.

I give my friend a loaded look, the wheels in my head already spinning uncontrollably. I know what she is working on, all the financial instabilities that Cavaglio Nero has left behind for someone to find.

"Well, we should sit down with Selene for coffee and catch up properly next time," Sasha says. "Anyway, we have to get going, but it was great seeing you!"

"I will see you around," Miriam says to Sasha, but her eyes are on mine.

"Hopefully," I answer with a devilish grin.

Sasha and I start walking away, but it's only after we've lost sight of Miriam that Sasha teases me.

"Do you want her number?"

"Not a single word," I warn, but I know it's too late already.

Sasha might cut me some slack now, but her eyes have already darkened, and I know that sooner or later, she will come back with a million questions. The problem is, I am not sure I have the right answers. I don't think I even know what that was. I enjoy women and have shared my bed with some amazing ones in the past, but never for more than a couple of encounters. My life is complicated enough as it is, and maybe that's why I have never been interested in more.

But whatever this spark is, it isn't normal. It's not what I feel when I see a desirable woman.

It's more, and I am terrified of that.

CHAPTER SIX

"Have you found something yet?" Elizabeth asks me over the phone not even three days after our meeting in that coffee shop.

"Good morning to you too, sunshine," I say cheerfully while stirring the coffee that has probably gone cold after sitting on my desk for way too long.

"Have you or have you not?" she repeats.

"I have not." The line goes silent. I can't even hear Elizabeth breathing. "Are you there?" I ask, looking at my phone.

"I'm thinking."

"Okaaay." I drag out the syllable.

"What is Conte doing? Who is he seeing?"

"Valine was here this morning," I whisper her name, hoping that none of my coworkers will hear the mention of it.

Everyone in the F1 paddock knows that the two of them are inseparable, they take "partners in crime" to a whole other level. However, I am pretty sure that Sasha's days of crime have come to an end.

"And you didn't think to mention that before?"

"It's not uncommon to see them together," I remind her.

"Of course it isn't, they are partners–"

"And lifelong friends," I finish.

"Your point?"

"It's not suspicious for her to visit a friend, who just bought the Formula One team. Plus, she's a reporter, she probably wanted a headline."

"Is this case too big for you, Miriam?"

I blink. Twice. Confused. "What? I don't work for you!"

"You don't, but you are helping me nonetheless."

"You owe me big for this, Elizabeth," I say.

"Big O's still count?"

"You can do better than that," I answer and hang up.

I don't like where this is going. Not in the least.

I didn't mind helping Elizabeth last year when I knew she was taking down the bad guys. But this time is different. Daniel is in fact the devil's spawn in my story, and I hate his guts, but I also know that he uses his abilities for good rather than bad.

After all, the devil was also an angel once.

I close my eyes and lean into my seat, taking deep breaths and trying to figure out what to do. I might not work for Elizabeth or Interpol, but curiosity has always been my biggest enemy.

When I open them again, I am possessed. My feet are moving of their own accord. Heels clicking on the marble floor. Hips swinging in full force.

I walk through the halls, almost running until I stand in front of the door which already has a new name engraved on it. I knock twice and then let myself in instead of waiting for permission.

When I make it inside, Daniel doesn't even seem surprised, he doesn't look up, doesn't flinch. Nothing. He doesn't even stop typing on his computer. It's as if he knew I was coming.

"Nice office," I comment, though my eyes are set on Daniel and the tattoos peeking out from under the blue dress shirt. When nothing leaves his lips, I move forward and take a seat in the chair in front of him. "Do your employers know that you are monitoring them with cameras?" I say with a grin on my face.

It only intensifies when he closes his laptop and looks at me. For a second, I am lost in his honey-brown eyes, then I force myself to recall how much I dislike the man, and how he has the power to hurt me.

"What do you want?" Daniel asks. But I know what he means to say is, *"Quit this bullshit."*

"I could ask you the same question."

Daniel lifts one brow, some sort of twisted amusement dancing in his eyes.

"What do you want with Cavaglio?" I ask.

He leans into his seat, crossing his arms over his chest, showing off his muscles in a ridiculously sexy way.

"That's why you came all the way here? To ask that?"

"It wasn't to enjoy the view."

"Then you have bad taste," he jokes, looking behind him, at the floor-to-ceiling windows that have a view of the most beautiful streets of London.

"I wasn't talking about that view."

"Even more of a reason to say you have bad taste."

"Narcissist," I huff. "Why did you buy the company? This time, I want the truth."

"Why would I tell you the truth?"

"Because the lack of it would mean that you have something to hide."

"And what happens if I do?"

"My patience is running thin, Conte."

"I can tell you." He pauses dramatically. "Or I can show you."

My smile grows. "Show me."

He grins at me, revealing his perfect smile, then proceeds to take a sticky note and write on it before passing it to me. I take it carefully, not wanting to touch him. Daniel is like kryptonite. The problem is, I am not sure how I react to it.

Can I take it?

Or will it be my downfall?

"What is this?" I mutter, reading the yellow piece of paper.

"An address. I will see you there on Friday at eight."

I raise a brow at him.

"You told me to show you."

I take a second, look at him, then back at the sticky note in my hand, then back at him again. My heart is racing. For a second, it feels like too good of an opportunity, a risky one at that. But one I am not willing to let go of.

"Fine. Dress code?"

"Business elegant."

"I'll see you there," I say.

The conversation comes to an end, and I don't linger in his office. I just stand up and make my way to the door, but just as I am about to leave, Daniel's voice stops me.

"How did you know about the cameras?"

I bite my bottom lip, but even that doesn't keep my smile hidden. Catching Daniel Conte off-guard is a bigger pleasure than I thought it would be.

"You didn't flinch when I came in, so you knew I was coming," I say, pausing for a moment before adding, "The question is, do you supervise all your employees or are you only fixated on me?"

And with that, I leave his office with the winning hand.

Miriam: 1

Daniel: 0

CHAPTER SEVEN

Blonde Dread: Someone paid a visit to the new owner.

Me: Huh… I heard the same thing about someone else…

Blonde Dread: …

Ginger Bestie: Please tell me they finally shagged!

Blonde Dread: Don't think so.

Blonde Dread: He is still his usual pissy self.

Me: He is the devil's spawn, it's part of his character

Ginger Bestie: And the appeal ;)

Me: Aren't you about to become a married woman?

Ginger Bestie: I have eyes.

Blonde Dread: Don't let Philip read this, he'll kill Dani.

Ginger Bestie: But my heart is for one man only.

Blonde Dread: You disgust me.

Me: Moving on… need help. ASAP.

Ginger Bestie: Coming.

…

I massage my temples, trying to keep the headache that I know is coming after a whole day of being on my laptop at bay. I don't have time to get sick. I need to figure out what I want to wear tonight. It's exactly what I have been trying to do for the past half hour, unsuccessfully so too.

My place is a mess, there are clothes scattered on the floor everywhere. Unpaired shoes are covering the ground, and my bathroom is an explosion of hair styling tools and shadow palettes. I huff loudly, feeling stressed, but I stay calm until Selene finally arrives.

Five minutes later, I hear a knock on my door, which I know is mere curtsey. My best friend got my spare key the moment I moved into the same building as her.

"Miriam?" she screams from the entrance.

"In my room!" I shout back.

Seconds later, my favorite ginger enters my bedroom. Selene and I have been friends since we met in college. It was friendship at first sight. We could not be separated after that, which led to both of us moving together to Monaco after our graduation. Life has changed a lot ever since. Selene achieved her life goal by the end of the 2023 F1 season by becoming the head of the marketing team at Cavaglio Nero, and it didn't hurt that in the process, she ended up dating Philip Burton, a three-time World Champion.

"What's the emergency?" she asks, out of breath.

It's then I notice her copper hair is completely ruffled, and some of her mascara is smeared under her eyes.

"What happened to you?"

"Two words. Philip. Burton."

I gag in disgust, regretting my question.

"Don't be dramatic, remember we used to live together."

I do remember the good times in our small Monegasque apartment, when we used to share every single sordid detail of our lives over coffee each morning. I am used to us talking about those kinds of things, but recently, Philip has become an esteemed member of our gang, and in a way, an older grumpy brother to all of us. So, I don't enjoy listening to the details of *his* sex life.

"If it makes you feel better, we were just making out." Selene pauses, and I know by the mischievous glint in her eyes what is about to follow. "And heavy petting."

"Disgusting."

"Why am I here instead of shagging my future husband?"

"Always so subtle," I answer, sitting down on the floor.

"It's Philip's influence." She smirks.

"I don't know what to wear," I say, trying to change the topic, not wanting to picture her husband-to-be doing the nasty.

"Are you going on a date?"

"I am not sure," I mutter. *Is it considered a date if two adults with a shared history are going out together at night?* "It's kind of a work thing," I answer instead.

"With whom?"

Nothing ever escapes her.

"Daniel."

"As in Daniel Conte, the new team owner?"

I nod.

"Are you guys going to finally give it a try?"

"It's not like that," I say to stop her, but the wheels in Selene's mind are already spinning out of control. "Focus, we can talk about that later. I need an outfit."

"Where are you going?"

"Some sort of boat party," I explain.

The address didn't show a lot on Google Maps, just a deck with some fancy boats, so I am working with assumptions, hoping that I won't be too far off.

"What about this satin dress?" she suggests.

"I will freeze this time of year."

"Right." The redhead scans my closet with her green eyes until something attracts her attention. "This one!" she practically screams, fishing a black cotton dress with an asymmetric cut out of my wardrobe.

I love it.

"Go put it on," she urges.

Never being one for modesty, I let my bathrobe fall off my shoulders and throw the gorgeous black dress over my body. Selene's shiny face is the only indication I get of how it looks before I see myself in the mirror.

This is the dress.

"Red lipstick," she says.

I obey and step into the bathroom, ready to search my make-up bag for the perfect shade of dark red. Then, Selene comes in holding probably the tallest pair of black stilettos that I own. I peek into the mirror once the look is finished and realize I look sexy but still elegant. I just wish my black hair was braided instead of straight.

"I will be disappointed if you don't bring Daniel home after dressing like that," Selene jokes.

I will be extremely disappointed if he doesn't at least grant me a look of admiration, I think to myself and notice my core clenching at my own thoughts.

"When are we going to get your wedding dress?" I ask, trying to change the topic, because I am afraid of what other thoughts I might conjure.

"I know what you are doing, but I am letting it slip. I was thinking before Christmas. Philip is announcing his retirement soon, and after that it will be hell with the press."

"Just let me know when. I will be there."

Through the mirror's reflection, I see tears pooling in Selene's green eyes.

"I love you." She sobs. "I can't believe I am getting married and get to share this with you."

"Oh, honey." I turn around and give my friend a hug. "Don't cry, dummy! Why would you cry?"

"Because I am so happy. My life is perfect," she manages to say between sobs.

"Of course it is. You worked your ass off the past years, and you deserve every good thing in life. I love you."

"Me too. I just can't believe this is our life now. We got our dream jobs, travel the world, I'm about to get married, and you are going out with the prince of hell."

"I could have done without the last part."

"Come on, you like him."

"I liked him until I realized he was Satan's spawn."

"Again with the dramatics." Selene rolls her eyes at me and then starts walking towards the door. "Anyway, my job here is done, you look gorgeous like always. Please text me when you get back home and let's meet for coffee this week."

CHAPTER EIGHT

After parking my motorcycle, I fling my leg over the machine to get off and remove my helmet. I am completely immersed in my thoughts, thinking about how soon spring will be here, and with it, the new F1 season will begin. The clock is ticking, and I have a team to deal with before the season starts. I want to change things and bring it back to its former glory. I want new drivers, a new team principal, and new strategists and engineers.

I lean against my Kawasaki while I wait for my demonic date to show up. Miriam has fascinated me since the day I met her in Monaco. Maybe if I was someone else, things would have played out differently for us. But I am not a good man, so things have taken another path for us. She dislikes me, probably even despises me, but I would take her hate over indifference any day.

I stare down at my outfit, noticing my shirt has moved out of place during the ride and my tattoos are peeking through. I rearrange my collar and sleeves methodically to hide them again. My tattoos aren't a secret, it would be hard to hide them given that my torso and arms are covered in them. But I don't love the idea of showing them off often. Only very few people know about their existence and even fewer know about their meaning.

Finally, a taxi pulls up nearby. I take a step away from the motorcycle, ready to open the passenger door, but Miriam is faster and opens it before I even get there. It takes a lot of effort to maintain my composure when she emerges out of the taxi, unapologetic as always. She's wearing a black dress that clings to her curves like a second skin, revealing a glimpse of her leg through an asymmetrical cut.

"Do you need a tissue?" I flinch at her words, unsure what she means. Miriam approaches me, then leans in, so close that I can feel the heat coming off her body. "You are practically drooling."

"It's not my fault you dressed to impress," I retort.

"It's not *my* fault you are so easy to impress," she says.

"Touché," I reply, forcing myself to look away. "Please, follow me."

I extend my hand in her direction, hoping she will take it without a fight, even if a part of me always needs her snippy and sarcastic comments. The thing that annoys me most about her is also the one I like the most.

Miriam looks at my hand as if it were a venomous serpent ready to poison her, but then finally, she takes it.

"Will you tell me where we're going?"

I stay silent, walking us through the dark street, while a *clickety-clack* sound echoes around us from her high heels. I control the urge to bend down and sweep her off her feet to carry her in my arms. I don't want her to feel uncomfortable having to walk in those high stilettos over the bricks of the city.

"That would spoil the fun," I answer.

"I didn't know you knew the meaning of fun." The sarcasm in her voice makes me laugh and, for whatever reason, the sound of it makes her eyes go wide. "I don't think I have ever heard you laugh before."

"That's because I *don't* know how to have fun," I tease.

"You don't always need to be broody and gloomy."

"Where should I invoice you for the therapy session?"

"Ask HR to share my bank account details with you."

I would laugh if I hadn't already asked for all those details. I found out everything I needed to know about her after our rendezvous in Monaco, but I also asked HR to send me her file yesterday.

We continue our walk in silence, accompanied by the distant hum of the city and the boats on the river, until we make it to our destination. In front of us, floating on the dark water, is an enormous boat, adorned with shimmering lights hanging everywhere and heating lamps all over the deck.

We can already hear laughter and music from where we stand. It seems like we are the last guests to arrive, and hopefully, we will be the first ones to leave.

"After you," I whisper in Miriam's ear, who is completely mesmerized by the magnitude of the boat.

"Where are we?" she asks, taking a step back at the same time she lets go of my arm.

"At a party," I explain.

"What kind of party?"

"A harmless one," I say, the corners of my mouth curling from amusement.

"Are there such things as harmless parties?"

"Nothing will happen to you while I'm here," I promise.

Miriam's mouth opens, then closes again, until finally she manages to muster the words, "I trust you."

"Do you?"

"For tonight."

She takes my hand and guides us onto the deck of the boat, where the security guard checks my ID before letting us in.

Miriam lets go of my hand as soon as we are cleared, and I feel the loss of her hand where it was pressing against mine only seconds ago.

The party is in full bloom. Men and women, personalities of the Formula One world, mingle, celebrating a life of excess. I scan the crowd, catching familiar faces, some of them good people, others not so much. In the distance, I recognize some racers from other categories, but it's the F1 drivers who shine bright in the middle of crowds like these.

Miriam's gaze follows mine, and I notice how her eyes light up when she sees the group of drivers as well. I tend to forget that not everyone works directly with these guys the way I have for the past few years. I can only imagine the way she feels being so close to some of the people she idolizes, so I don't tear her gaze away, even if I am slightly annoyed that she is looking at them rather than at me.

Guess it serves me well after the stunt I pulled in Monaco last year.

"Why are we here?" Miriam asks.

"You asked me why I bought the company," I say, smiling down at her. She's an intelligent woman, and I know curiosity is what gets her going, so why would I lay all the pieces of the puzzle in front of her when she can figure it out for herself instead?

She frowns at me.

"That doesn't answer my question."

"It does," I reply. "It's in places like these, behind the curtains where everything happens, *my little swan.*"

"Don't call me that." Her hazel eyes turn darker, probably remembering the first time I used that nickname. "What do you want to do with the team, Daniel?"

I smirk at her. "I thought you'd never ask."

"Answer my question."

A waiter passes by, carrying a platter full of crystal glasses filled with champagne. I stop him, grabbing two from the tray. I hand one to Miriam, who instantly chugs half of it as if needing to take off the edge.

"I want to bring Cavaglio Nero to its former glory days," I explain. "I am getting rid of everything that is corrupted in this team."

She frowns at me, probably thinking that I sound like a cynic. "What are you talking about?"

"Aren't you full of questions." I smile, then take the first sip of the golden liquid in my glass, enjoying the bubbles. But when the liquid hits my throat, I notice something different about the familiar taste of champagne, something in between plastic and metal. I try to smell the inside of the glass discreetly, but nothing sets off my alarms.

I really am a paranoid bastard.

"Answer my question," Miriam repeats.

"Why?"

"Why bring me if you weren't going to answer?"

"I answered your first question, didn't I?"

"You knew I was going to have more than one."

"You can't always have the winning hand, Miriam."

"You are so infuriating." She grunts and then takes another sip of her drink. I am tempted to take it away from her, not being able to shake off the strange feeling from my previous sip, but I decide against it. I can take care of her if anything happens.

Nothing will happen to her, not while I am here.

"I want to make the world a better place, that's why I bought the company." It's a vague answer, but it is the best I can do.

"Who needs to go?"

"You will have to find the other answers yourself."

Miriam gives me a full smile, showing me all her teeth.

"Challenge accepted," she says and finishes her drink in one more gulp.

The Cat

The Cat watched the events on the boat unfolding from the shadows, his eyes narrowed into slits, simmering with fury. For over ten years, he'd hunted the person he knew as Daniela, the one who slipped through his fingers and vanished into the night.

Memories of betrayal and lost alliances fuel his rage as he observes Daniel's every move, every gesture, every single action. He knew him as a little girl, but now he's a powerful man. A formidable opponent who took down his entire organization last year and one who will pay for that and more.

When The Cat first started his search, he thought it would be easier to find a girl from Argentina that had nowhere to go, but he was proven wrong when she did an excellent job at hiding for the past ten years. Daniel, however, made one mistake, and The Cat had been waiting for it for a long time.

Aligning with Sasha Valine has sealed his fate.

The destruction of The Red Horses last year was what gave him away. Both of them. Sasha once Natalia. Daniel once Daniela. Now a year later he finally saw an opportunity to take him down, to get his vengeance, and make Daniel pay for the past.

The original plan was simple. Spike his drink, snatch him from the party, and unleash hell upon him. But as The Cat watches, a glimmer of something unexpected catches his attention: the intensity in Daniel's gaze as he locks eyes with the woman beside him.

A flicker of uncertainty dances in his mind. Could it be? Does Daniel finally have a weakness, after all? The possibility is tantalizing, one that fills The Cat with hope and pleasure.

With a silent vow, he retreats back into the shadows, his anger smoldering beneath the surface. The hunt is far from over, but now, he is more determined than ever to claim his vengeance.

CHAPTER NINE

A cocky smile rests on my face when I walk away from Daniel. I love a good dare, and I know I can win this hand. I am fearless. I have always known that. There has never been a challenge that I backed down from.

Tonight isn't going to be any different.

He wants me to find the answers on my own. Fine.

I will get to the bottom of this, and once I am done, I will wave my victory right in front of his nose.

"Be careful," he warns with a deep voice, maybe even a hint of worry.

My eyes sweep over the faces of the people in attendance as I walk away. Some of them are familiar, colleagues from work or people I have seen around the paddock the few times I have been invited to a race. Most of them, however, are people I do not recognize, strangers who for all I know could be what is left of The Red Horses. A shiver runs down my spine as I recall the stories I have heard, things that are whispered because they are so atrocious, saying them out loud feels like a crime.

What if that is Daniel's purpose? What if he thinks there are still members of The Red Horses left in Cavaglio Nero? Is that what he means when he says he is getting rid of all corruption? Still, why would he buy a team?

Nothing makes sense to me.

My mind is spinning with all the possibilities, and I feel a little dizzy. I try to clear all those thoughts from my head and calm myself, but I can't. Daniel is on my mind. I have been able to stay away from me for over a year, but now it's almost impossible.

Hesitating, I take a step forward, trying to run away from my thoughts and determined to approach someone. Anyone. Someone who can shed some light on the dark uncertainty lingering in my head.

Just as I am about to make my move, someone bumps into me from behind, causing a splash of icy liquid to fall upon me. I whirl around in anger as soon as I feel it drenching my hair.

"You have got to be kidding me!" I grunt in anger.

"I am so sorry," the culprit says at the same time. "I didn't see you there."

My anger partly disappears as soon as I realize who the man standing in front of me is. I would recognize his dark-bluish hair anywhere, and I can't help but notice how his eyes are the color of polished mahogany rather than black like they seem to be on TV. Emi Saito is very different when you see him in person. He is more beautiful, his muscles more defined, his smile more seductive, it makes sense why he is one of the Casanova´s of the paddock. Okay, I might be getting distracted, but I'm a single woman in need of a good fuck, and he's a lovely specimen of a man. Someone I am sure could make me see the stars for a night.

"It's fine," I wave him off, avoiding a scene.

"No, it's not. I am sorry. Is there anything I can do?" he asks with a perfect British accent that doesn't suit him. There is something fake about it.

"It's fine, it's just hair," I lie. It's not *just* hair. It's hair that I styled for hours.

He looks down at me and raises a brow in disbelief.

"Hair as gorgeous as yours takes time to get done. I just hope that the alcohol won't impact it too much." *Is he flirting with me?*

"Your reputation precedes you," I answer simply.

"I hope that they only talk about my great manners."

"Sure," I answer sarcastically. "That and the trail of heartbroken women you leave wherever you go."

The driver laughs and shakes his head.

"Emi Saito." He slides a plain white card into my hand with his name and contact information written in extremely fine and elegant lines. "And what's your name, gorgeous?"

"Miriam Lefebvre." I blush.

"What brings you here, Miriam?"

"Work," I answer, then look around, trying to find Daniel, but he is nowhere to be seen. "What about you?"

"Work too," he states.

I raise one eyebrow, confused. Emi doesn't have a seat for next season, and Cavaglio seems to have two free seats now that Munguia has moved to Volpella and Senner didn't get a new contract.

Does that mean Emi is about to become a Cavaglio Nero driver?

"I am ready for a change of company," the man whispers.

"Aiming high, I see," I regret my answer the moment it leaves my lips. Truth is, Emi isn't a bad driver, he just isn't a great one, at least not yet. Cavalglio Nero is where the drivers go after winning a world championship. They are the team people dream of because everyone is a Cavaglio Nero fan.

"Sky's the limit," he jokes, but there is a glint in his eyes revealing how serious he is. Emi raises his glass in the air, ready for a toast, and I clink my glass against his. "To the dreamers."

"And to the ones who dare to dream," I add, then take another sip of my drink.

Seconds later, my head starts feeling dizzy and everything spins. How can I feel dizzy? I've only had two drinks. My tolerance is usually higher than this.

"Are you okay?" Emi asks.

I nod.

"So, you want to become a Cavaglio Nero driver?"

"That's the plan. Every child in karting dreams of becoming their driver when they grow up, and I am not immune to that particular dream," Emi says with a dreamy voice. "My results don't speak in my favor, but I had a shitty car, and I still managed to make it into the top ten this season. So yeah, I think I can bring glory to the team too."

"Well, Daniel Conte is around, so you might as well try to charm him," I suggest.

"I am not sure if I can work my brand of charm with men the way I do with women. I am straight in case you missed it," he jokes, "But he knows I'm here. He is the one who invited me to the party," he explains.

I try not to show him my surprise and leave my face as expressionless as possible, but I know that I fail miserably.

"My contract ended after Abu Dhabi, and he knows it."

"I thought João Querinho was the winning horse," I blurt my thoughts out loud and instantly regret it. It's not a secret that everyone wants to team up with the Brazilian driver, now that he has won two world championships at Volpella Racing. He is at the peak of his career, but that doesn't mean Emi can't secure himself a contract.

"Someone has to be his faithful squire," he says, the smile on his face radiating confidence and revealing his perfect set of teeth. "João is older than me, and I'm a patient person."

"Are you?" I tease.

"When needed." He smirks, and I can't help but mirror his expression. We fall into a short silence, and I use it to empty my glass. He does the same. "These things are loaded."

I nod again. "I didn't know champagne could be this strong."

"I am not sure it's only champagne." My eyes go wide. Am I being drugged? "Maybe there's some vodka in it."

My body instantly relaxes. I'd rather take my chances with Russian alcohol than some sketchy substances.

I start looking around once more, not really sure what I'm looking for when my head keeps getting foggier. I try to focus my eyes to see the people around me.

"Oh, look at that!" Emi screams with excitement, pointing at a couple standing in front of the captain of the boat. "Are they getting married?"

Almost as if they heard us, the couple loses themself in a passionate kiss right in front of the captain of the boat, while the people standing around them start clapping and cheering as if they were at a wedding.

What is going on?

"Miriam." Daniel's low voice comes from behind me, and it doesn't take too long before I feel his arm looping in around my waist. Usually, I would jump at his touch and try to wiggle out of it, but for whatever reason, my body decides to lean into him, my head almost resting on top of his strong shoulder.

"I didn't know you two were dating," comes from Emi. I feel so dizzy that I don't even bother correcting him.

"Have you thought about that proposal I made you?" Daniel asks Emi, not answering his previous question, and most importantly, never letting go of me.

"My manager will be in contact with you."

My jaw drops a little.

So, he really is next in line.

The sound of clapping hands distracts me. It seems like another couple has just gotten married, and more are surrounding the improvised altar, cheering for the fake newlyweds. I smile at their happiness and the gossip girl inside of me moves to the nearest corner, focusing to listen what the people are saying over there.

I listen to one of the older women talking to a man in a blue suit. "Everyone should get married!"

"I guess marrying can be fun when there is no pressure, no guest list to be drafted, and no commitment for the rest of your life," the man answers, and it's then I notice how Emi is also listening to the same conversation I am.

"What do you mean?" the lady asks exactly what I am thinking.

"This must be a fake wedding, almost like eloping in Vegas but without any real consequences. Most of these people don't even know each other," the man clarifies, and my heart drops a little. I don't really care what people do, but it seems sad to have a fake wedding without consequences and commitment. It defies the entire concept of getting married.

"You should do it," Emi jokes, looking at us.

"Do what?" I answer, trying to step away from Daniel, but his hold on me tightens, his fingers digging deeper into my flesh.

"I think we're going to head out now," Daniel announces.

Emi puts a hand to his chest, forcing him to stay put and robbing us of the chance of leaving this conversation. "It would be a hell of a good story."

"I am afraid we don't have time," Daniel insists.

"Do you have somewhere better to be?" I ask Daniel.

"It will take ten minutes." Emi smirks. "It's not as if it's a real wedding."

Daniel's jaw tenses, and then a breath of air leaves his nostrils, making them flare a little. "Move," he grinds out through his teeth, then drags me towards the captain. There are at least three other couples waiting in line, but he pushes them to the side, making us the next couple to get fake married.

"Do your thing and do it fast," Daniel barks at the captain.

"And they say romance is dead," I whisper, rolling my eyes at him.

"What can I say? My future wife drives me mad."

"Do you take him to be your lawfully wedded husband? Do you promise to love, honor, and protect him, to stand by his side in times of joy and sorrow, in sickness and in health?" the captain says, looking at me.

"I do," I answer, almost unwillingly, with the sole purpose of finishing this as quickly as possible. With my eyes blurry, I sign the paper standing in front of me without even bothering to read the ink on the fake document.

"And you," he says, looking at Daniel. "Do you take her to be your lawfully wedded wife? Do you promise to love, honor, and protect her, to stand by her side in times of joy and sorrow, in sickness and in health?"

"I do," Daniel answers firmly, his eyes locked on mine as he signs the same document as I did only moments before.

I am convinced he is finished speaking, but I am proven wrong when he turns to face me instead of the captain and his lips start moving again.

"I vow to love you, for who you are today and the person you are becoming. I promise to celebrate you, your successes, your achievements, and your victories. But I also promise to celebrate your losses. To stand by your side every step that you take. And I promise to protect you come what may. From this day on, you are mine, and I am yours."

It's only when Daniel finishes talking that I realize I have stopped breathing. My head is feeling dizzier and dizzier, and if I wasn't so stunned, what follows next would be the icing on the cake.

Daniel looks me straight in the eyes, but his hand is searching for something in the pocket of his jacket. The surprise gasp of the crowd behind us only foreshadows my own surprise. When I look down, I see his hand holding the most stunning ring I have ever seen. I only get a chance to properly look at it when Daniel slips the ring on my finger. The band is filled with stones, and the material is cold and slightly large. But it's when Daniel's hand has retreated that I notice the black diamond with a marquise cut rest at the center.

"I pronounce you husband and wife. You may kiss the bride."

Daniel is ready to go, but my head is so clouded that my control jumped out the window the moment that ring landed on my finger.

For the first time in over a year, I do exactly what I want to do every time I see Daniel. Taking a step towards him, I place my hand on his strong chest and proceed to do the unthinkable.

I kiss him.

I kiss him as if this was our first kiss, even if it isn't.

Daniel resists me at first, but something shifts inside of him when I tug on his hair. He becomes possessed, a wild animal who bites my lip and pulls with a fierceness on my hair like he has never before. All I feel is passion and desire, so much that I can even feel the hair on my neck rising.

We kiss for seconds, minutes, maybe even hours.

Time doesn't matter anymore. All I know and care about is Daniel and the way his hands are around me. I am barely even breathing, and he must sense it because eventually, he breaks the kiss. He's also breathless, but not quite as much as me.

"This was a mistake," he whispers.

What's the mistake? The fake wedding? The kiss?

I don't get a chance to ask because right after his words, I feel the world crumbling and blurring around me before everything turns black. I feel myself falling, ready to hit the ground, but someone catches me.

"Miriam." His sweet voice is the last thing I hear.

CHAPTER TEN

The party is in full bloom as soon as midnight comes around. Everyone is celebrating João's *win from earlier today. Surprisingly, even Philip is celebrating, though he only made it to P2. Who would have thought that all the eternally grumpy F1 driver needed was a crazy redhead to turn him into a tolerable human being?*

I have had fun all night long with my friend and enjoyed a negroni or three more than I should. But still, my mind can't stop thinking about that mysterious dark aura that Daniel Conte has around him. In fact, I haven't stopped looking for him all night long, hoping he will eventually grace the party with his presence.

Am I crazy for being this attracted by a man I have only spoken three words with? Probably. But delusion is my nature, and I am willing to take a little burn if the fire is as hot as Daniel is. It hasn't been long since I've been with a man, but he wasn't that good in bed, so all my mind can do right now is think about the amazing things I would let Daniel do to my body.

I am ready to forget about him and go live my wildest dreams with my vibrator when a platinum blond makes an entrance and finds her way to where the Brazilian driver is standing. I don't know whose eyes shine brighter. João's *or Sasha's. Whoever doesn't believe in love only needs to take a look at the way they adore each other to become a believer.*

But my eyes have more important things to do.

Where Sasha Valine goes, Daniel Conte follows.

He has to be here.

"I think your negroni needs to be refilled." The masculine voice I have been thinking about all day fills my ears, making the thin hairs on my neck rise, and my stupid heart decides to skip a beat.

I turn around, taking my time until I finally face him. Daniel is one of Formula One's most well-known people. He is on TV every weekend, narrating the races and qualifying sessions, but it's only now that it strikes me how incredibly beautiful this man really is.

"Make that two." I smile coyly. "You will need one if you want to keep up with me all night long."

"Your wish is my command, pequeño cisne*."*

"Little swan?" I ask, unsure if I understood the Spanish words right.

"You speak Spanish?" he asks, surprised.

"Un poco," I answer, biting my lower lip.

Daniel mirrors my smile, his eyes focused on my lips. The pull is undeniable. I have been with enough people to understand chemical compatibility, desire, and lust.

But this? This pull that I feel towards Daniel?

It's unreal.

He could be the sun I would still be willing to burn if I only got to feel whatever it is that I am feeling right now.

"Here you go," Daniel purrs, handing me a negroni.

"Thanks."

We clink our glasses and sip the orange liquid, never breaking eye contact. Once Daniel is done with his first sip, he licks his bottom lip oh so slowly. God, I could watch him do that all night long. But right now, I want his lips on my skin.

I am not going home alone.

And, by the look in his eyes, I know he is thinking the same.

Not wanting to drag this out, I take his free hand and lace it around my waist, forcing us both to move in the direction of the dance floor. I only stop when I find a semi-empty spot, then turn to face him and slide my arm around his neck.

Daniel moves us to the beat of the music, our hips moving in perfect synchrony. I close my eyes and tilt my head up, enjoying the sensation of his body pressed against mine. He doesn't long to figure out exactly what I want him to do, and a couple of seconds later, I feel his lips on my collarbone, making their way up my throat, leaving a trail of kisses behind that are making my core pound.

I can't take the slow and teasing pleasure anymore. Before I can stop myself, I run my fingers through his long hair and tug on it. Daniel's eyes lock with mine, silent agreement written all over them. Then he gives me a smile filled with anticipation, which I mirror right before pressing my lips on his.

The tension is palpable, and I can't resist it anymore. Our lips meet, and even though it's our first kiss, it's anything but shy. His hand finds his way onto the small of my back, pressing me impossibly closer to him, while our tongues tangle and I have to control myself in order to repress a moan.

The world around us seems to fade away.

I struggle to breathe through the intensity of the kiss, and after a while, I'm forced to break it, but before I do, Daniel bites my lower lip with an intensity that sends more need to my core.

"Let's get out of here," he suggests.

"I thought you would never ask." I smile.

CHAPTER ELEVEN

My head is pounding.

Worse even, it feels like it is being ripped off my shoulders.

I try opening my eyes, but I only see black dots. It takes me a couple of tries until I can finally open them, only to be blinded by the painfully bright morning light shining through my window.

It's only a couple of seconds later, when the blurry figures around me become sharp objects, that I realize I am not in a familiar room. Scared, I jump up with a plan to run away, but a wave of nausea stops me.

"Here." Daniel hands me a bucket.

It takes me precisely three seconds before I throw up everything inside of me. My entire body shakes, cold sweat drips from my neck, and my head feels dizzy. All kinds of disgusting fluids leave my body, and when I am finally done emptying my stomach, I drop to my knees, feeling cold sweat dripping down my forehead. An exhale leaves my lips as I look up at the man standing in front of me, looking slightly nauseated himself.

"Do you want some water?"

I shake my head and instantly regret the movement.

"Gatorade?" he insists.

"No. What happened last night?"

"You had too many drinks." He smirks.

My eyes go wide, and my mouth drops. "Did we—"

"Do you really think that low of me?"

"Actually, it feels like I can't think right now."

"I wouldn't even touch you with a stick under normal circumstances. I especially wouldn't when you are completely passed out and intoxicated, Miriam."

"That's not the vibe I got from you in Monaco."

"You were tipsy, not drunk. And I told you that—"

"That we would never talk about what happened," I finish for him. "Trust me, I don't like to think about that night either." My voice gets a bit shaky, betraying me.

Daniel stays silent, so I use the chance to rest my head against the silky pillow at the edge of the bed and enjoy the moment of silence. I am so tired of battling him every step of the way. I am tired of hating him so fiercely that I almost want him. I'm tired of admiring him when I should be scared of him. And, most importantly, I am tired of fighting and resenting him for what happened *that* night. I have never been one to get stuck in the past, but for whatever reason, I have never been able to move on from Daniel.

"Miriam," he starts, his voice sad.

"Don't," I warn him. "You said it. We are not talking about that night."

"Okay," he concedes. "Then let's talk about last night."

I don't protest, but only because I'm dying to fill in the blanks.

"I would like you to get tested."

The statement catches me completely by surprise.

"Excuse me?" I finally manage to say.

"For drugs," he clarifies.

"You think I was drugged?"

"I am confident you were. Strike that, I think we all were. You just had more to drink than most of us," he explains.

"Where the fuck did you bring me?"

"I'm sorry, I didn't think it would be a dangerous party, but clearly, someone had other plans for the night."

"Does this have something to do with the reason you decided to buy the team?"

Daniel looks me straight in the eyes, and his face goes completely still. "You are full of questions, and also of secrets."

I gulp. Even through my headache, I'm able to read between the lines. Does he know about me?

"Interpol is good, but I'm better." He smirks.

"Since when do you know?"

"Since the day Elizabeth recruited you."

Since the beginning.

A week before we met. Has Daniel been watching me since Monaco? Is this only a coincidence? It must be. He must have found me while he was working on getting Elizabeth on board with his whole plan. He couldn't have been looking into me. Could he?

"I don't have a secret agenda," he says. "I just want to right some wrongs. I love the sport, and I love Cavaglio, and after I was finished with my personal vendetta, I had some spare time and money for a new hobby."

"That's an expensive hobby."

"You can't even imagine."

"4.3 billion." I smirk because I know my numbers.

"Sometimes I underestimate you, Miriam."

"I suggest you don't make that mistake again. I am more capable than you think."

"Trust me, I know. Not many people would dare to assault me, especially if the weapon in question is a butterknife, but you seem ready to slice my neck if I give you a chance."

"Be a dear and get me a cab before I decide to try it with a real knife. Besides, the devil's layer is a hot place, and I have no desire to burn."

"Trust me, I have looked the devil in the eye, and he wasn't as good-looking as I am. Plus, his layer is far scarier than mine." I open my mouth to say that I am sorry, but Daniel is already on his way out of the room, and I am left feeling like the biggest asshole who has ever walked the earth. "I will send a nurse to your house to run the blood tests."

All this time, I have been comparing him to a deity of evil, when in reality, he has orchestrated the death of people who actually resemble the devil.

CHAPTER TWELVE

Once I'm finally home and showered, I allow myself to fantasize about dropping into bed again. I can't recall the last time I had a hangover like this. Life, however, is a cruel mistress, so right as I'm about to get into bed, someone rings my bell.

Wrapped in a hot pink bathrobe and with my hair looking like an untamable mess, I walk to the door and open it, convinced that my redheaded friend is the one intruding on my attempt to rest. Instead, I'm met with a woman in her mid-forties, with dark curly hair, and the kind of loving smile only a mother could give you.

"Miriam Lefebvre?" she asks.

I nod.

"Daniel Conte sent me to get some blood to be tested."

The sentence sounds creepier than it should, so I can't help but imagine Daniel drinking the blood of his enemies.

That's too much to process without having had coffee.

"Please, come in," I tell her, moving to the side to let her in.

"My name is Grace," the nurse says, walking into my home and towards the kitchen island. I don't need to ask her to make herself comfortable. Grace is already taking over my place, setting up all sorts of instruments and needles on the counter.

"I think I am going to pass out," I mumble when I see a huge needle next to some vials.

"Afraid of needles?"

"Nope."

Grace raises her brow at me.

"Maybe a little," I confess. "I can usually control my fear, but it's been a hard night."

"Daniel told me."

"You two are close?"

"In a way," she says in a tone that implies things I don't like.

I don't know what I hate more; whatever she is implying, or the wave of jealousy that hits me when I realize Daniel could be sleeping with other women.

Not could. *Is.*

Daniel *is* sleeping with other women.

Jealousy and sadness that I can't quite comprehend fill me in equal parts. I have done an excellent job keeping him out of my life for over a year, and now I am jealous because he sleeps with other women, sad even because he's not mine.

Unbelievable, Miriam.

"Daniel is my nephew," Grace clarifies. "No need to be jealous."

"I am not jealous," I blurt out, though a wave of relief sweeps through me.

"Sure." Grace doesn't touch the subject again. Instead, she focuses on her tools, and then points at the stool in the kitchen. "Take a seat while I finish this."

I try to divert my attention, focusing on a stain on my stove. I need to clean the house today. Yeah, that will help me get rid of all my problems. That and a three-to-eight-hour nap.

"Extend your arm," Grace orders.

I obey in silence, extending my arm and allowing her to put a rubber band around my biceps. Then, she turns around, grabs a cotton pad, and sprays it with some sort of liquid before she rubs it on the inside of my elbow. By then, my breaths are coming out in heavy pants because I'm terrified of the needle that's about to puncture my skin.

"I wish we had met under different circumstances," Grace says. "Daniel talks a lot about you."

The statement forces me to take my gaze from my elbow to look at the woman in front of me.

"I am not sure I know what you mean."

"Daniel is a complicated man. His life has been complicated too. But there is so much kindness in his heart. I just wish he would let people see it."

"I bet he will find someone—" I start, but she interrupts me before I can finish my sentence.

"He will. But my nephew is too stubborn sometimes. He needs a... what's the phrase in English? *¡Una patada en el culo!*"

"A kick in the ass?" I try to translate.

"Yes! He needs to be pushed out of his comfort zone. He needs someone that isn't afraid of him," she explains.

"I think there isn't a single soul on the planet that isn't afraid of your nephew, Grace."

"You aren't afraid of him."

"Are you suggesting something?"

"I am just stating the obvious."

"I —"

"We're done," she announces.

I look down at my arm incredulously. There is no needle there, but I can see vials filled with my blood on top of the kitchen counter. A droplet of blood falling from my vein is the only proof that there was a needle in my arm only seconds ago.

"How?"

"I have been a nurse for a long time." Grace winks at me. "And besides, Daniel is also afraid of needles. He isn't as strong as you might think he is."

I only wake up from my eighteen-hour nap because of the insistent sound of my phone ringing next to me. Somehow, after a couple of blind taps on my nightstand, I manage to retrieve the phone and answer the call.

"Miriam Lefebvre! ¡Tu es mort!" *You are dead!*

The French threat is all I need to fully wake up.

"I love you too, Maman."

"J 'ai eu tellement peur!" *I was so scared!*

"Why?"

"Why? Why?! Are you on drugs, Miriam?"

"No!" *At least not on purpose.*

"I have been calling you since last night. Sixty times!" I look at my phone while she continues to babble in French and notice sixty-three calls from her, ten from Dad, and another eleven from Selene. "I was so scared. Don't you realize that next to your dad, you are the only thing that makes me happy in this life? You can't do this to me, ma chérie."

"I am sorry, Maman. I went out on Friday for a work thing with the new CEO, and I was so exhausted after, I just passed out on my bed. I have been working so hard for the past few weeks, I guess my body just needed a break."

"Miriam, you are working too hard. Is this job worth it? Are you at least happy?"

For a moment, I stay silent. I have debated this for days. My job has always made me happy because there was a bigger picture to see. Numbers tell a story, but I am not sure if the story they are telling right now is interesting enough for me to stay.

"I am not sure," I tell her. "Things are changing in the company, and I think I am willing to give it some time before I make any decisions."

"How much time is that?"

"Half a year?" It's more of a question than a statement.

"Well make sure to visit your father and me in Paris before we move out. We've decided to go to Egypt next," she says cheerfully.

Mom and Dad moving around the world is nothing new. They have been doing it since before I was born, and my birth didn't stop them, it just made them settle down for a little bit longer to offer me some stability. But every couple of years, we would pack up and move to a new city or country, sometimes even a new continent. That's how I ended up with over seven languages in my head and an unresolved cultural crisis.

"I will try my best, Maman," I promise.

The truth is, I miss home quite a lot, whatever home means these days anyway. I miss my parents; they are my biggest cheerleaders. But I also love making a life for myself.

But what else do I need to prove?

After all, I built my first business in my early twenties. I sold it for a larger amount than I would like to admit and ended up working at a prestigious Formula One team, only to be recruited weeks later by Interpol, and I am only in my mid-twenties.

I have made a life for myself and a successful one at that.

But there is still more that I want to accomplish, even if I can't really put my finger on it.

Put my finger on it…

Suddenly, a flash from Friday night hits me.

A captain.

A ceremony.

A finger.

A ring!

I look down at my hand and find a black diamond ring wrapped around it.

CHAPTER THIRTEEN

The clock hasn't even struck eight in the morning, and I am already on my third coffee, going through emails and organizing the week ahead. I have been the owner of Cavaglio Nero for almost two weeks, and nothing seems to be working according to plan.

The contract with Emi should have been signed already and on my desk. Instead, I haven't heard anything from that bastard. João is also waiting for his contract, and I'm missing a team principal who can take care of the mess that is the team right now.

I have to hand it to them, they did an outstanding job during the 2023 season when Burton won his last Drivers'

Championship, and 2024 wasn't too bad given the situation – and by that, I mean Sasha's killing spree.

Last season, however, they had one of the worst cars, two unmotivated drivers whose contracts were coming to an end, and a team that was breaking from the inside out.

But that is what I am here for.

To fix it.

My phone rings with an alarm I know too well, a reminder of my doctor's appointment where I get my injection of testosterone. I'm usually not annoyed by it. I have been trans for over a decade, so most times I just go through the motions of it, and things like that are part of my routine. But not this time. This time, I'm annoyed by it. It's just a reminder that I am slightly different from most men. No matter how much I try, how many surgeries I get, how long my beard grows, I was born in a female body, even if I am a man.

I am torn out of this spiral when my door slams open, the glass vibrating after it collides with my wall. Miriam walks into my office, her brown hair curled instead of the straight hairstyle I have gotten used to for the past years. Her white pants are flowing around her long legs as she strides towards me. I think the worst has passed when she finally makes it to my desk, but I am surprised when she slams her hands on the table.

"I see you're not a morning person," I comment, forcing my eyes off her chest and the way her green satin blouse hugs it.

"What is this?" Miriam says, raising her left hand and showing me her ring finger.

Seeing that black diamond on her little finger makes me feel things I wasn't prepared to feel, but I keep my cool and just say, "That's what this is about?"

"Answer me."

"You really don't remember, darling wife?"

Her eyes go wide, surprise lacing her features. I am tempted to tell her the truth, but I enjoy her reaction too much to spoil the fun.

"Please tell me we didn't fly to Las Vegas."

"Why go to Las Vegas when there was a captain on the boat, ready to officiate our marriage?"

"Daniel!"

"You really don't remember."

Miriam stays silent for a moment. I can see fine lines appearing on her forehead as she takes a seat in front of me. It's almost painful watching her trying to recall the events of Friday night.

"I have to say it's a pity you don't," I mock. "After all, my vows were something to remember."

"Well, they couldn't be that memorable if it only took a couple of glasses of champagne to forget about it."

"Speaking of, Grace—"

"No. Don't you dare to change the topic, Daniel Conte! What the hell happened on Friday?"

I inhale deeply, ready to stop toying with her. "Emi Saito made us get married."

"Excuse me?"

Okay, now it's really time for the truth.

"The captain of the boat was officiating some sort of fake marriage ceremonies. You were really drunk by then, and I was trying to take you home, but Emi said it would be fun if we did it too, so we went through with it."

"And you just had a ring for me?"

I stay silent for a bit, not really knowing how to get myself out of that one. Saying I have had the ring for a while would be an understatement, but she doesn't need to know that. In fact, she doesn't need to know anything.

"I like having pretty things around," I answer.

"Who carries a black diamond around just like that?"

"I do."

"Ugh!" Miriam grunts, frustrated. "Did Grace at least come back to you with the drug test result?" she asks, massaging her temples with one hand.

"No, she hasn't. She needs more time."

"Will you let me know when you get them?"

"Who do you take me for?"

"An aggravating man with control and trust issues?"

"Is that the profile you made of me for Interpol?"

Her eyes narrow, and I know that in her mind she's planning ways to kill me. However, she gets distracted from planning my demise when my phone rings.

I look at the caller ID and proceed to ignore it.

"Side piece?" Miriam asks annoyed.

"Lawyer," I correct. "But your jealousy is cute."

"Please, don't mind me, I was about to leave now that I know I am not married to a psycho killer," I say, more hoping than knowing, given that he hasn't confirmed my worst fear yet.

Miriam slowly stands up, but I stop her before she can make it all the way. "Sit down."

She gives me a look of defiance but stays put, just like I asked her to.

"It will only take a minute."

"Daniel, this is Cedric, your lawyer."

I have always hated people who introduce themselves like that. As if I hadn't spoken to him at least fifty times in the past two weeks.

"How can I help you?"

"Help me? How can I help *you?*"

"Excuse me?"

"I hear congrats are in order!" the man says, but I am having a hard time understanding him. "How is the new Mrs. Conte doing? I must admit, the news caught me by surprise. I thought a person like you would have a prenup before getting married."

"Cedric, what are you talking about?"

"The wedding? It's all over the news."

"Which wedding?"

"Yours to Miriam Lefebvre..." Confusion laces his voice. "I saw the newspapers and the wedding certificate just got sent to my office. The wedding documents were signed by both of you..."

What is going on? Miriam mouths.

I turn around, ignoring her and trying to figure out what the hell is happening right now.

"So, you are telling me that those documents are valid and legal?" I ask, careful not to alarm the woman behind me.

"Weren't they supposed to be?"

"No."

"Oh." Silence fills the call for longer than it should, but Cedric breaks it again. "Do you want me to draft the divorce papers?"

I am about to tell him to do so before the sun sets. But through the reflection of the glass window in front of me, I see the woman sitting behind me, and that is the moment the craziest of ideas makes it through my mind.

Would it really be that bad to pretend for a while? Having a wife would give me an advantage over the arrogant men in the company. They would stop looking at me with distrust and start thinking of me as a family man.

Maybe being married isn't that bad.

And maybe for a while I can be selfish and enjoy the things I want in life before having to step back to my usual habits.

"There is no need for that, Cedric. I will call you later."

I haven't even hung up the phone when I notice Miriam giving me a suspicious look.

"What was that about?"

"We need to talk."

CHAPTER FOURTEEN

"We are what?" I scream at Daniel.

Possessed by fury, I take one of the cups filled with pencils on his desk and throw it at him. But he's too fast and somehow manages to dodge it, which only makes me more furious. I consider myself a non-violent person, but right now, I'm dangerous. I'm ready to slit Daniel Conte's throat. then push him out of his office window.

"We are married."

"Then let's get a divorce." My voice comes out in a high-pitched tone. Only two days ago, I was thinking about what I wanted to do with my life, but no part of me wanted to be married to one of the richest and most dangerous men in the world.

"It's not that easy."

"Yes, it is. Call your lawyer and tell him to draft the papers!" I scream like a mad woman, which is exactly how I am feeling right now.

I cannot be married!

"Again, Miriam, it is not that simple," he repeats.

I count to five, hoping it'll allow my mind to calm in some miraculous way, but I'm too angry right now. Everything feels like too much.

"How isn't it that simple?"

"I am a rich man and now I am also the owner of a Formula One team. You could sue me and get half of everything I own, so it isn't that simple."

"I am not going to sue you." *Is this what it's about?*

"You won't?" he says with a suspicious tone.

"What would I do with a Formula One team?"

"Destroy everything I am working on? For all I know, you could take it all away from me simply out of spite, fueled by the hate you feel for me. I am just protecting myself."

From me? I think.

"I don't hate you, not in the way you think."

"Then in what way?" he asks.

"I hate the way you make me feel," I start. "I hate the way I still think about Monaco. I hate the way you treated me, and most of all, I hate the way that I can't hate you, not truly, because a tiny part of me admires what you have done and what you are doing."

Daniel smirks. *He smirks!*

"If you don't take that smirk off your face this instant, I will be forced to stab you with your scissors," I warn.

"First the butterknife, now the scissors. What tool will you use next to attempt murdering me? A paper press?"

"Don't tempt me."

"Go home, Miriam. You have been through a lot over the past few days. Go home and enjoy a day off. I bet your boss won't mind."

"I hate you."

"You just said you didn't," he teases.

"I am allowed to change my mind."

"Go home and let me figure this out."

"You have twenty-four hours. I suggest you hide all sharp objects from the building and get rid of the paper press if you don't have a solution by then," I warn him.

I am exhausted.

No, strike that.

I am emotionally drained when I make it back to my apartment building.

Somehow, I have been able to avoid Satan's spawn for almost a year, and now I'm married to him and can't seem to get rid of him. What will be next? Adopting a kid? I shiver at the thought of kids. I've never wanted to have kids, especially none of my own. The world is overpopulated enough. I'd much rather adopt. But that is beside the point.

I don't want to share my life with Daniel.

End of discussion.

Right before I make it into my apartment, I spot a coffee mug on top of the kitchen counter that I am pretty sure I didn't leave there this morning.

"I've been waiting quite a while," Elizabeth says.

"Jesus Christ!" I say, bringing my hand to my chest.

"Don't use his name in vain."

"Ever heard about privacy?"

Elizabeth eyes me, and, instead of answering, she just walks past me and takes a seat at the kitchen counter. "I wanted to say congratulations. Shall I call you Miriam Conte now?"

"I can explain—"

"Save it," she stops me. "I am just here to tell you that I no longer need you to help me. Under different circumstances, it would have been beneficial to be married to the target, but you are too close, too involved. I don't know what your fascination with Daniel Conte is, but he will be your downfall."

"He knows I work for you," I explain, not wanting to hear any more of her painful words.

"What do you mean?"

"He knows I helped Interpol."

"You told him?" Elizabeth screams, enraged.

"Of course not. He told me he knew since you first contacted me."

The woman in front of me passes a hand through her short hair, lingering at the back of it to play with one of her short curls. I've learned that's her tick when she's stressed. She plays with that curl until it's almost straight.

"Fuck!" Elizabeth exhales.

"I'm sorry."

"All this time, he knew," she says, more to herself. "You could have been in danger, and we didn't even know it."

"Elizabeth, it's not your fault."

"Yes, it is."

I walk towards her and place my hands on the arms of my past lover, boss, and now friend? I have come to know her better than she would like me to, and I know that she is going to take this personally, even though there was no way she could have avoided it.

"I was supposed to be the one who protected you."

"You have protected me," I tell her.

"No, I haven't. You are married to the devil now."

"I think we should stop calling him that."

For some reason, the memory of how Elizabeth had approached me a week before I met Daniel comes to my mind. As soon as I said yes to her proposal, she gave me a file on everyone relevant to the case, but it was Daniel's file that caught my attention. However, there wasn't much in it: male, late twenties, a description about him, his talents and works in the deep web, and a picture of him in which he looked stunning.

But no real story about him, no parents, no sibling, no past life, nothing that could give him a motive to be linked to the case.

However, as the case unfolded, Elizabeth pieced the pieces of the puzzle together, and his story was the one that broke me the most. Little Daniel had felt different from his brothers growing up. He knew it and so did Ximena, his sister. So, she came up with a surprise for him and arranged for an appointment so Daniel could go to an expert in gender affirmation. The appointment went great, and they drafted a plan for Daniel's transition.

But when they left the doctor's office, both children, no older than seventeen, were kidnapped by the men of The Red Horses, and for two weeks, they endured all sorts of nightmares. Nobody will ever comprehend the horrors they went through, and the worst part is that Daniel not only lost his innocence, his dreams, and his childhood, but he also had to watch his sister die.

"The devil was an angel once. He was the Morning Star before he fell from the sky to rule over hell, and now he is keeping the monsters away," I say finally.

"You are too naïve if you think Daniel Conte is an angel."

"Maybe he isn't an angel, but he isn't the devil either."

CHAPTER FIFTEEN

Me: Sasha, are you in town?

Blonde Dread: Yes?

Me: Then please, both of you, come to my place.

Me: It's urgent!

Ginger bestie: Who died?

Blonde dread: I didn't do it.

Ginger Bestie: What do you mean, you didn't do it?

Blonde Dread: Sorry wrong chat ahaha

Me: Please just come.

...

The girls take their time to arrive, but when they finally do, Selene shows up holding a bag filled with all types of chocolate, candy, and a first aid kit. On the other hand, Sasha arrives with a huge bottle of champagne, and she doesn't even wait until she is inside my home to open it.

"Congrats!" she says as the foam rushes out of the bottle. "I thought we were planning one wedding, not two!"

"Sasha!" I reprimand her.

"Wait, what happened?" Selene asks, confused.

"Oh, you don't know?" Sasha replies.

"Know what?" The skin on Selene's forehead creases because she's completely perplexed by what is going on right now. To be fair, given her job, I thought she would have already known about it, but if she had, she would have been the first to call.

"She got married on Friday night," Sasha explains.

"Please tell me you married Daniel."

I roll my eyes at her.

"Oh my god. You did!" Selene vibrates with happiness.

"She did," Sasha confirms. "It's all over the news. I'll admit, it did catch me by surprise seeing Daniel getting married, but who am I to judge? I'm only the groom's best friend." I don't dig into that, but I make a mental note to let Daniel know how upset Sasha is.

Selene lifts an eyebrow, finally catching up with everything that is going on. "So, none of this was planned?"

"Not it wasn't," I say, but Selene is already far gone.

"He didn't even tell me you were dating," Sasha blurts out.

"Zip it, the two of you," I command in a low voice that I don't recognize. "Now sit down and listen to me."

I am pretty sure the girls are about to burst into laughter, but surprisingly enough, they stay quiet and take a seat on the couch. I take my time and grab some glasses from the kitchen cabinet. God knows I'm going to need some alcohol for this conversation.

"So, here is the thing," I say, pouring myself a drink. "It seems I am a married woman now."

With a subtle gesture, I extend my hand at them to show them the black diamond ring that's wrapped around my finger. Selene grabs my hand and inspects it carefully, looking at all the details. But it's Sasha's reaction that catches my attention. Her eyes glint a little more, and the corners of her lips are slightly tilted upwards.

"Don't you want to see it, Sasha?" I ask when she doesn't take a second glance at the ring.

"No thanks, I'm good."

"You know this ring," I accuse her.

"Maybe," she says without a second of hesitation.

"You didn't even have to look at it to recognize the ring."

"Honey, it's an Anna Sheffield *and* a black diamond at that. I would recognize those anywhere."

"Liar, you know *this* ring!"

"Focus, ladies," Selene stops me, knowing that we won't get far if we continue like this. "Please, I'm dying to know how it is that you got married before me."

"I was drugged?"

Sasha throws a dubious glance my way.

"Daniel thinks I was, but we are waiting for the test results to come in. But the thing is, it seems like there were some people getting married on the boat. The captain was officiating the ceremonies, and Emi Saito thought it would be a good idea to do that."

"Wait, Emi Saito as in the Japanese driver who will be racing for Cavaglio Nero next year?" Sasha asks with her journalistic tone.

"How do you know?" I ask.

"I am a journalist, it's my business to know these things."

"Plus, she's dating João, and he is going to be one of our drivers next season," Selene clarifies.

"When did this happen?" I ask, puzzled.

"This morning," Selene says. "Now, let's get back to our previous topic," she urges.

"Well, I thought it was a pretend wedding with no legal consequences, but as it turns out, I am a married woman now, and my darling husband wouldn't grant me a divorce."

"I get why you would want a divorce. But, at the same time, why *do* you want a divorce? There is a story there... And the chemistry! We have all seen the chemistry," Selene utters, puzzled.

"What you have seen is daggers flying each time I look at him. I hate him!"

"I think you are confused, Miriam."

Like a reasonable adult, I cover my face with my hands and grunt. This would be a great moment for the earth to swallow me and spare me all the trouble of coming to terms with my feelings for Daniel. Everything is so complicated when it comes to him.

"Whatever the two of you started in Monaco last year has had an impact on both of you," Sasha says, ignoring my current crisis. "I don't know what happened, but you obviously have a shared story, and you guys need to sit down like adults and talk about it."

"It's not that easy," I protest.

"'Hi Daniel, I think I hate you because of what you did,'" Sasha says, mimicking my voice. "'Miriam, I have issues. I like being alone but you, you make me want things—'"

"Do you know what happened in Monaco?" Selene mouths, looking at the blonde sitting on the other side of the couch.

"Nope," Sasha answers, emphasizing the *p*.

"Liar! You are his best friend," I say.

"Selene is yours and she doesn't know either," Sasha points out.

I don't say it, but that is an excellent point. Not even Selene knows what happened that night. Gosh, sometimes I feel like I don't even know it myself. Why did everything explode out of proportion the way it did?

"I don't know if I should feel insulted or relieved," the redhead says, and Sasha gives her a puzzled look. "I hate that she hasn't told me what happened, we are practically sisters, but at least Daniel didn't tell you either, which means whatever it is, they need to solve it without us."

"All I need are divorce papers."

"Why would that be a problem?" Sasha asks.

"I told you; he won't grant me the divorce," I repeat, starting to freak out. "He says that he is a team owner now and that I could ask for half of his assets. He is not willing to risk everything he's worked for."

Selene starts to babble something about how there must be a law written somewhere about this, but I am not listening to her. Instead, I am looking at Sasha. She is a master at ruling her expressions and covering her feelings, but I just know based on the way she is chewing the inside of her cheek that she knows more than she's willing to admit.

CHAPTER SIXTEEN

Burton: *Felicidades.*

Youngster: Why are you congratulating him?

Burton: He is a married man now.

Youngster: Who is the unlucky victim?

Youngster: OMG! I just googled it!

Burton: I thought you would have wanted your close friends at your wedding…How wrong I was…

Youngster: Wait, you consider us close friends?

Youngster: Philip, you have a heart!

Burton: I consider him one.

Youngster: You are just mad at me because I signed with Cavaglio for next season.

Burton: I am blocking you.

...

I leave the group chat on seen, not minding what the two drivers have to say about my new nuptials. However, I send a quick message to Philip, asking him to pay me a visit at the Cavaglio offices in the afternoon. Philip might be retiring soon, but I have an offer for him, and I know he's more than ready to take it.

The wait isn't long. My agenda is filled with boring meetings all morning long, and for lunch, instead of treating myself to a delicious meal, I go to my doctor's appointment. When my doctor kindly reminds me to pay a visit to my gynecologist, I answer him with a polite smile and ignore his recommendation like I have done for the past two years. Everything feels fine, and I don't feel anything strange going on in the place where my breasts used to be, so I am skipping it again.

With the sun hiding behind the buildings, Philip Burton strolls into my office as if he owns the place. I will give it to him, he has probably been here more often than I have. It doesn't matter which team you like or what driver you support, any person who has been following the sport has heard his name. He is one of the oldest drivers and one of the greatest in history. Philip only has four world championships, but he could have won more if luck had been on his side more often.

"Straight to point, Conte. My soon-to-be wife is at home picking out flower arrangements and I am eager to go back to her."

"I see Philip Burton can be tamed, after all. It only takes one determined woman to do it," I tease, knowing I'm playing with fire.

"Why am I here?"

"I hear you are retiring."

"Does it matter?"

"It does to me."

"Why? You just signed two drivers."

"And I am a team principal short."

Philip opens his mouth, then closes it.

I smirk.

Not many people manage to make the villain of Formula One feel uncomfortable or out of place, but I have, and it's only taken me three sentences.

"You're crazy, Daniel."

"No, I am just building a new team, and I only want the best in it. *You* are the best, Philip. You are ancient in the sport and, paired with your good results, it grants you the status of a legend."

"Drivers don't become team principals, at least not right away," his lips say, but his eyes tell a different story.

He wants this. A new challenge.

"Tell me you can't direct a team and manage drivers. Tell me you can't make strategic decisions and read races better than anyone else. Tell me you don't know every single word in the regulations better than your wedding vows."

"I don't do media and public relations," he points out.

"Let me worry about those."

"Can I think about it?"

"Do you really need to think about it?" I ask, challenging him.

"No." I don't need to be a fortune teller to know what comes next. "Congrats, you got yourself a team principal."

"You aren't the only one who enjoys a challenge."

"Be ready for the press shitstorm," Philip warns.

I have known for months that Philip was retiring. It's been the worst kept secret in the paddock, and that has given me time to prepare. It's no secret that the press viciously hates Philip Burton, or at least they act like they do. Because making him the villain has sold them more headlines than they care to admit.

I flash Philip a devilish smile. "Let them come for us."

"You are a sick bastard, Conte."

"I enjoy righting people's wrongs."

This is an unorthodox way of doing things. No driver wants to become a team principal right after they retire, they usually take some years of sabbatical, try out other racing series or simply enjoy their family and well-deserved rest.

Philip Burton isn't like any other driver.

He is made to smell fuel every weekend, to order, to command, and, most importantly, to compete. He might be ready to step out of the car, but he isn't ready to leave the garage.

"Welcome to the team, Philip."

"Not so fast," Philip halts me, right as I'm about to shake his hand and seal our deal.

"Are you going to complain about the paycheck?"

"No, but since you insist on bringing up the topic, I won't do it for less than six million."

"I'm a generous man."

"Talent costs money."

As far as team principal paychecks go, this isn't the highest. But it's a hefty amount, especially for a team that is reconstructing itself. Lucky for Philip, I am willing to pay that much to get him on board.

"What other conditions do you have?"

Philip grins with satisfaction. "I want to race during the off-season. Nothing huge, I already have a triple crown, but I would like to do the race of champions with João next year," he explains, and I can't help but think how lovely it is that after almost twenty years in the sport, he has finally found someone he likes in his teammate.

"Anything else?"

"The Dakar, since it's during off-season." I give him a skeptical glance. "You said this was an unorthodox move, and it is."

"If the calendar allows it, you can do those two," I give in without much of a fight. "We can review other series on a yearly basis."

"You are a crazy man," Philips declares.

Any other team owner would probably try to find better outcomes that fit their interest more: lower their paycheck, cancel their plans of racing, get someone more experienced as a team principal… I don't plan on doing any of that. Philip works best in an environment that treats him well, and I am willing to provide that. I am willing to create an environment that takes care of others, where people feel secure and equal. But most importantly, I want an environment of winners, and Philip craves the same thing.

"I am an optimistic person, and I expect the best of you, Burton."

"You got it."

CHAPTER SEVENTEEN

I decide to work from the Cavaglio office on Thursday, but I only go there in the afternoon, which is way later than my usual working hours. Given that, right now, there is no mystery to be solved, I won't need that many hours to get my job done. Now, I just need to figure out what I am going to do with the extra time and my life.

The first thing I notice when I walk up the steps of the subway station and cross the street to the office building is a crowd of people standing in front of it. It's not strange for people to pass by and stay at the entrance, hoping to see their favorite drivers, but it's usually smaller crowds during business days. Unless there is someone important here today.

"Excuse me," I call out, trying to move towards the door.

"Do you work here?" a young child asks me.

"She's a woman," his friend, a kid standing next to him, cuts in. "She is probably a secretary, or she is married to someone in there."

My jaw drops at the statement of the boy who can't be older than ten. I am fairly used to these types of comments coming from fifty-year-old men, but he is just a child. He shouldn't say things like that, but it looks like he hasn't been educated on the topic of sexism yet.

I can spare five minutes to teach the child the basics.

Bending down a little so I am at eye level with him, I tell him, "I promise if you study enough, you might get a job in one of these companies. It doesn't matter whether you are a man or a woman, it's all about what's up here," I say, pointing at my head.

"Really?" His eyes glint with excitement. "I want to be a driver like Philip Burton when I grow up."

"Sure," I encourage him, hiding a smirk. "But first you need to learn to treat women well. We are all equal and deserve to be treated the same way, no matter our gender or background. Besides, if you treat someone badly, no matter if it is a man or a woman, they could stop you from becoming a driver. I could stop you."

"How?" the kid asks with skepticism.

"Women make big decisions behind closed doors. Now, be a good kid and cheer for women too," I tell him as I stand up, ready to leave.

It takes me some time to make my way through the crowd and walk through the glass doors leading into the building. My eye catches a familiar figure before I have a chance to get to my office.

"I see Emi Saito is gracing us with his presence today," I say cheerfully while I walk in his direction.

His face lightens up when he sees me.

"Miriam," he purrs. "You are a ray of morning sunshine."

"What are you doing here?" I ask, suddenly in a good mood.

"I had my seat fitting," he explains. "And I thought I would stick around and wait for you to make an appearance." Emi is a shameless flirt, and he is known for approaching both single and taken women. That's not my style but to each their own.

"Why were you waiting for me?"

"Just wanted to give you a new contact card."

I give him a confused look.

"To replace the one you lost," he explains.

"What makes you think I lost it?" I tease him.

"I gave it to you on Friday. It's been almost a week, and you haven't contacted me. It's obvious that you lost it."

"I didn't."

"I don't believe you," he says, offended.

Instead of answering, I grab the card from inside my phone case where I stored it and show him that it's still with me. "I am sorry, but I have your card."

"You know you could have told me you lost it. Now I know you don't like me enough to go out with me."

I blush a little at the effort he is making, but the truth is, I am not interested in him. Not like that. Not enough. My head is filled with confusing thoughts about someone else. I look down at my hand, right where Daniel's black diamond rests. I might not be in a serious relationship with the man, but whatever is going on between him and me feels more important than the possibility of dating an F1 driver.

Emi is about to open his mouth, but I stop him before he can even start.

"I am a married woman now."

"So, the rumors are true?"

I show him my ring finger. "Seems so."

"I don't know about Daniel, but I am not a jealous man, and I am willing to share if you want to be shared. Anyway, I must leave now. It was a pleasure seeing you, Miriam."

In a swift move, Emi puts on a black pair of shades and throws a cap over his dark-bluish hair, an attempt to be able to leave the premise unnoticed. However, the masses outside are already waiting, so when he walks out the door, chaos reigns, and not even the noise-cancelling doors can do anything to keep out the screams.

I am ready to turn around and finally make it to my office, but I bump into something behind me before I can do so.

"The ink on our marriage certificate hasn't even dried yet and you are already flirting with other men."

"That's because I haven't signed any papers."

"Still, there is nothing more sacred than the 'I do's' shared between a husband and wife during their wedding vows."

"You mean the ones I can't remember?"

I am certain that Daniel is about to snap at me, but instead, he inhales sharply and waits a moment, almost as if he was counting down to ten to soothe himself.

"Can I help you with something?"

"Yes, pack your bags. We are going on a trip tomorrow."

"I am not going on a trip with you."

"Yes, you will," he insists.

"You will have to take me screaming and kicking."

I don't like the look in Daniel's eyes when I say the last part. It's a look that screams 'try me,' and I know he will drag me to the end of the world if that's what he wants to do.

CHAPTER EIGHTEEN

One would expect that Miriam would know when to pick a fight and when to drop one that she can't win after the events of the past week. However, when she opens her door still in her pajamas and with her hair wrapped in a satin scarf, I know she has picked the wrong fight.

"Please tell me you've packed your bags." I decide to give her the benefit of the doubt at first, but I know by her sleepy face that she literally just woke up.

"I told you I wasn't coming with you."

"Very well."

I let myself in, walking past her and somehow finding my way into her room where I expect the closet to be.

"Hey!" I hear Miriam call out from behind me.

I don't really care. I'm a man with a single objective in mind, and that is packing my wife's bag for her. I open the closet and find some basics for her to wear: a pair of jeans, a blue satin blouse, and some neutral tops. After all, we are only going for a night. Then, I open multiple drawers.

"Stop!" she demands.

"Why? Afraid I might find your vibrator?" I tease, opening one of the drawers painfully slowly to give her a chance to stop me.

Miriam doesn't disappoint and sprints in my direction, only to shut the drawer. She doesn't notice it, but her hand lands on mine, and I am forced to realize this is the first time she has touched me since I put my ring on her finger.

"That's my underwear drawer, you perv."

"It's nothing I haven't seen before."

Miriam grunts, frustrated.

"Pack your own bag if you don't want me to see what's inside your drawers, *my little swan.*"

"I told you; I am not going anywhere with you."

"And I am warning you, stop pushing."

"Or what?" She always defies me.

"Or you won't like what happens next," I warn.

Miriam lifts the corner of her mouth, then falls on top of her bed, crossing her arms over her chest. It's obvious that she won't go down without a fight, but neither will I.

We make it to the airport an hour later. Miriam is still dressed in her pajamas after throwing a series of tantrums that I did not want to deal with. During that hour, I have thought multiple times about whether this is really worth the hustle, but I know it is, and I am willing to make her feel uncomfortable if I get to see her smile by the end of this.

The chauffeur parks in front of the private jet and opens the backseat passenger door. Miriam makes no attempt at stepping out of the vehicle, so I do what any sane person would do. I push her out of the car, and she practically falls to the floor.

"Daniel!"

"You keep saying my name in such an aggravated manner, but it sounds a lot prettier when you are moaning it."

I know she is about to throw another tantrum, but I don't give her a chance. I bend over and lift her off the ground, only to throw her small body over my shoulder. It takes her three seconds before she's screaming, kicking, digging her nails into my back.

"Honey, if you want to mark me, then at least dig your nails in deeper," I encourage her.

"I am going to kill you," she threatens.

"I would love to see you try."

The flight attendants try to conceal the surprise written all over their faces when they see us boarding the jet.

"We are newlyweds," I try to explain.

At the same time, Miriam screams, "Someone save me!"

Instead of getting furious and losing my temper, I spank her ass, "Behave, darling. People are watching us."

"Drop me," she insists.

"As you wish," I answer, letting her fall on top of one of the seats. "Are you going to behave now?" I say, leaning over her, my hands on either side of her seat.

"I will never forget this, Daniel."

"I would be disappointed if you forgot any of our moments together."

One of the flight attendants approaches us. "We are ready to take off as soon as you are."

"Please don't let us keep you. I promise my wife will be on her best behavior," I reply, taking the seat next to Miriam, whose satin scarf has fallen off her head, allowing her locks to fall all over the place.

"Where the fuck are you taking me?"

"Istanbul."

Miriam's eyes go wide, shining with a mix of emotions. "You are taking me to the FIA Prize Giving Ceremony?" she guesses.

I nod.

"Are you joking?"

"Nope."

Then, Miriam does something I wasn't expecting. She grins, and almost instantly her smile turns into laughter.

"You should have started with that."

"It was supposed to be a surprise."

"You wanted to surprise me?"

"Yes."

"Thank you," she says and plants a kiss on my cheek, and my stupid broken heart decides to go ahead and skip a beat, maybe even two.

CHAPTER NINETEEN

It's only when we make it to the hotel room that I realize my darling, loving husband's plan has two flaws. I give him the benefit of the doubt and hope the queen-sized bed in the hotel room was an honest mistake and not a plan to get me into our marital bed. But the second and most important error is that I don't have a gown for the gala, which we're attending in less than six hours.

"I can't believe you took me here and forgot to tell me to bring a dress," I reprimand him. At the same time, I scroll through my phone, trying to find stores nearby where I can find a last-minute dress.

"Who says I forgot about the dress?"

"The lack of a dress in this room would suggest none of us brought one on the trip."

"Do me a favor, Miriam." I look at him expectantly. "Get ready and let me worry about the dress."

"Do you even know my size?"

"You are 5'8, but usually you say that you are 5'6 because it makes you feel smaller and more feminine. You would fit a 36 size in jeans but buy them in 38 because you are more comfortable in those. You like tight fits to accentuate your figure, unless you are working, then you opt for loose shirts, size M." My jaw almost drops. "Did I get it right?"

I move my head up and down, nodding.

"Then, it's settled. Get ready. I will be back with a dress before you are done."

I want to throw a shoe at him, but I contain myself instead. A part of me is furious at him, at the trip, and at the one bed situation that I will have to deal with later. But I am also thrilled to be here. To be attending this event.

When it comes to F1, I've been lucky and enjoyed more commodities than most fans have. Being best friends with a woman who works in the sport has its perks. I have been getting an insight into what happens behind the curtains through Selene, got to visit the garage, go to the GPs and afterparties, and spend time with some of the drivers. But I was never allowed to take part in the more formal events, the ones I have always wanted to attend.

As much as I like a good party and some careless fun, I also love these galas because at events like this one, alliances are built.

If only it weren't for Daniel…

Now I will have to experience another first that will be forever linked to him.

First gala.

First marriage.

First obsession.

First rejection.

In an attempt to distract myself from the fact he's the only man to ever reject me, I take a peek at my suitcase, trying to find the make-up bag Daniel so kindly decided to toss in there. And that's when it hits me, the third flaw in my husband's plan.

"Fuck's sake!" I blurt out, absolutely enraged, and before bothering to take a second look at the suitcase, I rush out the door, grabbing my white sneakers and sprinting towards the elevator. I am still trying to put on my second shoe when the doors open to the lobby. With my one shoe unlaced, I rush towards the reception, skipping the line.

People complain behind me, but I am a woman on a mission.

"You see this hair?" I ask, pointing at the curly mess. "It needs to be straightened, and I forgot my hair straightener. Please tell me your hotel has one," I practically beg.

"I am sorry, the only thing I can offer you is a hair dryer." My eyes start tearing up, and I am so close to losing it. "Is there anything else I can help you with?"

"No."

By sheer will, I manage to pull myself together and avoid becoming a crying mess in the middle of the hall.

Two hours later, Daniel comes back carrying a giant bag, which I assume holds my dress. I am still sad about my lack of a hair straightener, but curiosity to see what is inside the bag cheers me up. I jump out of bed, ready to sprint to the door, but Daniel puts it behind his body.

"Give that to me."

"You look divine," he says, then places a kiss on my forehead. I am startled for a second, not used to his lips on my skin, and most importantly, the way it makes me feel. I would love to say that I hate it, but the truth is, I feel comfortable, safe even, and the butterflies in my stomach jump happily at the warmth of his touch.

"You are my husband; you have to say that even when my hair is a mess," I say, trying to shake off my feelings.

"Nobody forces me to say anything I don't want to." Daniel leans down. "You look divine, whether my ring is on your finger or not."

"Thank you," I manage to muster.

Daniel doesn't answer, instead, he hands me the red bag carrying the dress I am supposed to wear. "Here is your dress. Selene picked it out."

"Selene knew we were coming?!" I ask, even though I know that Philip almost always attends this event, be it as a champion or vice-champion.

"Of course she did. We are sitting at the same table."

For a moment, I am speechless. It's hard to be mad at him for not granting me a divorce, and it's even harder to pretend I hate him when he compensates by taking care of me this way.

"Don't be shy. Try it on," he encourages me.

"Wait here."

CHAPTER TWENTY

Instead of wearing the white, crisp shirt everyone will be wearing at the gala, I put on a black one underneath my suit. Then, I wait for what feels like an eternity.

"Miriam, it's been half an hour. Do you need help?" I ask.

"One more minute."

"You have had thirty of those," I call back, leaning against the door.

By some miracle, the door finally opens, and I almost fall. Somehow, I manage to avoid the crash, but my heart doesn't. It lands right at Miriam's feet, where her golden dress cascades around them. My eyes travel up her body, enjoying the peak of her leg through the slit of the dress. And the view keeps getting better. The satin dress hugs her curves perfectly, and the corseted part at her chest makes her small breasts look exquisite.

"You like it?" she says, spinning once to let me see the back of the dress, which is low-cut with a golden cross identical to the one tattooed on my back hanging down her spine.

I am so lost in her, I can't answer the question. Her hazel eyes are surrounded by some accents of golden makeup, and her brows are a rich brown that makes her features sharper. Then there is her hair. I have always loved her hair, but the way some loose curls fall down her forehead, right under her eyebrows, is doing things to me that I cannot explain.

"Daniel?"

"I love it."

Her eyes shine bright, and a part of my heart softens at the pure smile she gives me. Miriam doesn't know it, but she holds all the control. She is the one in power and the only thing keeping her close to me is a marriage contract.

"Really?"

I nod.

I notice her eyes scanning me, confused for a moment when she sees the black shirt.

"Shouldn't you be wearing a white shirt and a tie?"

"I enjoy breaking the rules." I wink at her. "Besides, gold shines best against black, and I like it when you shine."

Because that is exactly what I want her to do. Shine.

I want her to shine as brightly as the sun when she is next to me, more than she already does on her own. I want her to be happy when she is with me, but also to contradict me every single step of the way, to scream and shout. Most importantly, I also want her to feel safe.

I want everything. But I will allow myself nothing.

Miriam

The gala is more stressful than I anticipated.

Hundreds of cameras are pointed at us. We have managed to catch as much attention as the drivers. Everyone wants to know about us: our wedding, our romance, Daniel's plans for the team....

The only time I feel any sort of relief is when I see familiar faces in the crowd of people. Philip and João make an appearance, side by side, with Sasha and Selene strolling in front of them. The first is wearing a long silver dress with millions of shiny rhinestones attached to it, making her look like an ice queen. Meanwhile, Selene wears a pale pink flowy dress that makes her look like a tiny forest fairy, especially because of the way her red hair is styled into perfect braids.

"Let's take a picture together," Selene suggests.

Everyone takes their designated positions next to their partners. Selene and Sasha fit perfectly against their significant others, while I struggle to find my place next to Daniel.

"Breathe," he instructs.

I am ready to do so, but when his hand slips onto my waist and his breath hits my neck, I become hyper-aware of him. It's impossible for me to breathe, but against all odds, I make it through and almost run towards the table in search of some bubbly alcohol to calm my nerves.

Luckily, I am sitting at the same table as the girls, and even if there are a hundred cameras around the room, it feels like any other Friday night out with the group. It's just fancier and people are getting shiny trophies in the background.

I don't pay much attention to them until it is João's and Philip's turn to go on the stage and receive their F1 trophies. This is Philip's second season in second place since he came back to the sport, but by the smile on his face, you would think he just won his fifth world championship.

The host hands him the trophy and then a microphone, and for the second time in his career, Burton doesn't shy away from the cameras, and is ready to blurt his heart out like he did when he won his third World Championship.

Looking at Selene, he says, "I was a reckless kid when I started karting and enjoyed giving my mother heart attacks whenever I found ways to make my kart go faster than it should.

Sadly, she isn't with us anymore, but my soon-to-be wife has a similar reaction whenever I come up with crazy ways to overtake my competition during a race."

The crowd laughs, and a tear slips from Selene's eye.

"I love this sport and have given almost two decades of my life to it. At this point, all of you are probably bored of seeing me on your TV every other Sunday. Years ago, I decided I needed a break from the car and the circus that F1 can be at times. Now, I think it's time to leave room for the younger generation and become the best at something new." Philip pauses and looks at João. "It's time for you to break my records." The crowd bursts into laughter, but João looks up at him with admiration. "And it's time for me to become the best husband."

I stop looking up to the stage when I notice Selene trying to hold back her tears next to me. "Don't cry," I whisper.

"I am so proud of him," she whispers back.

I pet her arm, trying to offer some comfort until Philip makes it back to our table, but my attention is stuck on Sasha, who is looking at João the same way my friend looks at Philip.

Is that the look of love?

"Are you growing feelings?" Daniel jokes.

I would like to say that his comment doesn't bother me, but it does, and I don't even know why. Forcing a smile, I excuse myself and make my way to the bathroom. My blood is boiling, and my mind is spiraling because of Daniel's words. I have feelings, I know that. I am a sentimental person. But am I growing feelings for him?

Did you ever stop having them?

Breathing exercises don't calm me, and my heartrate only increases when the door opens, and Daniel makes his way inside.

"What are you doing here?" I ask, confused.

"I was waiting for you," he says, taking a step towards me, forcing us inside the bathroom again. With a swift move of his hand, he locks the door, never taking his brown eyes off me. I gulp, noticing how the energy in the room shifts.

"You didn't have to."

"You are driving crazy, my little swan."

"Grant me the divorce and you can get rid of me," I taunt him. My heart is beating so hard against my chest that it's becoming harder and harder to breathe.

"No way in hell am I letting you go without a fight."

I look at him with anger in my eyes, knowing damn well there is nothing that can force his hand. Daniel has set his mind on this marriage, but I am not willing to give up my freedom so easily.

"What is it you want from me?" I say, anger lacing my voice.

Daniel takes a step towards me. "Everything."

I have heard how certain things trigger people into madness. Perhaps, my marriage is my trigger because I do what only a crazy person would. I grab Daniel by his jacket and push him towards me. For a moment, I am sure he is about to push away, but then I see the way his eyes lock onto mine, and even though I started this, it's him who puts his hand on my neck squeezing it in that perfectly balanced way that blurs the line between pain and pleasure.

Our lips meet with an intensity that has been building for way too long. The kiss isn't a stolen or one that I will forget. It's raw passion, a storm of unspoken emotions, desire, and longing that neither of us will ever recognize.

Daniel tugs on my curls in that delicious way that forces me to tilt my head up, giving him better access to my mouth. We kiss for what feels like an eternity, my hands moving across his chest and biceps, and Daniel does the same. His touch is soft at first, caressing my arms, leaving a trail of goosebumps where his fingers meet my skin, only to then find his way to my cleavage.

"More," I moan with need.

Daniel obliges, and with a soft pull from his hand on the fabric, my bare breasts slip out of the corset.

Daniel's eyes glint with desire.

"These are new," he announces with a low voice and then tugs playfully from one of my nipple piercings. I want to answer, but my mind gets foggy when his wet tongue licks the sensitive spot on my breasts while his other hand squeezes my other nipple hard enough to send a wave of pain through my body. "Makes me wonder what else is new," he says between licks.

There is a spot on my breast glistening with his saliva and the look of that makes my core clench with anticipation.

"A lot has changed since Monaco."

The air shifts again, and I can feel Daniel tensing, and very slowly, he distances himself from me, both physically and mentally, leaving me to wonder what the hell I have done this time.

"This was a mistake," he declares, already moving away from me and towards the door. "I will see you at the hotel."

CHAPTER TWENT-ONE

Daniel doesn't lose time. As soon as we make it past the threshold into his apartment, his mouth lands on mine, and I moan at the pleasure of his hands over my body. We kiss for a little while, and then he takes my coat off, throwing it on the floor.

His lips leave my mouth and move towards my ear, biting on my lobe while I make quick work of the buttons of his white shirt. It surprises me when I notice his entire torso is filled with colorful tattoos.

When I am done unbuttoning his shirt, I allow the tip of my finger to explore the art on his body, but my eyes are focused on the eagle in his chest. The wings are spread in a way so the upper part of the design covers the scars underneath his breast.

Daniel's muscles flex as soon as my finger caresses his stomach where the word "damaged" is written along the left side of his V-line, while the other has the word power on it. I am lost in the tattoos on his arms, neck, and legs. But what catches my attention the most is the reflection of his back in the entry door mirror. His back is completely tattooed, a cross covering the biggest part and the words, "It is mine to avenge; I will repay" written across it. The words remind me of a quote I once heard in Sunday school. There is a line like that in the bible, about God's wrath and how he would make sinners pay. It's fitting. After all, Daniel might be a god like that, making people pay for their sins.

The man holding me stops kissing my ear and looks me in the eyes. For a second, I am sure he's just catching his breath before devouring my mouth again, but instead, he guides his hand to my throat and squeezes, lightly chocking me. The sensation is so inhibiting that I can't help but smile at him. Then, his thumb presses inside my mouth, and like the good nasty girl I am, I suck, biting slightly on his digit, enjoying the look of desire he gives me.

Finally, he kisses me again, but he doesn't linger at my mouth. With a swift move, he gets rid of my clothes and as soon as there is nothing but my lacy black bra in his way, he starts moving his fingertips towards my breast. Daniel knows exactly what he is doing, gracing my skin with his fingertips, and leaving a trail of goosebumps wherever his skin touches mine.

My core tenses in anticipation and a soft moan escapes my lips when he finally tugs on my bra, letting my breasts bounce free. The feeling of his tongue against my nipple is pure ecstasy, and I have to bite my bottom lip to keep from screaming.

"Lista para una noche inolvidable?" he asks if I am ready for an unforgettable night in Spanish.

"How come you speak Spanish?" I ask, my voice faltering.

"I was born in Argentina," he explains.

Usually, I don't care about the men I sleep with, not their background, not their origin, not their past, that is a story for breakfast, but with Daniel, it's different. I need to know everything about him, I crave the information, no matter how stupid it is to do so right now.

But Daniel doesn't give it to me, I sense the switch in the mood between us. We have gone from passion and heat to something cold and undesirable, but both of us try to do our best to ignore it.

"Is your family from there?" I ask, ignoring the signs.

"I don't speak about my past," he says, and then kisses me again, trying to rekindle the spark.

"Sorry… I didn't know it was a touchy subject."

"It isn't," he snaps.

I stay silent, but my face gives me away.

Then Daniel gives me a look, and he doesn't need to say the words for me to know that whatever we thought would happen tonight, won't be happening at all.

Sex used to be a problem when I first transitioned. I knew I was attracted to women even before I transitioned, that never changed. But I used to be afraid of intimacy with girls, thinking they would reject me as soon as they found out that I didn't have a dick.

I have overcome all those fears almost a decade later. God only knows the perversions I have indulged in, and the things I have tried. However, all those relations and experiments were with people I had no strings with, and most of those women agreed to only have a one-night-stand.

Nobody has ever dared ask me about my past, my roots, my family, or my origins, and that is for the best. I am not willing to commit to anyone, and most importantly, I am not willing to share my scars.

Miriam is threatening that.

The worst thing is that my stupid broken heart is bouncing inside my chest, willing to share my entire story with her. Why her? Why is she special? I have known her for less than twelve hours and not for a single minute since this morning have I been able to get her off my mind. It's ridiculous.

I don't do the obsessive and possessive boyfriend thing.

Strike that. I don't do boyfriend.

There is always a first time, *my stupid heart screams, but I know best. There can't be a first time for me. I can't open up, not to her or anyone. Damaged doesn't even come close to how fucked up I am.*

I have a hundred scars on my body. That's what my tattoos cover. But they can't cover the most painful of them all. They can't cover the one my family left in my heart. Simply ripping that organ apart would have been less painful. If your family can treat you the way mine treated me, then how can a person you meet on a random day be any better?

The answer is that they can't be.

That's why I can't stand the idea of a relationship. That's why I do sex, not intimacy. It's the reasons why a night like tonight has gone from pleasure to pain.

"We don't need to do anything you don't want to do," Miriam starts, but I am too far gone in my own thoughts.

"You need to leave."

"Excuse me?"

"I said leave," I repeat.

"Are you serious?" Miriam says, incredulous.

"Yes."

"What the fuck is wrong with you?" she says, working on assembling the clothes that are scattered on the floor, making sure she doesn't leave anything behind.

"Everything," I answer in an attempt to scare her away.

I try not to look at her while she rushes to get dressed. I try to get rid of her lingering smell in my nose, but I know that's the least of my problems. I might have met her only hours ago, but something inside of me longs for her, and I know that no matter how hard I try, I won't be forgetting her any time soon. Miriam doesn't know it yet, but I do.

She holds the keys to break me harder than my family did.

"Don't ever talk a word about what happened tonight."

"Is that a threat?" she asks.

"It's a demand."

"Unbelievable." She sighs.

"It's for the be—" I don't get to finish the sentence.

Miriam is already making her way out of my apartment and slamming the door so hard, the walls tremble once she's gone.

I am doomed to an eternity of loneliness inflicted by myself.

CHAPTER TWENTY-TWO

The clock ticks while I wait in the dark. Seconds pass, then minutes, then hours. The later it gets, the more nervous and worried I am. It's well past two in the morning when Miriam finally strolls into the hotel room with the grace of a newborn giraffe. I am five feet away, but the smell of alcohol makes it to me.

"I thought something had happened to you," I reprimand her.

Miriam jumps in place and squeals with surprise when I turn the lights on.

"Jesus Christ!"

"Where were you?"

"Don't you have ways to know that?" she counters, taking her heels off and throwing them my way, across the room.

"Well, I'm asking you," I reply. Of course I ordered my security team to stay near her and call me in case something happened. I knew where she was every second, but I want to hear what she was up to from her lips.

"Grant me the divorce and I will tell you."

"That's not going to happen, little swan."

Suddenly, Miriam turns around and walks towards me so quickly that I don't see what is about to happen. In the blink of an eye, she is in front of me, her hand raised in the air, colliding with my jaw a second later.

"Don't ever call me that again."

She is already turning around, but I grab her wrist before she can get far. Tugging on her wrist, I force her to spin until she is only millimeters away from me and forced to look me in the eyes.

"You don't complain when I call you *my* little swan."

Miriam gives me a defiant look.

"Talk to me," I encourage her.

"You don't want to talk about what happened in Monaco? Fine. But then I don't want you to use the nickname you gave me that night." She sounds exhausted, and her usual flame is almost extinguished. "I am going to bed," she declares.

I am left in the room alone while Miriam takes a quick detour to the bathroom. In the meantime, I take my clothes off and make my way to the master bedroom where the bed is. It feels almost criminal to move the pillows out of the way to slip into the perfectly made bed, but I do it anyway, for the second time today destroying something beautiful.

"What do you think you are doing?" Miriam asks.

"Trying to sleep?"

"Not in my bed."

I sit down, pushing the comforter to the side. I don't miss the way Miriam's eyes trace my torso, inspecting every single one of my abs and tattoos, reminding me of the night we spent in Monaco and how her finger traced them, becoming the first and last person to ever do so.

"There is only one bed in this room, Miriam."

"You can take the couch."

"Just go to bed."

"I am not sharing anything with you, let alone a bed."

"Please," I hear myself begging.

"If you won't take the couch, then I will."

"Very well," I start.

"Then—"

"Take the couch," I finish.

Her mouth opens, then closes, and opens again. I am about to burst into laughter, but I am pretty sure Miriam will kill me if I do that, so I contain myself and remain silent. She grabs a pillow from the bed and one of the blankets, and then tries to arrange them on the tiny couch in front of the bed, attempting to get as much comfort as she can. Eventually, she gives up and falls asleep curled up with the blanket covering everything but her tiny feet.

It's almost painful looking at her like that, curled up in a tiny ball so she won't fall out of the couch. Regardless, I still wait a couple of minutes in the dark, waiting for her breath to change before I go over to her corner and carry her into the queen-sized bed. Miriam is exhausted enough that she doesn't notice the shift from the hard and uncomfortable couch to the softness of the mattress, and I am thankful for it, not willing to engage in another pointless fight.

I stay there, sitting on my side of the bed and looking at her sleeping form for a while. I don't know how long I stay there, watching her sleep without a care in the world.

"I am sorry, little swan. But I promise, I will make it worth it for you."

CHAPTER TWENTY-THREE

I wake up between the softest and warmest sheets, but that isn't even the best part. The best is the smell; that manly scent that has become painfully familiar.

"Conte," I say, suddenly waking up to the realization of my own thoughts.

It doesn't take a genius to realize I am in bed and not lying on the ground where I fell asleep last night. Moving at a painfully slow pace, I turn around, expecting to see the man from my nightmare on the other side, but, luckily, I am alone.

"I didn't sleep with you." Daniel's voice comes from the other room. "I just carried you to bed. You looked painfully uncomfortable in that corner last night."

Slowly, I stand up. The morning cold grazing my naked legs makes me shiver. I feel better than I expected after last night's countless drinks, the only side effect a slight headache.

Small wins, Miriam.

"We need to talk," Daniel says, strolling into the room.

"I don't have anything to say to you."

"Well, I do, so sit down and listen."

I open my mouth to object, but he puts his thumb under my chin, forcing me to keep my mouth shut. I hate to admit it, but the contact of his skin on mine makes me shiver again, flashes of last night's kiss filling my mind at the same time.

"Please, give me five minutes."

I take moment to look at his glassy eyes, the red around them, an indication of his sleepless night.

"You have two minutes."

"I suggest an alliance," he says, instantly catching my attention. "One year, that's all I ask of you. One year of us pretending to be a loving couple in a happy marriage."

"Why?"

"I just bought a company that is on the verge of breaking, and the last thing I need is instability on my side," he starts. "The people on the board already doubt me, coming from new money and a background in journalism. They dislike me for many things and one of them is me being a transsexual man, who doesn't fit into the box of what they want a team owner to be. But, with your help, I can fit the box a bit better. I can be a man who believes in marriage and is in love with a *woman*."

"You are missing something."

"Trust me, I am not."

"Yes, you are missing that I am a black woman. If they don't like you for being trans, what do you think they will think about you being married to me?"

"It's too late for that. We are already married, darling."

I stay silent for a while, trying to wrap my mind around the words he just uttered. I have known for a while that he was born a woman; Elizabeth told me as she pieced the puzzle together. Still, it catches me by surprise, because this is the first time since I have known him that he has referred to himself as a transexual person.

To me, it changes nothing.

Daniel is Daniel, no matter the sex he was born with. No matter what genitals he was. Hate him. Love him. The line is thin, but that part of him changes nothing about the way I feel about him.

Over a year ago, he was a crush.

Two weeks ago, I hated him.

Now? Your guess is as good as mine.

"What do I get out of this?" I ask, indulging him.

"What do you want?"

What do I want? That question has been taunting me for weeks now. Who am I? What do I want? What am I doing with my life?

My whole adult life, I have been surrounded by money, it's part of my job, but I have never been one of those people who only think about how much they have in their bank account, nor do I stress about it. I have been lucky and comfortable enough that I didn't have to worry about it. But things could be better, and money means many things. It means time. Time to become myself again. Maybe to discover what truly drives me.

"My time is worth a million."

"Done," Daniel says without hesitation.

"And," I continue. "Twenty percent of Cavaglio Nero."

"Why?"

"You bought the company to make a difference. I want to make a difference too. A team where people like us feel safe and valued. A team that pushes for more female drivers on the grid, and a team whose monetary transactions don't end up tearing families apart."

Daniel takes a moment, but not as long as I thought he'd need to think about my demand.

"Seven percent," he counters.

"Thirteen."

"Deal."

"Imagine the faces of the board members when they see a trans man and a black woman making the decisions," I add, extending my hand.

Daniel gives me a devilish smile. "The older ones might get a heart attack."

"Exactly."

"It's settled then."

Daniel extends his hand towards mine and shakes it, sealing our new partnership. It might be the rest of the alcohol from last night making the decisions and maybe tomorrow, I will regret it, but right now. I don't care. It feels like maybe I'm getting back on track.

It might take blackmail and an unorthodox marriage of convenience, but I am on my way to do something that matters and something where I can help people again.

CHAPTER TWENTY-FOUR

Two weeks have passed since our trip. Miriam has been flying low the entire time, not wanting undesired attention. She comes in and works her scheduled hours, then leaves again. I have noticed that she has been working from nine to five, rather than pulling twelve-hour shifts, since our arrangement. She has been smiling more recently, taking breaks to get coffee with her friends, and the dark circles under her eyes are gone. I am relieved to see a glimpse of the old Miriam again.

Rumors are already spreading around the office. Thankfully, nobody has accused Miriam of fucking her way to the top, or else I would have had to figure out a way to fire them without getting a complaint from Human Resources. The rumors are more about my lack of competence, considering I was willing to give a share of my company to my new bride, but the heart wants what it wants, and mine might be broken, but it does need Miriam nearby anyway.

These few weeks have also been productive for me. All new contracts have been drafted and sent. João and Emi are officially on board with us, and the new car is already looking beautiful. The boys have been testing it in the simulator, and the engineers have made some adjustments to tailor the car perfectly to their respective driving styles.

Now there is only one last contract waiting to be signed, and that's the one that makes Miriam the owner of thirteen percent of my company. It's been sitting on top of my desk for two days now, and still, I cannot bring myself to call her into my office and make her sign the paperwork. A part of me feels like I am buying her and I don't want that. I want her to be free and independent, just like she is, but the cold and more analytical side knows this is only business and it will benefit her in the long run.

She gets a million and a part of my company.

But I won't get her. Not in the way that matters.

I pick up the phone and dial my assistant's number.

"Bring Lefebvre in," I instruct him.

"Your wife, sir?"

"Yes."

I hang up the phone, ready to write my last email before Miriam comes into my office, but the damn device rings again.

"What?" I ask, hoping to hear my secretary on the other end.

"She will get hurt. Everything you love gets hurt."

A distorted voice fills the room from the phone speaker, and before I can say anything and demand answers, the line goes silent.

"What the fuck?" I curse through my teeth.

Unease settles inside my body. I have never been afraid of anyone in my life, except for that one time. That's what being kidnaped as a child and sold to rapists does to you. I don't negotiate with criminals.

I kill them.

And whoever is behind this macabre joke will pay the consequences of their own actions. They are fucking with the wrong person.

Finally, Miriam makes it to my office. The first thing that strikes me is that her natural locks are on full display. I love it. The curlier her hair, the freer and more herself she feels. Miriam is still a long way from where she used to be, but the fact that she is styling her natural curls in the office shows she's feeling comfortable and secure.

And if her hair wasn't enough to do undecipherable things to me, her outfit does the rest. A short pink dress that makes me feel jealous of every man who has seen her in it, paired with an oversized blazer that hides her figure only slightly.

"See something you like?" she teases.

"Yes." Miriam smirks, so I add, "The painting behind you."

Her cocky expression disappears, and she turns around to face the new Cabanel hanging on my wall.

"Please tell me it's a replica of the Fallen Angel and not the original painting."

"Why? Are you going to tell Elizabeth?"

"Tell me the real painting is hanging in the Fabre," she insists.

I smile.

"Please," she begs.

"I like the way you look when you beg, *my* little swan."

Miriam rolls her eyes at me. "You have until the count of three to tell me the truth."

"This is the original one." Her mouth forms a perfect O-shape, and my mind drifts to the things I would do to her if only I gave myself the chance. "I bought it from the museum yesterday."

"How much money do you have?"

"More than enough to last generations."

"How?"

"I am not willing to share all my secrets."

"Not even with your wife?" she says in a seductive tone.

Miriam leans over the table, and her dress falls in that perfect way, granting me a peak at her lacy bra. If I were a different kind of man, this would be all it took for me to share a couple of secrets with her, but I am not.

Alas, I come up with a different answer. "Not even with her."

Miriam doesn't take no for an answer, instead, she walks around the table and takes a seat on top of it, right in front of me, distracting me when she closes her legs extremely slowly. I don't break eye contact, but I wish I would.

"So, why did you bring me here, if it's not to share your secrets with me, darling husband?"

"I called you to share my company with you."

"Are you serious?"

I nod.

"I thought you were backing out," she admits.

"I am a man of my word, and a deal is a deal."

I stand up from my chair and tower over her. Miriam tilts her head up. We are so close to one another that I can feel her breath on my skin. It's almost painful being this close to her and not being able to touch her. It's even worse when her lips open involuntarily, her body taking the reins.

"What are you doing?" she whispers.

"This," I say, leaning even closer and bringing my hand behind her, only to grab the folder she has been sitting on this entire time. "You are sitting on the contract."

Embarrassment covers her features.

"You could have asked me to move."

"Why? This is much better."

She doesn't answer. Instead, she tries to snatch the contract out of my hand, but I am faster than her and bring it behind my back.

"Not that fast, señorita," I tease. "You are getting thirteen percent of my company as soon as you sign, and a million once 2026 comes to an end."

"Am I doing the next week for free, since you only asked for a year of my time?"

"A man could only wish that his wife wanted to be with him out of love," I mutter, pretending to be offended.

"A man could, but you are so much better than other men. You are Daniel Conte," she reminds me, and I can't help but smile at her words.

Damn right I am.

"So, what is the catch?" she asks.

"There are terms and conditions for both of us."

Miriam raises a brow at me.

"It's three simple rules. First, you are required to attend formal events and some races with me next year. Second, things are staying platonic unless we are required to kiss in front of cameras and such."

"And third?"

"For the time being, we are not allowed to be seen with other people." There is more than one reason why this is important to me. For one, people wouldn't take us seriously if we were seen dating other people. But, more importantly, I don't think I can see Miriam with anybody else.

"What if I am dating someone else?"

Jealousy hits me hard. "Are you dating someone else?"

"Do you care?" she taunts me.

"As your loving husband, I do."

"Jealous, Conte?"

"Are you or are you not?" I drag out the words.

"Maybe."

"Answer the question, Miriam."

"Why is it so important to you?"

I move closer to her. So close that there isn't a single inch of space between us. Then, with my right hand, I grab her chin, forcing her to look right into my eyes. There is a slight tremble in her lips. Good, she knows I am serious.

"As long as that black diamond ring is wrapped around your finger, nobody but me gets to touch you."

Miriam gulps.

"Have I made myself clear?"

"Yes."

"Good girl. Now sign the papers."

Miriam

My inner voice is begging me not to sign these papers and run away. The other is looking at the contract in Daniel's hand with desire.

One year. One million. Thirteen percent of Cavaglio.

It takes me a minute, but when I snap out of my trance, I snatch the contract out of Daniel's hands and scan every single word carefully, especially the part where the three rules are stated.

1. Attendance of Events:

1.1 Party A agrees to attend formal events and specific races of the Formula One 2025 season with Party B over the next year.

1.2 If Party B cannot attend an event, they will promptly inform Party A with a valid reason.

2. Platonic Relationship, Except for Public Occasions:

2.1 Both parties agree to keep their relationship platonic.

2.2 However, in situations requiring public display of affection, such as in front of cameras, Party B agrees to engage in activities required in the moment such as kissing, holding hands, and gestures of affection.

3. Exclusivity:

3.1 During the term of this agreement, both parties agree that they shall not engage in dating or romantic relationships with any other individuals. This includes, maintaining any romantic, intimate, or exclusive interactions with other persons, whether in public or private settings, for the entire duration of the contract.

3.2 This exclusivity is effective until the agreement ends.

If I do this, I am committing to a fake relationship for an entire year, and that isn't even the worst part. It's the person I am committing myself to and the way I feel for him.

Do I hate him? Do I like him? Check and check.

The distinction between love and hate is blurry, like a hazy horizon. Lust only adds more complexity to my feelings for him. That's where hate fucks come into play, which is exactly what happened during the gala two weeks ago. I was ready for it, almost begging. Maybe all I need to do is hate fuck him to get him out of my system…

No, Miriam.

Focus.

Desire and lust must be the logical reasons why I feel so drawn to him. Why when he leaned into me before, showering me with his rich cologne, I felt like I needed to kiss him. It's intoxicating in a way I have never felt before, but I won't give in. I am afraid that if I do it, I will lose myself in him, and I am on the path to rediscovering myself.

"Any questions?" Daniel murmurs from behind me, and a shiver runs down my body. He is so close that I can barely breathe, but my decision has been made. I turn around and grab a pen, then sign the contract. "I knew you were a smart girl."

"Congratulations. You have gotten yourself a wife."

No snarky reply leaves his mouth and when I look up at him, I notice he isn't even looking at me. Instead, his attention is on the building outside his window, and he looks focused and almost worried. The air between us shifts and Daniel seems more cold than usual.

"I don't think ignoring your wife is the best way to keep her happy," I announce when he doesn't pay me any attention.

Still, Daniel doesn't move. His hand is pressed against the window and his eyes are filled with concern.

Then, all of a sudden, he turns around and screams, "Get down!"

Things move too fast. Before I know it, Daniel is jumping, throwing himself on top of me, and rolling us underneath the desk. Then, the most terrifying sound I have ever heard penetrates my ears.

Gunshots.

The windows explode after the third shot, and a wave of crystal rains through the office space, none of them hitting me though. Daniel's body is covering mine entirely, protecting me from the glass.

My body is shaking uncontrollably, and fear dominates me, but in the middle of the terror, Daniel manages to press his lips to my forehead.

"Nobody will put a finger on you," he whispers.

I manage to nod, or at least I think I do.

The alarm goes off in the office and through the now shattered windows, I can hear police sirens. My mind knows help is on the way, but my heart is still beating against my chest uncontrollably fast.

"Look at me," Daniel instructs, but I am still to shaken up too follow any instructions. "Little swan," he says with a sharp tone. "I wasn't asking. I was demanding."

Miraculously, his demand works on me, and I fight out of my trance of fear and look up, instantly getting lost in the richness of his brown eyes.

"Now breathe." I obey and take a big breath. "Good girl," he praises, still standing on top of me, and I can feel my core clenching at his words.

What a terrible moment to be horny.

"Distract me, please," I beg him.

"Are you having a panic attack?"

I want to fuck you and I can't so I need a distraction, is what I want to say, but instead, I say, "I might be."

"Do you really think I will let anyone hurt you?"

I shake my head.

"The world will be diminished to fire and ashes if someone ever lays a finger on you without your permission."

I gulp at the intensity of his words. "What if you are the one who hurts me?"

"I would never hurt you."

I lift a brow.

"Not intentionally," he clarifies.

"We might need couples therapy then," I joke. "I think we keep hurting each other in unintentional ways."

Our conversation comes to an abrupt end when someone slams the door to the office wide open and three cops make their way inside, their big bulky boots crushing the glass spread on the floor.

"They are alive!" announces one of them.

"And it's not thanks to you," counters Dani, standing up and lifting me off the ground with him. "Why has it taken you so long to come?"

"We were securing the perimeter, sir."

"Next time, secure the permitter and send a team upstairs. *My* wife and I could have been killed. Did you find whoever is responsible for this?"

"No, sir. Our team is still scouting the zone."

"Then scout faster!"

"Yes, sir."

The officer doesn't get a chance to answer and before I can stop Daniel, he is pulling on my wrist and leading us out of the office and into the elevator.

"What are you doing?" I ask.

"Taking you somewhere safe," he replies.

"Where is that?" I press, hoping for some clarity.

"We have to add a new clause to our contract," he declares out of the blue.

"Don't ignore me and answer my question!"

"You are moving in with me," he states matter-of-factly, his eyes looking at me with an intensity and determination I haven't seen before.

"Like hell I am." Defiance fuels my response.

"Someone just tried to kill us. I am not taking any chances."

"So what?" I shoot back, incredulous. "Your solution is to make me a prisoner in your house?"

"At least until I have a permanent solution."

"Please tell me you are joking," I plead.

"Do I look like I am joking?" he challenges.

"I will escape you, Daniel."

"You can try, little swan, but I will cuff you to my bed if I need to."

"You wouldn't dare."

"I would if that is what it takes to keep you safe."

CHAPTER TWENTY-FIVE

I never thought I would hate Miriam's screams, but it looks like I do. The woman has the lung capacity of a professional diver. No matter what I say or do, she doesn't stop screaming as I take her to my apartment.

Let me put it this way, it usually takes me twenty minutes to get home from my office. Today, it's taken me almost an hour. Kicks, screams, a police officer stopping us on the way because Miriam insisted she was being kidnapped, and a slap in my face from her later, we made it home. I'll admit that it surprised me she resorted to the slap as a last resort, rather than doing it while we were leaving the office, but I won't question her logic.

"I am so going to kill you!" Her eyes flash with fire.

"I bet there are laws against killing your husband," I retort, a smirk playing on my lips as I meet her anger head-on.

"At least I will be free from you in prison," she snaps back.

"Are you willing to change your jailor for another?" I provoke, enjoying the twisted dance of power between us. She is mad, I get that. I understand she wants her freedom, but I am willing to take it away from her if that's what needs to be done to keep her safe.

"Anything to get rid of you."

"You hurt me, little swan."

"You don't have feelings," she says, dismissing me.

"Lies, my heart bleeds for you." I mock.

"Then let me go!"

"You can be free inside these walls." Miriam grunts with frustration, but I ignore her. "Now, come. I will show you the penthouse and your room."

I start walking towards the penthouse. Every corner is bathed in pristine whites, creating an ambiance that feels almost clinical. Crystal accents catch the light, casting delicate reflections that dance across the polished surfaces, adding a touch of opulence to the minimalist space. The open kitchen is also white, like the rest of the house, featuring marble countertops that look as if they have been untouched, as if waiting to finally be used. Then, there are the four rooms, each adorned with sleek furniture. The beds are crisp and neatly made.

"Are you sure you live here?" Miriam asks.

"Why would you ask that?" I ask, even if I know exactly what she means with that question.

This house isn't a home. The absence of personal things or sentimental touches says as much. I haven't grown attached to anyone – except Sasha – or anything, and this house is a testament to that. It doesn't show signs of life, even if I have been residing here for almost a year now.

"Do with it whatever you want," I state.

"What do you mean?"

"Make it look like you live here."

"Why? I don't."

"Do you really want to go there again?"

"Don't you?" she teases. "Are you tired of my screams?"

"Those aren't the kind of screams I want to listen to, Miriam," I say, not thinking twice about my words before they make it out of my mouth. It seems my life has become a constant contradiction whenever this woman is concerned. I say something and then do the opposite. I draft a contract that prohibits us from having any romantic relations but then I am also dying to be with her. That is the kind of power she has over me.

"Then those are the only screams you will get from me."

A devilish smile makes it to my lips. "Is that a dare?"

Miriam takes a step back, but she clashes with the wall behind her, and I use the chance to cage her in, putting my arms right over her head.

"You wouldn't put a finger on me."

"Not unless you beg."

"I won't beg."

"Your body is telling a different story. But, don't worry, I will only touch you when you beg with your body, mind, and soul, little swan."

"That will never happen."

"The game has already started," I state matter-of-factly.

Miriam's face turns red, anger in her eyes. For the first time since I have met her, I am afraid that maybe I am pushing her too far. Why do I keep doing these things to us? I keep taking steps forward, even when I know I will never be able to give her what she wants. Then, I take seven steps back, and the game starts again.

"You are a toxic asshole," she states, as if finishing my line of thought.

"I am sorry," I say sincerely.

Miriam blinks, confused. "Say that again."

"I am sorry."

"Do you have a fever?" she asks, raising her hand to my forehead.

Now I'm the one who is confused.

"Are you okay? Do you need me to call Grace?"

"Ha. Ha."

"Excuse me for worrying about you. Daniel Conte is known for being ruthless and unapologetic."

"You sure you aren't confusing me for Philip Burton?"

"I guess you boys have been spending too much time together."

"You know what? Let's go to the kitchen, have coffee, and talk like civilized people," I suggest.

"I didn't know you could do that."

"Neither did I." *At least where you are concerned.* "But I am willing to try."

Miriam

I glance at Daniel as he brews the coffee, the smell of the toasted beans filling my nostrils, while my eyes follow the trail of his tattoos over his muscles. Then, he places the mugs on the pristine white countertop of his kitchen, and I'm grateful for the distance the island provides. Now that the adrenaline from the gunshots has completely faded, and I have managed to partly tame my anger, I find myself confused and unsure of how to process my own emotions, which shouldn't be a surprise given this is my new normal around Daniel.

For the first time, I was desperate for him and his touch, and I couldn't even blame it on alcohol. It was all me, and that's the part that scares me the most.

"Speak," I say.

"You are not a prisoner, Miriam."

"A golden cage is still a cage, Daniel."

Daniel huffs, tired of the constant sparring. I don't blame him. I feel the same. I am tired, so tired that all I want is to give in and cease the fighting. But stepping down isn't in my nature.

"You are not my prisoner," he insists. "I just want to keep an eye on you. Keep you safe. You are free to roam the house, go to the office, meet your friends, do whatever you want."

"And couldn't I have done it from the comfort of my own house?"

"No. Someone just tried to kill you, Miriam!" he screams at me. I jump, surprised at his tone and the look in his eyes. He's usually so stoic and void of feelings, but now, fear is painted all over his features. "I can't let anyone hurt you, and if your sense of freedom is what has to be paid for your security, then this is what has to happen."

"Do you even hear the bullshit you're saying? You won't let anyone hurt me, but you have hurt me countless times over the past year, Daniel. You are the one hurting me now, incarcerating me because of what?"

"Because I can't handle the thought of you being dead."

The pain in his voice is so palpable that even my heart skips a beat. I only know half of Daniel's story, but I can imagine this need to protect me has something to do with it.

Against my better judgment, I stand up and close the space between us to hug him.

"What are you—" he says, but I cut him off.

"Shhh."

We stay there for a couple of minutes. At first, Daniel feels stiff in my arms, but eventually, he loosens up and slides his arms around my waist, resting his chin on my head.

"I will stay here if that helps you sleep at night," I start, still pressed to his chest, trying to soothe his fear. "But I have conditions. You will give me a key so I come and go as I please." I feel him nodding against my hair. "You will grant me space whenever I need it. I mean it. You don't get to follow me around all day long. I am more than happy to take a security guard or Sasha with me from time to time, but I will need space."

"Thanks," he finally says.

"That's what friends are for."

"Is that what we are?"

"Yes. It's what we are now. No more games, Daniel."

I take a deep breath, my words hanging in the air between us. An unexpected revelation that manages to surprise us both. Friendship is not a choice I make lightly, it's not even the choice I want to make right now. But for the sake of this fake marriage and making it to the end of this year completely sane, it's a necessary step.

"Friends it is, little swan."

CHAPTER TWENTY-SIX

"*Donde* están, *meninas?*" the familiar voice asks.

My body convulses, limbs tangled in an agonizing torment. A cold sweat grips me. My heart races, its erratic beats echoing the chaos in my mind. I try to scream, but my mind traps the sound. Every nerve in my body feels like it is on fire, and I am suffocating in the darkness of the same closet I was in when I was a child.

"RUN!" my sister screams.

"*La puta madre!*" our captor curses.

"Run, Daniela! Run!" my sister repeats.

Everything inside of me wants to run. To do what she's asking, but I'm paralyzed, stuck in place. The fear of death isn't what's holding me back; it's the fear of what comes after. The child from the nightmare wants to escape so badly… But the adult I am today can't.

Why would I escape? There is nothing but misery and death waiting for me. Going back home isn't an option. My sister won't be there to protect me from my parents. They labeled me an aberration, banished me like I was some kind of monster when my father couldn't beat the man out of me.

The pain of those thoughts is suffocating, more than enough to jolt me awake in the middle of the night. My heart pounds, and I gasp for breath, clawing my way out of the darkness. Sweat rolls down my forehead as the room comes into focus, and the echo of my sister's desperate plea lingers like a ghost in the corner of my mind.

Another night, another brutal reminder of the worst day of my life.

The door to my dorm slams open, and Miriam bursts in, looking like she just ran a marathon.

"What happened? Are you okay?" she asks.

I can't answer right away, still trying to shake off the nightmare, and, just when I am ready to answer, my focus slips away as I realize Miriam is standing in front of me in *nothing* but an oversized t-shirt, the moonlight making her dark skin glow.

I'm momentarily entranced by her beauty, her legs shimmering in the silvery light, and the buds on her nipples making an appearance under the soft cotton shirt.

Snap out of it, I tell myself, but my mind takes a minute to catch up with the command.

"Just a nightmare," I finally manage to mumble.

Miriam strides towards the bed with a slow, almost seductive sway, and I can't help but notice every enticing detail of her - the graceful movement of her hips, the shine in her hazel eyes, the way her dark curls cascade over her shoulders, and those fucking piercings on her nipples.

I stay still, my heart pounding as she gracefully settles on the edge of the bed near me. She looks at me with a worried glint in her eyes, and the residual fear from the nightmare fades away.

"That doesn't answer my question. Are you okay?"

"What does it matter if I am not?"

"It matters," she whispers, tugging a strand of hair behind my ear. "You matter, Daniel."

Her words take me by surprise and, for a moment, I feel vulnerable. Miriam doesn't have the slightest idea of the hold she has over me. If she did, she wouldn't say that.

"You don't mean that."

"I do. Friends matter."

That fucking word.

Friends... That's not what we are.

That's not what I want us to be.

"Friends take care of each other," she continues.

The warmth in Miriam's eyes takes on a mischievous glint, and a sly smile plays on her lips, signaling that something is about to happen. Before I can fully grasp the situation, she leans into me, her hand pressing against my chest and her pointy fingernails scratching my bare skin. Gently, she pushes me backward onto the mattress.

My pulse quickens when she gracefully swings one of her long legs over me and sits on my lap. I am filled with anticipation, and the playful spark in her eyes is enough to send my heart into cardiac arrest.

"I thought you wanted to stay friends."

"I told you. Friends take care of each other," she repeats, leaning towards my ear, then she bites my lobe, sending a wave of pleasure over my entire body.

Out of reflex, my hands find their way onto her legs, and my fingers dig into the flesh of her ass.

"Miriam," I groan.

"I know you want me."

"You don't want me," I answer, frustrated.

"Lies," she says, leaving a trail of kisses on my jaw.

My eyes roll back, and I clench my teeth with so much pressure that it's almost painful, but not enough to distract me from the sensation of Miriam on top of me.

"You have three seconds to stop me," I warn her.

Miriam ignores me and plants a kiss on my chest instead.

"One…" Her lips keep trailing down. "Two…" I warn.

"Let me help you," she says again.

"Fuck it," I curse.

I can't resist Miriam's particular brand of mischief. Desire that lingers in the air. I can practically smell the lust and need coming from both of us. Miriam doesn't stop me when I press my hands against her neck. She is eager and smiling when our lips finally clash. Desire and longing explode inside me. I can't stop myself from enjoying the soft moans that come out of Miriam's mouth whenever I bite her bottom lip.

The world fades away, and all I can think about is the sensation of her. The way her hands move over my body, one tugging on my hair, while the other explores my torso. Or the way she very softly humps my leg, rolling in circles with her hips.

"Daniel," she moans.

The way she tilts her head up with her lips slightly parted is one of the most sensual images I have seen in a long time. This woman is going to be my fucking death.

"Daniel," she moans again, but this time, my name is more urgent. Suddenly, she stops kissing me, stops trying to get satisfaction from my body and instead, she shakes my shoulders. "Daniel!"

The worst thing happens.

I open my eyes.

Daylight filters into the room through the window.

Miriam isn't on top of me.

She isn't kissing me.

"Wake up. We are going to be late for work, Daniel."

She's waking me up.

CHAPTER TWENTY-SEVEN

Me: I am pretty sure I just woke Daniel from a sex dream.

Ginger Bestie: Did you join him?

Blonde Dread: I hope she did.

Ginger Bestie: The sexual tension between them is unbearable.

Me: You are seeing things.

Ginger Bestie: Am I?

Blonde Dread: I am seeing the same thing…

Me: Then go to the same therapist, you two are crazy.

Ginger Bestie: You are the only delusional person here.

Blonde Dread: Just fuck. It will solve the problem.

Me: I am very content with the way things are right now, thank you very much.

Blonde Dread: When was the last time you had sex?

Me: Why does that matter?

Blonde Dread: Six months?

Me: I am leaving the chat.

Blonde Dread: I will ask Daniel to buy you a vibrator.

…

The office becomes my sanctuary, which might seem strange considering there was a shooting here less than twenty-four hours ago. The entire staff has been allowed to work from home while the police investigate what happened and the glass in Daniel's office gets replaced.

Daniel…

That man is going to drive me crazy.

My mind wants to hate him with every single fiber of my body, and there are plenty of reasons for me to do so. I have spiraled in them since the day he came back into my life. It's almost impossible to keep him out of my head at this point. The blood on his hands should be reason enough for me to move to another country and enter a protection program. And if that wasn't enough of a reason, the way he imposes rules over me, like making me move into his apartment, could be another red flag. But then, there is the way he keeps going hot and cold on me, kissing me fiercely one second and pushing me away the next.

And what bothers me the most is that I don't even mind. I keep going back for more and taking the crumbs he gives me. I keep daydreaming about what comes next. Will it be the bad or the good side he shows me, and will he give me another memory that I will treasure in secret for the rest of my life, or will I have to find a way to finally tune him out of my thoughts?

What makes Daniel so special that even if my mind wants to hate him, my body can't stop feeling the pull?

"You suck," I whisper, looking down at my heart.

"Just if Philip's standing in front of me," Selene says happily, strolling into my office as if it was the most casual thing ever, Sasha walking behind her.

"Fuck's sake!" I whisper-scream. "You almost sent me into cardiac arrest, you sneaky, little pervert."

"You will be fine, and if you really have a heart attack, then it's a good thing your husband is one of the richest men in the world and can afford the best doctors."

"Look at you, talking about my husband, when your fiancée is Philip Burton," I tease her.

"And mine is João Querinho," Sasha announces. She raises her left hand to show her ring finger displaying a gorgeous and elegant emerald stone that might be the exact same shade as João's eyes.

"Shut up," Selene says, grabbing Sasha's hand to take a closer look at the ring.

"When did this happen?" I ask.

"Last night. We were talking about what happened to the two of you," she explains, looking at me. "And everything that happened two years ago and then suddenly, João popped the question!"

"How long has he been planning it?" I ask.

"He told me he bought the ring a couple of months ago. Apparently, he saw it at a jewelry store during the Brazilian GP race weekend and has been carrying it around ever since."

"That is so adorable," Selene swoons. "Do you have a date?"

"Nope, but I want a winter wedding, so we will do it next year."

"Well, since we are talking wedding dates… I have something to tell you," Selene starts. "Philip and I have decided to move up the wedding and have it on the twenty-first of December before the season starts again."

"You really are in a rush to get married. The twenty-first of December is in like ten days," I point out.

"Well, there is another human being pushing for that date," she says shily.

"Who? Just say the word and I will take care of them."

"Sasha, "I reprimand her.

"What?"

"Stop! Nobody is hurting mini-P," Selene replies.

"Mini-P?!" Sasha and I ask in unison, confused.

"Mini Philip. I am pregnant," Selene announces.

"Shut up!" I say, standing up and throwing myself at my best friend. "I am going to be an aunt?"

"Yes." She laughs, a single tear of happiness escaping her eye.

"How long have you known?" Sasha asks.

"It's still very early, but with the stress of the wedding, we wanted to share the news with you already."

"Philip is going to be such a great girl dad." I laugh.

"Well, I don't know the gender yet."

"Congrats. You are going to be amazing parents," Sasha tells her.

The hours fly by after Selene's and Sasha's announcement. I have tried to keep my mind occupied all day long, trying to escape some uncomfortable thoughts. In fact, I have been so focused on my work that it's not even five in the afternoon, and I have already finished everything on my To-do list.

What do I do now? I have been successfully escaping my thoughts and avoiding Daniel so far. I need to do something that will keep me away from them for a little bit longer.

"Mrs. Conte." The voice of Daniel's assistant drags me out of my thoughts. "Mr. Conte would like to know when you are going home?"

"Max, right?" I ask the blonde guy who can't be older than twenty-three.

"Yes."

"I am still using my maiden name, and you can call me Miriam." I smile at him. "Also, tell my darling husband I will go back home when I feel like it."

"Miss."

"Yes?"

"Would you mind if I rephrase it? I would like to keep my job, even if Mr. Conte is almost as scary as a serial killer when he is angry."

What does that man have that makes all of us want to stay close to him?

"A wallet dreams are made of? Charisma? Power? Good looks? I am guessing you married him for at least one of the above, if not all."

"Shit, I wasn't supposed to say that out loud."

"Your secret is safe with me, Miriam," Max says. "You might not have figured out why just yet, but it's obvious that Mr. Conte and you have a deep connection. You just had to see the way he was protecting you yesterday. A real prince charming, if you allow me to be so frank."

I laugh at the last part, flashes of Daniel protecting me yesterday filling my mind. The way his voice calmed me, and his touch made me feel safe even if there was a gun pointed at us.

My marriage might not be perfect, or even a real one. I probably shouldn't have any feelings for my husband, and, to be fair, whatever feelings I have are, at best, complicated and confusing. The man makes me question my entire existence whenever he is around.

This entire day, I have been trying to escape feeling pity for myself. My friends are falling in love, getting engaged, and having babies in a conventional way, and those are things that I won't have. Not with Daniel. He has robbed me of falling in love conventionally with my partner, of the possibility of having a marriage full of happiness and experiencing that perfect honeymoon phase the movies talk about. He has robbed me of dreaming with my partner about the future and looking forward to the endless possibilities of our life together.

But he has given me my bite again. Life was in black and white for a while, and maybe, right now, I am not seeing it through a rose-colored lens. But life's colors are shining bright, and, even if I hate Daniel, he makes me feel like nobody has ever made me feel before.

"Tell him I am on my way home."

CHAPTER TWENTY-EIGHT

Youngster: I am getting married!

Burton: We are pregnant!

Youngster: Why does everything have to be a competition?

Burton: We are F1 drivers, our life is surrounded by competition.

Me: You are a team principal now.

Burton: You can take the car away from me, but you will never take the fuel from my veins.

Me: Congrats on the marriage and the baby!

Me: If you hurt Sasha, I will kill you.

Me: You will make a great dad.

Youngster: Why does Burton get a compliment?

Me: Do you think he won't be a great dad?

Youngster: Won't you tell me I will be a great husband?

Burton: Congrats. Don't mess it up João!

...

The news of Sasha getting married doesn't catch me by surprise, but still, it's capable of bringing out a smirk on my otherwise stone-cold expression. I knew it was coming since the day João showed me the ring. I am only surprised he has been able to keep it a secret from her for so long.

I close my laptop and lean against the comfortable leather chair, closing my eyes and taking a deep breath. Working from home today was a terrible decision. The penthouse has always felt like a cold and empty space, but I can't help but feel the coldness ten times more now that Miriam has spent a night here. Sure, she has been around for less than twenty-four hours, but there are already signs. The smell of her perfume is still lingering in the house, and there is a cup with a lipstick stain on the kitchen counter that I have not even dared to clean away.

I open my eyes again, trying to shake the uncomfortable feeling, only to notice the velvety box of Miriam's black diamond ring on top of the desk. It feels strange to see it there and not feel its weight in the pocket of my jacket after having been carrying the damn ring for almost two years.

"Devil darling! Your wife is home," I hear Miriam shouting from the entrance.

Out of instinct, I hide the box the ring used to live in before Miriam's finger became its new residence, then leave my study. I go down the stairs and find Miriam in the kitchen, cleaning the cup of coffee she left there this morning.

"I know I forgot to clean the cup this morning when I left for work, but you have been home all day… You could have taken care of it," she says in a soft voice, even though I can hear a tint of fake indignation in it. However, my brain is stuck somewhere else. She called my apartment home. "If you are the kind of man who thinks women should do the cleaning, let me tell you, you are very wrong, and I will not be putting up with that kind of shit."

"Do you really think *I* would think that?" I say, taking the cup out of her hand to clean it with a sponge and soap. Miriam looks wide-eyed at me, without words. "Exactly."

"I didn't see you at the office today."

"Sharp as always, Mrs. Conte."

"Don't call me that."

"If I can't call you by my name, my little swan, then tell me, Miriam," I say. towering over her, the water still running over my hands in the sink. "How should *I* address you, because you are sure not giving me many options."

I notice goosebumps appearing on her arms, and I can't help but feel some satisfaction from it.

"Miriam. Just Miriam," she finally answers.

"Couples usually have pet names for each other."

"Then you can use 'little swan' in public."

I nod. "How was your day at the office?"

"Selene and Sasha came by. One is pregnant and the other is getting married." I notice a glint of sadness in her eyes, but I decide to ignore it for now. We both have had a hard week as is, and I don't enjoy seeing her in any kind of pain, but the emotional one is even worse because I don't know what to do to help her, and that breaks another piece of my heart.

"I know," I reply.

"How do you know?"

"The boys and I have a group chat."

"Wait. You are telling me Philip Burton is in a group chat with you and João?"

I nod.

"You're kidding?"

"Why would I?"

"Philip hates people, especially the press. You are people and you used to be a journalist. When did you two become close enough to be in a group chat?"

"You know he's also my new team principal, right?"

"Ha! Ha!" She fakes a laugh. "Spill it, Conte."

"I've always liked the guy. He is one of the greatest of all time, but he has also had the worst luck and worst career choices when it came to choosing teams and getting teammates. Besides, I've never faulted him for hating the press, in fact, I understood him. Most people don't know how to act like a normal compassionate human in this industry. They don't see a face, only benefits and headlines."

"So, you have a heart, after all," she notes.

"I don't play nice with people who don't deserve kindness."

"Do I deserve it?"

I don't hesitate. "Yes."

"Then, you should stop hurting me. I know you don't do it on purpose, but I can't keep up with your mood swings. You are worse than me during my period, and, trust me, I am a very hormonal gal. Start stocking up on chocolate, junk food, and tissues."

"That bad, huh?"

"Wait and see, roomie."

"I never meant to hurt you, Miriam," I almost whisper, looking down at her gorgeous face. I can't help but see a glint of hope in her eyes.

I will never be able to give her everything she wants.

"I realized that today. A part of me knows you don't hurt me on purpose, that's why I still haven't drawn a line, but I will if you keep crossing my boundaries, Daniel."

"I am trying my best to be a good friend and make this year bearable, after all, a year with an unhappy wife can pass very slowly."

"On the note of happy wife, happy life, I am going to my apartment now to grab some things if I am to live here permanently."

"No," I say.

"Happy wife, happy life," she reminds me.

"My answer remains the same. You can't go now."

"Why?" she demands.

"How do you know you won't be followed? That someone isn't waiting for you there? That you won't be harmed?" I ask, paranoia getting the best of me.

"You are being overprotective."

"And I will continue to be exactly that, if it allows me to ensure your safety, Miriam. Someone tried to shoot us yesterday. I am not taking any risks where it concerns you."

"But I need my things," she protests.

"Grab my credit card and replace them with new things," I reply, and in a swift move, I grab her phone from the pocket of her trousers.

"What are you doing?"

"Putting my credit cards on your phone," I say, adding the American Express I know by heart into her wallet app.

"Daniel, you are being unreasonable," she points out.

"What do you want me to do?"

"Meet me halfway."

I sigh. Then, I massage my temples with my fingers, trying to come up with a solution. I know I am being unreasonable, but I can't help myself. Not where Miriam is concerned. Especially now that I don't know whether it's her or me being targeted.

"Sit down," I order.

"Don't order me around," she replies, pointing her finger at me.

"Please." I sigh. Thankfully, she does as I ask and takes a seat. "Remember Grace?" She nods. "She called me with your test results today."

"Were they positive?"

"Yes," I start. "Someone put Rohypnol in your drink."

"What is it exactly?"

"It's a sort of drug known as benzodiazepines. It produces drowsiness, sleep, and amnesia, amongst other things."

"So, it's a rape drug?" she asks, her face turning three shades paler and worry covering her eyes.

"Yes."

"Were we all drugged at the party?"

"Emi Saito was negative. I asked the nurses from the team to run a full blood test with the excuse of him needing to be clean of any substance abuse before joining the team since he is a newcomer, and Grace tested me. I was positive too."

"So, whoever did it was targeting me?"

"I can't be sure. Maybe you just had more drinks than us, or maybe they were just targeting women at the party. Whatever it is, I am not letting this repeat itself. Nothing bad is going to happen to you, got it?"

"Don't make promises you can't keep."

"It's not a promise. It's a statement."

CHAPTER TWENTY-NINE

Sleep doesn't always find me at night, and when it does, it's restless and plagued by my nightmares of the past. Last night, however, it completely eluded me. The entire bottle of whiskey I consumed after Miriam left the apartment didn't help one bit. I am so drunk that I haven't even had a hangover yet.

And that's when the best of ideas hits me.

I grab my phone and unlock it, quickly passing my fingers over the blurred screen until I find the messages app and write to Sasha.

Me: I am conmning ovrr

I don't waste time trying to correct the spelling errors, nor taking a shower and getting ready to leave the house. I just grab my keys and wallet, and throw a pair of shades and a cap on to hide my identity. It's a sunny day outside, and the streets of Monaco are still crowded with fans. The last thing I need right now is for one to recognize me when I am smashed and in terrible shape.

I decide to take a walk and clear my head. Sasha only lives a couple of blocks away, normally it should be a fifteen-minute walk. In my state, I will probably take half an hour, but time is the only thing I have right now.

I stumble through the narrow, glamorous streets of Monaco, the blend of wealth and opulence swirling around me. I am too drunk to notice the people until I make it to one of the main streets.

There is the sound of laughter and the clinking of glasses, a stark contrast to the shadows within me. My blurry vision fixates on a couple, hand in hand. She is a blonde, probably Miriam's age, and he is a young man who seems to have a wallet big enough to satisfy her expensive tastes. In one hand, he carries designer bags probably filled with trinkets and excess.

It's like a slap in the face.

People are starving, lives are getting wrecked, children are being kidnapped, and, here they are, living in their stupid bubble of glamour and excesses. I hate them.

I hate that I hate them, but not for being excessive.

The more I soak in the scene, the more I realize my rage isn't about their dumb spending—it's my own damn jealousy.

I'm here, all alone, stewing in regret for treating Miriam like garbage last night. The truth's eating at me, and I can't escape it. I shoved her away because I'm a coward, scared as hell of getting close to anyone, terrified of falling for someone who might actually matter.

I tear my gaze from the nauseating display of love, determined to avoid drowning in their happiness and my misery. A few steps ahead, a jewelry store catches my attention.

Normally, I wouldn't give it a second thought, but something about the glinting ring in the showcase grabs my attention. The band is a shiny, silver one, adorned with stones that I assume are diamonds. Yet, what really catches my attention is the black diamond in the center. Its marquise cut. The dark elegance standing out in contrast to the gems surrounding it.

I stride into the store, the employee offering a sharp yet friendly greeting. I can't be bothered with pleasantries and cut to the chase.

"How much for the ring?"

"Which ring?" she asks, displaying a full smile.

"The black diamond in the showcase," I point out, impatient.

"Oh, that's an Anna Sheffield. It's—" she begins.

I interrupt her, my tone demanding. "How much?"

"Fourteen thousand euros." She barely finishes the sentence before I'm speaking again.

I hate spending that kind of money on material things, but this ring is calling to me and it has Miriam written all over it. I need to have it.

"Pack it," I order, my brusqueness evident.

The woman disappears momentarily in the back of the store, and, while I wait for her, I send double the amount of money I just spent on the ring to Sasha's organization 'White Horse,' which takes care of women and children who have been victims of human trafficking. I don't like throwing money at my problems, but at least I can help someone after my excessive purchase.

Eventually, the woman returns with a black velvet box that she opens in front of me. Her hands tremble slightly, her nervous energy palpable. It's no wonder, given what an insufferable jerk I'm being. God, I hate myself for that.

"Perfect," I say, masking my internal turmoil.

She closes the box and walks behind the counter, deftly packing it into a bag. With a wave of my card, I pay and snatch the bag out of her hand before I continue to make my way to Sasha's place.

I stumble into Sasha's place. The alcohol is slowly starting to fade, replaced by the weight of the ring inside the bag. Sasha doesn't pry, but her eyes catch the bag and my hangover. No questions are asked while she brews us a cup of coffee before joining me on the white couch.

"That's an expensive jewelry store," she observes, nodding with her chin towards the bag.

"It was an expensive purchase," I mutter.

"What did you buy?" she asks, her curiosity evident.

"A ring," I reply.

Sasha almost spits out her coffee. "You bought what?"

"I bought a ring."

She sits in stunned silence for a moment, trying to discern if I'm being serious or playing some bizarre joke. "And for who, pray tell, did you buy a ring?"

"Miriam," I answer matter-of-factly.

"I don't believe you."

Instead of arguing, I pull the velvet box out of the pricey paper bag and pass it to her. Sasha doesn't hesitate and opens it in a heartbeat. Her expression remains impassive, but I know her well enough to see the gears turning in her mind. She thinks I have gone mad. Maybe I have.

"It's an Anna Sheffield," I comment.

"Why is it black?" she asks, cutting straight to the point.

I take a moment to consider Sasha's question, my mind retracing the impulsive steps that led to this peculiar choice.

"Black diamonds symbolize flawless, eternal, and unchanging love." I laugh at the irony, knowing I am not capable of loving or being loved.

"Was the fuck fest so good that you fell in love?"

I laugh bitterly. "We didn't even do that."

Her eyes go wide.

"I threw Miriam out before we could get to it."

"And you decided to buy her an engagement ring after that?"

"She is the only woman I will ever consider marrying,"

"And you say you are not in love." She huffs.

"No. I am not in love," I pause. "I am obsessed."

Love, as I have experienced it, is a fickle creature. It doesn't always stand the test of time. It crumbles under the weight of expectations, or it simply loses its luster. Love is what my parents were supposed to feel for me when I came into their lives, but they couldn't even pretend to care for me when I became less than perfect in their eyes.

Obsession, on the other hand, is a different beast.

It's fueled by an intensity that borders on irrational. The kind that blinds you to the flaws of the other person. Obsession clings to the soul with a tenacity that surpasses love, and I am never going to stop being obsessed with Miriam. Not even once I have drawn my last breath.

My little swan will be mine.

Even if she doesn't know it yet.

CHAPTER THIRTY

The week passes by in a blur. Now that I am free of tracking money trails from questionable sources, I can redirect my focus towards more meaningful projects, the ones that I have been dying to get my hands on.

I've been delving into the budget for the women's sports section the entire week, looking at the numbers and figuring out how we can do more to make a difference in a sport that has had so little space for women in the past. With the budget that Cavaglio has, and the historical meaning of the team, they should be doing more to support women in motorsport, and I'm hoping Daniel will agree with me this once.

Daniel… The person who seems keen on being my personal protector. I haven't wrapped my head around the fact that he showed me a slightly vulnerable side of him, one that cares about me.

I rise from my desk, clutching my laptop, and walk across the familiar halls towards Daniel's office – a route that's become too familiar for my taste. I went from wanting to avoid him at all costs, to living with him, in less than a month.

While I walk, I notice my locks swaying freely around me, and I can't help but enjoy the sight of how much healthier they've become in the weeks since I ditched my straightener. I haven't touched it since late November, that's when this madness started, and now it's past mid-December

When I finally make it to Daniel's office, his assistant, Alex, is stationed at the door, typing away with a headset on his head.

"Is he in?" I ask.

Alex nods, glancing over his computer. "Yep, he's in there," he replies, covering his microphone with a hand.

"Thanks," I whisper.

My legs are trembling and my heartbeat picks up speed with every step I take towards the door. Summoning all of my courage, I push it open only to find the office empty. Disappointment washes over me. Then I realize I was really looking forward to seeing him.

Suddenly, I sense heat behind me, a familiar presence.

"Miss me already, darling?"

"You wish," I counter with half-parted lips.

A raspy laugh escapes Daniel, who's now standing in front of me. I realize he must have been sitting in the area behind the door, which explains why I didn't spot him. What a stellar ex-Interpol agent (if I can call myself that) I am – all that training for nothing.

"Are you here to discuss my credit card bill?" he jokes. "I noticed you went all out."

"You told me to get anything my heart desired."

"I don't recall using those words."

"Don't worry, I can recall it for both of us," I quip. Daniel smirks, causing my heart to skip a beat and my legs to tremble even more.

"Since you're not here to apologize for the astronomical sum of money you spent, what can I help you with, wifey dearest?"

"Cavaglio's budget," I declare.

"What about it?" he asks.

"You're not doing enough to support women in motorsport."

"I am listening," he says, taking a seat in his leather chair.

"The female rep in the Cavaglio Nero's young drivers' academy could use some help. The company could be that help," I explain.

"Make me a pitch."

"Now?" I ask incredulously.

"What better time than the present?"

"I don't have a presentation," I mutter.

"Use your mouth." The innuendo doesn't escape me, but I decide to ignore his words and the ache in my core.

"Okay," I mumble, feeling nervous and excited. "Cavaglio, as a motorsports legendary team, holds a unique opportunity to help women into racing. First, we should establish driver development programs that include more women, not just one every three years. Also, you should include training and mentorship from one of our drivers. The boys have been doing it for a while with their karting pupils, and most of these girls haven't had a chance to have a mentor. This could inspire the next generation, and it wouldn't cost us more than it does when we're supporting men.

"We could also encourage motorsports as a career through karting programs. Most girls quit karting because of the bullying they face. We could afford to generate a new racing series to foster equality and progression for talented female drivers.

"Your women quota on the team is also something we could work on. I understand if we don't want a woman to carry a ten-kilo wheel during a two-second pit stop – even if I could argue against that. But I don't see why we are not working on educational programs that have a higher female quota. Almost all your aerodynamicists and engineers are men, and I haven't checked the percentage of female university students, but I bet there are at least a hundred girls out there dying to learn how to build a car. Find the next Aiden Nowey, find the best car designer and engineer ever seen in F1! But this time, let him be a girl."

Daniel places his elbows onto his desk, and, although my heart is racing and my mouth feels dry from the nerves, the smile on his face is impossible to ignore. I nailed it.

"How long have you been thinking about this?" he probes.

"A while. Why?" I reply, not being able to hide the smile building on my face.

"I like it when you are passionate," he answers.

"So, are you going to help me?" I ask, urgency creeping in.

"I will always help you, Miriam," he assures me.

My smile disappears at the intensity of the tone. Weeks ago, I would have dismissed this as a simply flirty and annoying comment. Now, I know the answer is filled with honesty, and I can't help but appreciate how much this man has given me, even when he has taken so much from me.

"I have conditions," he declares.

"Name your price," I respond with determination.

"I want a deck and a budget sheet by the end of the week with a firm plan on how we are going to use the resources. I also want you to call the talent scouts and ask them to see what's out there. I want only the best; I don't care about their sex."

"You got it," I reply, commitment driving my response.

"And," he starts, "you are having dinner with me and Grace tonight."

I pause for a minute, surprised.

"Your aunt?" I ask, remembering the nurse.

"Yes."

"Does she know we are pretending?" I ask, waving a finger between both of us. "That this marriage is a sham?"

"No."

"Why?" I press.

"Why would I tell her?" he retorts, a hint of defiance in his tone.

"Maybe because you aren't supposed to lie to family?"

"Grace has gone through a lot. She has seen *me* go through a lot. It seemed nice to have her stop worrying about me for once and let her think I am in a happy, loving marriage, even if my wife acts like a cheetah sometimes."

A genuine laugh escapes my lips. "You like my paws," I joke.

"Can't say I don't, especially when they draw blood on my back." The sway with which he says the words catches me by surprise, and I can feel my jaw dropping to the floor.

"When and where?" I ask, trying to recompose myself.

"At home. Eight o'clock."

CHAPTER THIRTY-ONE

Monthly dinners with Grace have become a ritual of my adult life. No matter in what part of the world I am, she will demand we meet at least once a month for dinner and will make sure to feed me an insane quantity of her homemade empanadas. Sasha has been my rock, but Grace holds an important spot in my heart in a different way. The woman who was once my nurse has filled the empty spots that my family left behind. She has been more of a mother to me than the woman who birthed me ever could have been.

Grace's insistence on meeting Miriam formally has escalated to an annoying level that I can no longer ignore. She's heard about her endlessly for the past year, and now that we are in a sham of a marriage, I can't avoid her request any longer, especially not after Grace had to run Miriam's blood tests.

I can hear the soft rhythm of Miriam's steps descending the staircase before she even asks her question.

"Do I look good?"

Turning around, I'm met with a vision that steals my breath away. She's draped in a stunning white dress that hugs her curves in all the right places, a stark contrast against her glowing dark skin. The memories of my dream flicker in the back of my mind, and I struggle to contain my desire.

"Ravishing like always," I manage to reply, tearing my gaze away before I do something I know we both will regret.

"You barely looked..." Her voice trails off, disappointment laced in it.

"I don't need to look twice to know how delectable that dress looks on you."

I thought living with her would be a great idea. But it's becoming my own personal hell. She is so close and yet I cannot touch her or look more than once at her without my mind coming up with images of what I am willing to do to worship her body.

Miriam's mouth opens, but no words emerge.

After a moment, she simply murmurs, "Thanks."

"Are you vegetarian?" I ask, trying to change the topic, even if I already know the answer to all her food preferences.

Miriam shakes and nods her head all at the same time. “I try to consume as little meat as possible, but I am not opposed to eating it every once in a while.”

“I see,” I answer simply. “Grace will bring her meat empanadas, and I am making the rest.”

Miriam's footsteps draw closer, a gentle rhythm that breaks the silence of the kitchen. I can sense her presence behind me before she speaks.

“What's all of that?” Her voice is soft and filled with curiosity, her eyes taking a peek over my shoulder, the warmth of her body enveloping mine.

I turn to meet her gaze, a smile tugging at the corners of my lips.

“Chimichurri to go with the empanadas,” I explain, gesturing towards the vibrant green sauce that sits in its bowl. “And Provoleta,” I continue, pointing at the golden slab of cheese sizzling on the grill, filling the room with a savory smell.

“What is Provoleta?” Miriam's curiosity peaks, her eyes flickering with interest.

I reach out to point at the cheese, my finger lingering on its molten surface. “It's an Argentinian appetizer,” I explain. “It's a thick slice of grilled provolone that goes with the chimichurri and some bread."

“It smells good.”

"Do you want to try?"

"Can I?" Miriam answers eagerly.

I nod, a grin spreading across my face as I reach for a spoon from the drawer. With precision, I dip it into the creamy cheese, then carefully spread it onto a piece of bread, generously drizzling chimichurri sauce over the top.

Instinct guides my hand as I raise the piece of bread and cheese towards her mouth. Miriam's lips part, a silent invitation, and I can't resist the urge to feed her. Our eyes lock when the food touches her lips, and time seems to stand still. The air crackles with electricity, charged with my desire that only grows more intense when a soft moan escapes my wife.

It's a sound I've heard before, but this time, it resonates within the deepest parts of me, stirring something bigger than mere pleasure. This time, it feels more intimate than the previous times when my lips were touching her skin. This time, it's more than mere carnal connection.

"Look at you two!" Grace's sudden intrusion startles us, and Miriam jumps slightly, her eyes wide with surprise.

I forgot my aunt has a key to the apartment...

"How does the saying go? Barefoot and married in the kitchen. All we're missing is a baby." Grace's words hang in the air, laced with humor and affection.

Miriam covers her mouth, a blush creeping up her cheeks as she tries to swallow down the food, while I roll my eyes at my aunt for her comment.

"Grace," I warn, stopping her before she scares my wife away.

"I'm just teasing," Grace says with a mischievous smile.

She places a glass container covered with tin foil on the kitchen island, then envelops me in a bear hug that squeezes the air out of my lungs. With the affection only a Latin aunt can muster, she plants a kiss on my cheek, leaving behind a lipstick stain.

"Miriam, you look divine!" Grace exclaims, turning her attention to my wife. For a second, Miriam's expression is a mix of amusement and confusion, caught off guard by Grace's affection.

Latin aunts…

While I watch Grace and Miriam share a moment, warmth spreads through me, and a part of my heart I'd long considered frozen, seems to melt. This marriage might not be real, but in a way, Miriam fits perfectly into my broken family. I can see in Grace's eyes how she instantly falls in love with her. But again, who wouldn't love my wife? Well apart from me, of course. I won't let myself love her.

At least not how she deserves to be loved.

Never again will I let my guard down, allow myself to be hurt. The inevitable heartbreak isn't worth it. But for now, I can pretend and enjoy this glimpse of what life can be. For once in my life, I can let myself enjoy these moments with Miriam while my walls are still intact. For one evening, and only with the woman in front of me, I want see what a normal life could look like.

"The table is already set," I announce, breaking the comfortable silence. "Do you want wine?"

"Of course," Grace replies with a grin. "Make it red."

"Wouldn't have it any other way," I chuckle, pouring the wine.

We sit around the table, the aroma of freshly baked empanadas filling the air, mingling with the scent of the dishes I've prepared. Dinner progresses smoothly, and I find myself fascinated with the way Miriam and Grace start bonding, discovering shared experiences and interests. They're more alike than they might realize, both having explored the world. Between the two of them, they have probably seen each corner of the globe.

"Sorry, but I need to ask," Miriam starts tentatively.

"It's coming," Grace jokes, casting a playful glance in my direction.

"How old are you?" Miriam finally asks, her curiosity genuine.

"Guess," Grace chimes in, a mischievous twinkle in her eye.

"I wouldn't go past forty."

"I am forty-seven," Grace answers with a wide smile.

"And you are his aunt?" Miriam asks, her brow furrowed in confusion, looking back and forth between both of us, while doing the math and trying to spot similarities between us both.

"She isn't my aunt by blood," I explain, feeling a surge of nervous energy as I reveal a part of my untold story.

Miriam's eyes widen with surprise, but there's also a glimmer of understanding there, and as Grace shoots me a knowing look, I realize that this moment marks a turning point, a step towards embracing my past and sharing it with those I hold dear.

"You know about my sister Ximena, right?"

Miriam nods.

"Before we were kidnapped, Ximena took me to a doctor that specialized in gender affirmation therapies and surgeries." A knot forms in my throat and I force myself to hold the pain of the memories at bay. "Grace was the nurse assisting the doctor that day."

A tear escapes Grace's eye as she holds my hand on the table.

"I had nowhere to go when I escaped The Red Horses, no family who would take me in, no sister that would help me become myself and protect me from the hate my parents had started to give me. I lived on the street for a bit, until an opportunity presented itself and I got my hands on a computer at a public library. I quickly discovered how good I was with technology and started doing my first under-the-radar work for people who needed my help and were willing to pay for my services.

"When I had enough money a year later, I decided to visit the doctor again. After all, the whole story would have been even more painful if Ximena's efforts had gone to waste. I started the treatment, and Grace was my nurse. She took pity on me and took me in. She was the first person after my sister passed away that I ever opened up to, and she was the first person after Ximena to accept me the way I was."

"You could say I adopted him," Grace says with a smile on her face and tears running down her cheek.

Those early days were especially painful.

Becoming Daniel wasn't easy. It wasn't easy to transform my body into what it was always meant to be.

It's not uncommon for people to have a hard transition, to be abandoned by their family when they go through it. But mine had an extra layer of pain after having been kidnapped and trafficked.

And Ximena's death made the pain even worse.

My sister had given her life for me.

I felt guilty for her death. If she had never taken me to see the doctor she wouldn't have been kidnapped, wouldn't have been raped, wouldn't have died.

It took me almost a year before I considered changing my gender again. And finally, I did it. I also visited a therapist who helped me deal with the pain, the loss, and all of the trauma I had endured.

"Grace became like an aunt to me," I say, knowing that the woman who took me in never liked the term "mother," and I didn't either. A mother should protect you and ensure your well-being, but mine didn't. "She stepped in and took care of me during my transition, never judging me."

"I still need to take care of you…"

"Not always."

"Sure, you can take care of yourself until it comes to making your doctor's appointments," Grace scolds me.

I laugh, and then I notice a tear rolling down Miriam's eyes.

"You are a wonderful human being," she whispers.

"No, I am just a human being," Grace corrects, and then continues with the story. "Eventually, we moved to Colombia.

I didn't know about Daniel's plans back then, but things became clear when he found Sasha, which wasn't an accident like I thought at the beginning."

"I tracked The Red Horses while I was transitioning. I became obsessed with them, then I found Mancini and his gang… and somehow, I stumbled across the tapes from Sasha that Mancini kept hidden. The horror she lived equaled my own, and it was then I decided I needed to find her. I convinced Grace to make us move to another country, saying that I needed distance from my past and my ghosts. She didn't question it and as soon as we landed in Colombia, I searched for the woman who would change our lives. Grace took her in too," Daniel finishes, a mix of nostalgia and sadness mixed in his voice.

"Of course I took her in! But even if Daniel saw me as family, Sasha never saw me as more than a caregiver until recently," Grace explains. "She was thankful, there is no doubt about it, and she made sure to show how grateful she was, but when we found her, she was broken in her own way. She didn't see paternal authorities with fondness after finding out her father was one of the worst monsters this world has seen. She also lived with the guilt of having abandoned her mother, and I knew if she let herself love me or get attached to me, she would never recover from the guilt, so I let her be and waited for her to heal those wounds."

The air shifts. It's no longer a happy family dinner but a gloomy one, filled with the pain of the past. I try to cast the memories away. After all, life has been rather nice the past few years. We did take down The Red Horses, we killed the people that wronged us. And we were able to start a new life.

“Pour me some more wine,” Grace says.

“I think we need something stronger.”

“Negronis?” Miriam asks, and I smile at her.

CHAPTER THIRTY-TWO

Time flies when you're drinking Negronis and sharing stories with good company. Boy, I am either very drunk or things have really changed in a few weeks if I'm considering Daniel *good company.*

You always have - the traitor voice in my head says. Tonight, my mind's been full of intrusive thoughts, and the more I drink, the harder it becomes to shake them off.

Sure, blame it on the Negronis. It's not as if you never had dirty thoughts about Daniel before. I have to hold back a grunt of frustration and involuntarily squeeze my thighs harder together under the dinner table, trying to find some relief, but it's impossible to do so when he laughs at the stories Grace has been sharing. The sound of his laughter vibrates in my bones and travels down to my core. Every time he lets me see that smile of his, I can't help but picture his teeth biting me.

How can I be horny right now?

"I think it's time for me to go home," Grace announces.

"I'll call you a taxi," Daniel offers.

"Oh, I came with my car," Grace explains.

"Hand over the keys, señora," Daniel insists, extending his hand to her. Grace rolls her eyes but obliges, fishing her car keys out of her purse and handing them to Daniel. "Mañana *lo llevo de vuelta a tu casa.*" *I will bring it over tomorrow,* he says in Spanish, in that Argentinean accent of his that makes my legs ache.

Breathe, Miriam. Focus. You can't be thinking that.

"*Portaté mal, mi rey,*" Grace teases him. "The same goes for you, Miriam. Don't be shy to misbehave and let your hair down."

"I'll try my best," I say, offering her a smile.

"Well, time for me to go. Have a nice night, you two," Grace says, planting a kiss on Daniel's cheek before leaving the apartment.

"Finally, we're alone," Daniel murmurs as soon as the door is closed. His voice is thick and raspy, and I'm already struggling to keep my mind off my dirtiest desires. Him talking doesn't make it any easier.

"I'm going to bed," I announce, trying to escape him before I do something I know I will regret in the morning.

"Not so quickly, *my* little swan." The emphasis on the "my" doesn't go past me, but I decide to ignore it instead of fighting it.

When I turn around and look into his eyes, I notice how desire and lust are drawn all over them, and I have a feeling those feelings are mirroring my own right now. His honey-brown eyes make me feel like I'm drowning in need for him. I am so lost in them that before I realize it, Daniel crosses the space between us, and then he corners me against the wall.

His arms are above my head, his knee parting my legs, and the way he looks down at me is sin incarnated. My breath grows heavy as desire pulses through every cell of my body. It's as if I've been holding my breath for an eternity, every part of me yearns for him, but I can't give in. Things are complicated enough as they are.

"We're friends," I remind him, but my voice betrays me, and breaks midway through the lie. "Friends don't do this."

"What if I don't want to be your friend?" he counters, his words sending a jolt through me.

My lungs stop working, and my heart races even faster. What if he gives in? I'm not prepared for that. I have never thought about the possibility that one of us would finally give in to this twisted game of ours. Would I let myself give in or would I hold my ground, cling to the stupid boundaries we've set?

"That's something you need to decide when you're sober," I manage to reply, though my voice trembles with longing.

He smiles down at me, and I force myself to look away, shutting out that dangerously enticing smile of his. I know the effect it will have on me. But I'm doing just fine. I just need to hold on a little bit longer, find a way to make my escape.

Escape. That's it. Escape before you do something dumb!

I try to assess the situation calmly. His hands still linger above my head and his knee is positioned between my legs. With a surge of adrenaline, I remember the night we first met in the office and how I was able to overpower him.

If I did it then, I can do it again.

Quickly, I twist my body to the side, attempting to slip out from under his grasp, but his hold remains firm. I don't give up. I grit my teeth, then push against his chest, trying to create enough space to wriggle away, but his strength overwhelms mine.

Adrenaline fuels my movements, and with a sudden burst of energy, I arch my back and thrust my hips upward, leveraging my weight to break his hold. For a fleeting moment, I feel victorious. I twist and turn, trying to slip out from under him, until I manage to slide off to the side, breathing heavily as I put some distance between us.

But Daniel is quick to react, reaching out to grab my wrist and trying to force me again into his hold. In a split-second decision, I pivot and twist, but my move backfires, and we tumble to the floor in a tangle of limbs. At least I am the one landing on top.

My heart pounds in my chest as I straddle him, pinning his wrists above his head with a firm grip. Our eyes lock in a heated exchange, the air thick with tension and desire. But as I hold his gaze, I know that I've won this round, escaping the intoxicating pull of his touch.

"Make up your mind when you are sober, Conte."

Daniel smirks and his mouth opens, but before he can say anything I stand up and press my white heels on his chest. His smile only grows wider, and I can't fault him for it, the sight of my stilettos holding him down is even turning me on.

"Good night." I finally say and walk towards my bedroom.

I'm not running, but I might as well be sprinting up those stairs trying to escape my fake husband. When I finally make it onto the upper floor, Daniel's raspy laugh echoes through the place, so infectious that a smile involuntarily spreads across my lips as I finally reach my bedroom.

Closing the door behind me, I press my back against it, feeling the weight of the moment settle around me. With a sigh of relief, I allow myself to breathe, my chest rising and falling in sync with the rhythm of my racing heart. I slide down the wall and feel the coldness of the floor seeping through my clothes as my ass meets the hard ground.

The intensity of the evening rushes over me, wrapping me in a blanket of emotions I can hardly contain. But, for now, I try to focus on getting rid of the most intense feeling of them all.

The one between my legs.

I scan the room, looking through the many packages I have ordered over the past twenty-four hours. Express delivery is my biggest ally in this house. Finally, amongst another twenty things, I find what I was looking for. Intact and still unopened is a box with a neon pink toy printed on top of it.

Please be charged.

I crawl towards the spot where the box is and almost break my long nails as I try to open it. Without a second thought, I free the pink toy from the plastic holding it hostage and turn it on.

"Yes!" I practically scream when it starts vibrating.

I don't hesitate. Trembling with need, I make it into the bed and open my legs. With shaky hands, I push my drenched underwear to the side. The touch of my fingers already sends shivers of pleasure through my body so intense that I know I won't last long.

With my right hand, I turn the vibrator on and then press it over the sensitive nub of nerves at my center.

A moan escapes my lips.

Definitely not going to last too long.

My hips start moving in circles, matching the vibrations, trying to rub myself harder against the toy. With my free hand, I push down the neckline of my dress, pulling my white bra down as well. My breasts jump free. My nipples are already hard when I tug on the silver beads, remembering Daniel's face when he saw them last time.

"Fuck."

I try to whisper, but I am aware it comes out as a scream instead.

I go up the stairs, ready to go into my room when a sound distracts me. At first, I think the vibration sound comes from a phone, but then I notice the constant pattern and how the sound grows louder at Miriam's door.

Without hesitation, I press my head against her door and then I hear the sweetest sound from her mouth.

"Daniel," she moans just as the vibrations get more intense.

"Fuck," I whisper to myself.

On the other side, the vibrator hums with an erratic flutter. A wall might be separating us, but I can sense how this setting is teasing Miriam when a soft chuckle escapes her lips. I would give anything to be in there with her and watch her pleasuring her clit, but I stay outside and listen closely while my hand flies against the front of my pants.

I don't know how long I stay in that position, but eventually, the setting changes again, more intense, and so do Miriam's screams.

"Fuck, yes!" she cries out.

I bite down on my lip, trying to hold back my own sounds, but it only gets harder when I hear her bed starting to shake under the movement of her hips and the headboard pounding against the wall.

I know she has reached the last setting where her little desperate cries grow louder and the pulse between my legs is out of control. Might not get blue balls, but I am really close to exploding from whatever condition Miriam is giving me.

"Ah." Another moan that forces my hand to press itself harder against my pants.

Then, the grand finale. Fast moves, loud moans. The headboard pounds even harder. Her hips meet the mattress in circle patterns right before she screams, "Daniel!" The vibrator turns off, and I know she has reached her orgasm.

My name coming from her lips does it for me.

Without thinking I slam the door open, a side of me instantly regretting the intrusion into her safe bubble, but the most primal side of me… Oh, that one is loving the vision that Miriam is post-orgasm.

"What the fuck?" Miriam screams, trying to cover herself. I get a quick glimpse of her glistening pussy and her perky breasts before she covers herself and takes a seat at the edge of the bed.

Soon, I tell myself. *Soon, you will be mine.*

"What the hell is wrong with you, Conte?"

"It's fucking rude to scream someone's name during an orgasm and not invite them to the party," I retort.

"You were listening?" Miriam's cheeks flush with embarrassment, her eyes burning with embarrassment but also lust.

"Just the grand finale," I lie, trying to spare her the embarrassment and hoping she won't hate me more than she does already. "My name sounds divine when you moan it. It would have been a pity to miss it."

"You had no right!" Miriam's voice trembles with indignation, her fists clenched at her sides.

"Oh, but I had, my little swan," I say taking a step towards her and holding her chin between my fingers, forcing her to look into my eyes. "Next time you scream my name, it will be because I am the one playing with you."

"In your dreams," she states, but there is a defiant glint in her eyes, daring me to test her, and I know it's not in my mind when a hint of a smile reaches her lips. It's only a corner that lifts, but it tells me everything I need to know.

"You just made my dreams come true," I tease her. "Now, it's time to give life to yours."

CHAPTER THIRTY-THREE

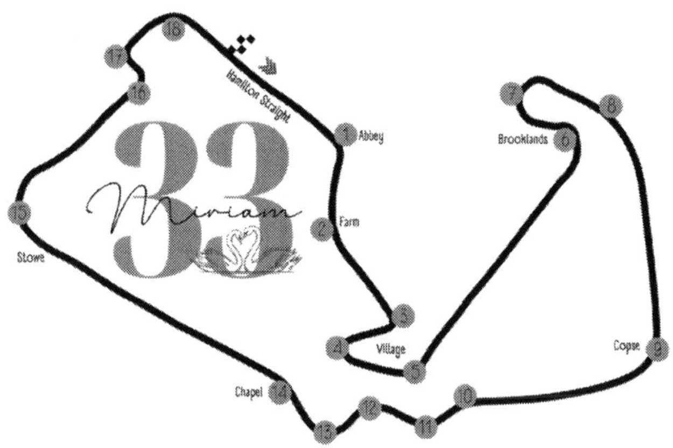

Devil's spawn: Where are you?

Devil's spawn: You are not in the office.

Devil's spawn: You can't hide forever, little swan.

Devil's spawn: You will have to come back home eventually.

Devil's spawn: I am getting tired of this game, Miriam.

Me: I am getting tired of this game too, Conte.

Devil's spawn: I am ready to play a new game.

Me: Who says I want to play with you?

Devil's spawn: Your screams.

Me: I know many men named Daniel.

Devil's spawn: You do?

Me: Yes.

Devil's spawn: Great.

Devil's spawn: I will kill them all.

Devil's spawn: My name is the only one you will scream.

Me: Jealous much?

Devil's spawn: Nobody touches what's mine.

…

The brisk air of winter bites at my cheeks as I make my way to the empty race track in Silverstone. The familiar scent of coffee wafts up from the cup clenched tightly in my hand, offering some solace against the damp chill that seeps into my bones.

It's a stark contrast to the warmth I feel whenever I am in his presence.

I am still mortified about last night, and I know I won't be able to hide from Daniel forever, and, most importantly, I can't hide from myself for much longer. Eventually, I will have to confront the truth, no matter how much it hurts.

I make it onto the track and into the empty garages of Silverstone. I've been here before. In a way, this place has marked a major change in my life. It feels like the first domino stone fell here when Selene met Philip. Over three years ago, I came to Silverstone, full of hope and excitement for the future.

Now, my best friend is moving forward with her life, building a family, while I feel stuck.

I shake my head, trying to keep the negativity at bay. It's time to start acknowledging my own accomplishments. My life might not have gone the way I wanted it to work out, but I have been doing quite well.

“Mrs. Conte,” the familiar voice of the man I spoke with on the phone greets me as I arrive. “All the arrangements have been made as per your request.”

“Thanks,” I reply, feeling the buzz of my phone in my pocket. I don’t need to look at the screen to know the messages are from Daniel. “Is it ready?” I ask.

The man nods. “It was on short notice, but yes.”

“Thanks, next time, I'll make sure to organize it more in advance.”

“We can always accommodate a Conte.”

I resist the urge to roll my eyes. My husband’s name does open many doors, but I have accomplishments of my own.

“Might I ask why you decided to come?” he says.

“My husband isn't the only one with a passion for motorcycles,” I explain. “Besides, adrenaline usually helps clear my head.”

“I see.” The judgment in his tone is palpable. “Anyway, this is the bike we have prepared for you.” He steps to the side and gestures with his chin towards the orange Aprilia RSV4 Factory 1100 parked behind him.

It's the bike of my dreams, one of the top-class superbikes; 1,099cc, V4 engine, and an Öhlinssuspension. It's not the best bike on the market, but it's one I've been obsessed with for a while. Now, I even get to try riding it.

My parents loved bikes, and they even collected them when I was a kid until they realized it was pointless to keep a collection given how much we moved. But Dad would always schedule a yearly bike tour, and in one of those, he taught me how to ride them. I fell in love with bikes too and took my driver's license test as soon as I could and have been visiting different racetracks ever.

My phone buzzes again, distracting me from the bike.

"Do you want to check your messages, Mrs. Conte?"

I smile at him and then take a quick look at my phone. The screen is filled with messages from Daniel. The last one summarizes our relationship perfectly:

Devil's Spawn: I'm coming for you, little swan.

"How much time do I have on the track?" I ask.

"Ten minutes. Some teams have booked the track as they have a filming session scheduled, so I couldn't give you more time"

"That's fine," I assure him. "I'll get changed and then take it for a spin."

Entering one of the nearby cabins, I retrieve the suit I secretly burrowed from Cavaglio Nero out of my bag. It's time to drown out the noise of my thoughts, but I fail miserably at that. However, I am able to redirect them into something more positive and stop thinking about myself as a failure for the first time in a while.

I am not even near the end of my twenties, and I already created and sold my first consulting company, chased my dreams to the city I've always envisioned myself living in and established myself as one of the best financial consultants in Formula One. I have even collaborated with Interpol, and now I am working on a project to empower women in motorsports. My personal life might be in shambles, but I have done well in my career. And I'm damn proud of it.

"Little swan," my husband's masculine voice comes from the outside of the cabin where I am putting on my racing suit.

"You have got to be shitting me!" I sigh.

"Not my kink," Daniel says as I slam the door open. Surprise doesn't quite encompass my feelings when I watch him standing in front of me in racing leathers. "Stealing from my property?"

"Our property, darling," I say, showing him my ring.

"Told you I would find you."

"You found me. Now go," I demand.

"I think I will stay," he counters, passing a hand through his unruly brown hair, a long strand falling against his forehead.

"And do what?" I say, my voice sharp with disbelief.

"Race with you," he replies, his tone daring and playful.

"Excuse me?" I ask, incredulous.

"Darling, do you need a hearing aid?" Sarcasm drips from his words.

"I am not racing you," I protest.

"Afraid of losing?" he jokes, a smirk on his lips.

"Never," I answer, my pride stinging at the suggestion.

"Then we can have a quick race," Daniel insists.

"What happens if I win?" I challenge, crossing my arms over my chest.

"What do you want?" he asks, his gaze locked on mine.

"Answers," I say firmly.

"Okay. Three laps, the first to cross the finish line gets three questions," he declares, a smirk playing on his lips as he lays down the terms of our impromptu challenge.

Someone brings a second bike, identical to mine, into the garage right when Daniel pulls his helmet on his head, the dark material of his suit and helmet making him seem ten thousand times hotter than usual, which is saying something giving the sex appeal that this man has every other hour of the day.

"See you at the race track, little swan."

"The only thing you will see is my rear!"

"There are worse things to see than your ass," he jokes, mounting the bike.

Before I can come up with an answer, Daniel storms out of the pitlane with the bike. I follow him, warming the tires. But unlike Daniel, who is storming off to the start and finish line, I take my time driving around, testing the bike and the conditions of the track. I have driven in Silverstone before, probably over a year ago, but always with a car, never with a bike, so I want to make sure I am ready for this.

Eventually, after longer than I anticipated, I make it to the start of the track, where my husband is already waiting for me.

"Ready?" Daniel asks, raising the visor of his helmet.

"Yes!" I call back as we approach the start line.

"GO!" he screams loud enough so I can hear him.

The roar of engines fills the air, drowning out all other sounds as I rev the motorcycle underneath me.

The wind whips against my helmet.

We approach the sweeping curve of Copse, and I lean my bike into the corner, feeling the tires grip the asphalt beneath me. Adrenaline surges through my veins, fueling my resolve to conquer every inch of this track. Through Maggots and Becketts, I push harder, my body instinctively finding the perfect line through each twist and turn.

Daniel is relentless, always next to me as we drive through the corners effortlessly on our bikes. The traces of his bike are messier than mine, but he somehow still manages to be slightly faster than me. He drives with an intensity that is hard to match, more erratic and impulsive, while I am more conservative.

With laser focus, I try to get as close to him as humanly possible. I refuse to let him win. As we barrel into Chapel, I release the full power of my bike to pass him by the exit of the corner, but his bike goes faster as we approach the final sequence of corners — Stowe, Vale, and Club. I give everything I have, but Daniel is faster and passes me effortlessly when the second lap starts.

Our engines scream in harmony as we drive down the Hangar Straight. My eyes are fixed on Daniel's figure ahead of me.

My husband.

My adversary.

And the person I have been yearning for.

Maybe what I need isn't distance from him as much as I need closure and to solve our problems. Our relationship has always been messy. A failed one-night-stand. A forced marriage

I never wanted. The friendship we both dread. Perhaps it really is time for us to sit down and talk like adults.

With newfound clarity in my mind, I push my bike to its limits, leaning into each corner with precision, but Daniel is a blur of black ahead of me. As we approach Stowe at high speed, I try to close the gap between us. But Daniel truly is relentless. I push and push. Harder. Faster. My heart is pounding in my chest as I fight to keep pace with my husband. But as we cross the finish line, it's Daniel who crosses it first.

Again.

One last lap.

One last chance.

With gritted teeth, I try to push myself to the limit. Daniel maintains the lead as we drive through the twists of Abbey, Farm, and Village. We race through Aintree, a left-hander, followed by the high speed into Brooklands. And finally, I find my rhythm again and feel the harmony between the motorcycle and me. Understanding the vibrations of the engine and the way it needs to be treated.

Daniel is good.

But I am better.

And, now, I have the speed and the skills to overtake him.

When we make it to Luffield, I see my chance. With a burst of speed and adrenaline, I surge ahead, passing Daniel with precision, my knee softly grazing the asphalt as I make it into the corner.

You are almost there, just a few meters left, I keep telling myself, while pressing my foot on the pedal, conjuring all the speed the bike has to give. My eyes are narrowed, and I am chewing the inside of my cheek so hard that I can taste blood in my mouth.

But it's all worth it when I am the one to claim the win, seeing the chequered flag first. Technically, there isn't anyone to wave it in the air, but I still celebrate my win, zigzagging across the straight and doing a wheelie, the front tire lifting in the air for a couple of meters. I'm enjoying the burst of adrenaline and happiness in my body.

I slow down, noticing how Daniel does the same behind me. It's when we make it to Abbey that I stop the bike, breaking in front of Daniel so hard that a print is left on the track.

"Ready to answer some questions?" I mock.

CHAPTER THIRTY-FOUR

We go for a short walk along the Silverstone track; our shoulders shily touching here and there. Each time she comes closer to me, it's an effort to not press my lips to hers, especially because her sweet perfume is driving me crazy.

Eventually, we find a patch of grass near the track. Miriam throws herself on it without a second thought, not bothering to check if the grass is damp from the morning rain.

"Sit down," she commands.

I roll my eyes but comply and sit down next to her.

"You have three questions. Use them wisely."

"I'll ask whatever I want," she protests. I meet her gaze. She is so transparent to me that I can see the wheels turning as she musters the courage to ask what's really on her mind.

"Don't be shy," I urge her.

"When did you buy my ring?"

A range of emotions wash through my body. At first, a cocky smile makes it to my lips; I have been waiting for her to ask that question for weeks and, finally, the day has come. But then, I hesitate, reluctant to tell her the truth. Being vulnerable and opening up isn't in my nature. It doesn't come easy to me, and this time is no different.

"I want the truth," she presses.

"The morning after Monaco," I confess.

"Why?" Her voice trembles.

"I was on my way to Sasha's place and saw it in the window of one of those luxury jewelry shops. It reminded me of you because they are some of the rarest and most precious diamonds on Earth. Like you are one of the rarest and most precious people on Earth. You are a rare woman, unique, if I dare say so. There aren't two of you, and the same goes for this diamond," I say, taking her hand in mine, feeling the coldness of the sharp stone.

"Are you in love with me?" Miriam asks with a cocky grin.

"Is that your second question?"

"You are driving me crazy as it is, I don't need to know how twisted your mind is when it comes to love, but I would like to know why you call me 'swan'?"

"*My* swan," I correct her. "When I saw you the first time, I had the same feeling, I was obsessed and couldn't take my eyes off you. You were a shining beacon of light in the middle of a dark and scary world. It was like watching a white swan gliding in a dark pond." I pause and take a deep breath, gathering the courage to say what I want. "I haven't been able to take my eyes off you ever since. Even if you spent over a year trying to avoid me. I was there, watching you from the shadows, little swan."

Miriam gulps at the intensity of my words. God, even I need a break from them. I wasn't planning on saying any of that, but that's the effect Miriam has on me. She tears down my walls, one by one. And she doesn't stop, she never does. I don't think she will ever stop until she makes it to the remaining pieces of what once was my heart, and I have a feeling she will try to piece them back together.

Would it be so bad if she did?

"Since the day I met you, I felt protective of you. Loyal in a way that, until then, I had only felt towards Sasha, but it feels more powerful, more intense with you. If something were to happen to you, Miriam, I would set the world on fire. I would make every single person on this Earth pay for it."

"I think I'm missing the point?" she manages to utter, though her words sound out of breath.

"Swans have an extremely protective behavior towards their partner, in fact, they are monogamous creatures and only mate once in a lifetime."

"Are you asking me to be monogamous?"

"You already signed a contract for that," I quip.

"You are always three steps ahead, Conte." She laughs.

"That's the worst-case scenario. Usually, I am ten ahead."

Miriam's gaze remains fixed on the track, her eyes tracking the cars as they speed past in a blur. It takes her a moment, a couple of minutes perhaps, before she speaks again. But I'm in no hurry; I find solace in the silence, enjoying the chance to drink in her presence.

"Why do we keep trying to be friends with each other when it's obvious that it's not working out?" she finally musters the courage to ask, her tone laced with a hint of vulnerability.

"I don't know what you mean," I lie.

"The truth and only the truth," she insists, her voice firm and unwavering.

"I'll take whatever you're willing to give, Miriam," I answer with resignation. I don't know when things started to shift, but they have been for a while.

I will always keep my distance, but for her, I am willing to make an exception and take a step towards her rather than one back. I am willing to risk the tiniest piece of my already damaged heart, only for her. That is the kind of effect she has on me. She makes me question everything I've ever convinced myself of.

Was it a lie when I told myself that I would never let my guard down ever again?

"And you're not ready for anything more than friendship." I finish.

Miriam takes her eyes off the track and looks straight into mine, while her chest rises and falls with each ragged breath, her eyes flashing with a fierce intensity that sends a shiver down my spine. I've seen her angry before, but never like this – never with such raw passion.

"Stop doing that! Stop making decisions for me! Stop making decisions for both of us," she continues, her anger palpable. "The last twenty-four hours have proven that we are anything but friends."

"Then what are we?" I challenge.

"I don't know," she admits, her voice softening slightly. "But friendship isn't supposed to feel like this – it's not supposed to be this hot and cold, this confusing. It's not supposed to leave me longing for something more, something deeper. Friendship is tender, it's supportive and genuine."

My heart pounds in my chest as her words hang in the air between us, heavy with unspoken longing and desire. And then, in a whisper barely audible above the sound of the racing cars, she utters words that send a jolt of electricity through my veins.

"It's not supposed to be you coming into my room when you hear me orgasming, that was a boundary you crossed, Conte. And if that happens again, I promise you, the world isn't large enough for you to hide from me. This thing between us, it borders madness. It's raw and passionate and so many things I can't even describe. I can't get you out of my head, no matter how hard I try, and you keep giving me these crumbs and then pushing me away again. Whatever this fake marriage really is, it's starting to become toxic, at least for me."

"I can never give you my heart, Miriam," I confess, my voice heavy. "I don't have one to give. That was taken away from me a long time ago. But what I can offer you is my undying loyalty and a maddening obsession for you. I can promise you that as long as I'm breathing, nothing will ever harm you."

Her eyes search mine, a mixture of confusion and hurt swirling in them. "You're the one who's been hurting me," she says softly, her voice tinged with sadness.

The words hurt the deepest part of me. It's not the first time she has said them, but it hurts just the same to hear them again.

"I know," I murmur, unable to meet her gaze.

Heavy and loud silence settles between us, the tension crackling in the air is just as palpable as the pile of my regrets and unspoken emotions, but there is something there too, a glimpse of hope. I might have a million more things to say, and so does she. But this is probably the first time since we got married that we are actually talking and understanding each other.

"I have a feeling that after this conversation, things are going to change," I tell her after a while.

"How can you tell?" she asks.

"Don't you feel it?" I ask. "The change?"

A shy smile plays at the corners of her lips. I can't help but smile in return, relief flooding through me at the realization that she feels it too.

"I feel something," she admits, her voice barely a whisper.

"Besides the ache between your legs," I joke, a cocky grin spreading across my face.

Her laughter fills the air, a sweet melody that washes over me like a warm embrace. In that moment, I know that whatever lies ahead, we will stand together, and maybe, just maybe, there's hope for us yet.

"I can never give you my heart," I repeat, almost unintentionally.

"I don't need your heart, Conte. Mine works just fine."

CHAPTER THIRTY-FIVE

Ginger Bestie: Have you gotten laid already?

Blonde Dread: No news on my side

Me: I don't know what you are talking about…

Ginger Bestie: I don't know… Sasha, do you?

Blonde Dread: The looks of longing?

Ginger Bestie: The tension in the air?

Ginger Bestie: The shy smiles exchanged in the office?

Blonde Dread: The movie nights every night this week?

Me: How do you know about those?

Blonde Dread: Kind of my job to know things…

Me: Depends on what job we are talking about.

Blonde Dread: I retired from my other job.

Ginger bestie: What other job?

Blonde Dread: Making friendship bracelets, of course.

Ginger Bestie: You never gave me one!

Me: You should do them for us before the wedding, Sasha.

Blonde Dread has left the chat.

...

Time flies after Silverstone, and Daniel and I slip into a rhythm that works for us. Our days blur together in a whirlwind of work, office meetings, and the relentless hustle of wedding preparations for Selene and Philip.

Conte was right, something shifted between us. Ever since Silverstone, there has been a tension between us, different from the one we felt in the weeks before. It has turned into something electric and charged with the intensity that I felt that time I first saw him in Monaco.

Even if it's a good thing, it's also terrible.

What happens if I give in to those feelings and that lust?

I tried to keep my emotions at bay, stay clear from those feelings, after all, he said it himself, he can't give me his heart. But it's hard to stop longing for him when the smell of his cologne lingers in the bathroom each morning after he's done getting ready. Or the way my heart races whenever our eyes meet across the room. And, most importantly, what is hardest to ignore is the way I have been aching with insufferable longing whenever he's nearby. I can't stop thinking about his hands on the most intimate parts of myself.

I am desperate for him.

But I keep my feelings buried beneath a facade of normalcy and use my vibrator more than I care to admit, making sure he is at the gym whenever I turn it on in my room. But nothing works, and I keep getting more lost inside my head, scared to confront my own truths.

I can't have his heart, but he might have mine.

I carry on with my life, trying to ignore that particularly scary thought, and luckily, before I even realize it, the twenty-first of December sneaks up on me, and the wedding becomes a welcome distraction. With the surprise pregnancy, we had to rush everything, but money has a way of smoothing over any inconvenience that might arise. Philip and Selene have already spent a couple of days in Spain, while the rest of us arrived in the city this morning.

The wedding is taking place in Granada. Philip has spared no expense in giving Selene the wedding of her dreams; he even went so far as to rent *el Palacio de los Cordoba,* so he could give her the perfect Spanish wedding and have the Alhambra light up in the background while the sun sets on the horizon during the wedding ceremony.

"Oh my god," I say as I step into the villa they've rented for the weekend, spotting Selene in a silky white robe with the word *bride* embroidered in golden letters. My friend glows under the Spanish sun, her strawberry hair catching the sunlight in a cascade of silky strands, and her green eyes shining with a myriad of emotions.

"You're here," she squeals, launching herself at me in a bear hug that nearly knocks me off my feet.

"Don't you dare do that to me, Selene," Sasha warns.

"Always so friendly," Selene teases back.

"They don't call me the blonde dread for nothing," Sasha retorts with a smile before enveloping Selene in a gentle hug. Sasha might be one of the most intimidating people I've ever met – right up there with Daniel – but beneath her tough exterior, she has a heart of gold. When Sasha loves, she loves fiercely and without reservation.

Maybe Daniel could love like that too, I think before I can stop myself.

"Okay, we don't have a lot of time. Let's go inside and get ready," Selene tells us, grabbing both our hands and walking inside the house.

"The wedding is at five," I say.

"Your point?" Selene counters.

"It's twelve," Sasha reminds her.

"Wait and see! The day is young, and I have surprises for everyone," Selene tells us. Sasha throws me a look, asking what she's talking about, but I shake my head, not having a clue.

"Aren't we supposed to be the ones surprising you? It's your special day," I say to my best friend.

"I have had a special day every day since I met Philip." A sort of positive jealousy courses through my body. I long to have what they have, that sort of pure and kind love. "Today is about celebrating my love with our friends and making them happy too."

"Well then, show us what you have in store," I say.

"Ç'estmoi qui est en magasin." *I am what is in store, a* familiar voice echoes from behind me.

"Maman?" I gasp, turning around to find my mom standing there. Tears of joy and sadness blur my vision as I take in her familiar face. It's been months since I last saw her, and until this moment, I hadn't realized just how much I'd missed her.

"What are you doing here?" My voice is shaking.

"First of all, come give your maman a hug," she urges with her arms wide open. I don't hesitate and run into her embrace, feeling her arms wrap around me in a tight hug that makes me feel safe and brings back memories of my childhood.

"I missed you," I manage to whisper.

"Not enough considering you didn't come to visit me!" she replies.

"It's not like that—" I begin, but she cuts me off.

"Ah yes! You got married," she says. "Did you think I wouldn't find out? Why didn't you tell me? You're married to a fancy CEO."

"It's complicated—" I start.

But, at the same time, Conte's voice interrupts me. "It's my fault she didn't tell you," he says as he approaches us, extending his hand to shake my mom's. "Daniel Conte, your son-in-law."

My mom eyes him up and down, assessing him with a critical gaze. "Fine specimen," she muses. "Why didn't you tell me you were getting married?"

"We weren't planning to get married," I explain. "It was a Las Vegas kind of situation."

"We had been dating for a while and got carried away in the heat of the moment. We thought what better time than the present to get married," Conte explains, sort of.

"We got married at a boat party," I finish for him.

"Why doesn't that surprise me coming from you, Miriam," my mom says, rolling her eyes at me. "But why didn't you tell me? We are so close! You always tell me everything."

"I wasn't sure if it was the right decision. Like, yeah, we had been dating, but marriage? You know me..."

"I do," my mom says softly. "And seeing Mr. Conte here, I can understand why you decided to settle down. You look good together., but are you happy?"

My mom's words strike me.

Am I happy in a marriage that doesn't fit any conventional mold and that I was kind of forced into?

Daniel and I are a complicated puzzle, each piece refusing to match with another. Our relationship is a combination of longing and frustration, passion, and exasperation. We fight all the time, but despite all of it, there's a sense of contentment that settles over me when I'm with him, of safety, of happiness.

I might never experience the kind of love that my friends have. Daniel might never be able to love me the way I've always dreamed of being loved. But in his own imperfect way, he makes me happy. Even when he infuriates me and pushes all my buttons, even when he makes my blood pressure rise to sky-high levels, I am happy.

"Yes," I finally answer, my gaze locking with Daniel's. And, in that moment, surrounded by the warmth of my family and the beauty of Granada, I know that it's true.

Despite all the complications and uncertainties, I'm happy.

CHAPTER THIRTY-SIX

After the high of seeing my mom and introducing her to my husband, the girls and I retreat to one of the salons in the villa while the guys play a round of soccer outside in the courtyard. Granada's weather is unexpectedly warm for this time of year – a lovely nineteen degrees instead of the usual fourteen. So, when I look out the window, I spot Daniel, alongside Philip and João, with his shirt off. My eyes involuntarily fixate on his tanned muscles, glistening with a sheen of sweat covering the colorful tattoos on his torso and arms.

"Do you want your phone?" Sasha interrupts my daydreaming, her tone teasing. "To capture the moment since you seem to be enjoying the view."

I shoot her a deathly glare. "Shut up."

"Whatever." She chuckles, unperturbed by my reaction.

"Okay, ladies, I'm coming out!" Selene's voice rings out from behind the curtain where she's been getting ready.

I don't need to look at Sasha to know that her jaw is on the floor – mine right there with hers. As Selene emerges into the light, my breath catches in my throat at the sight of her in her wedding dress. It's a delicate, balloon-sleeve gown adorned with lace flowers cascading over the tulle fabric. The train trails behind her, and the V-neckline creates an ethereal aura that makes her look as if she had just stepped straight out of a fairytale, a modern-day nymph with otherworldly beauty. Her strawberry-red locks cascade in a half-up, half-down style, waves effortlessly hanging around her shoulders. Some strands are framing her face, held in place by the crown on top of her head.

"What do you think?" Selene asks, her voice trembling.

"Don't you dare cry," I snap, not knowing if the words are for her or for myself. My own emotions are bubbling dangerously close to the surface.

"I can't make any promises," she replies, dabbing at her eyes with a tissue. "But I saved the mascara for last, just in case."

"Has your dad seen you in the dress already?" I ask, knowing how close Selene is to her father.

"Nope," she says, shaking her head. "It's going to be a surprise."

"He's going to sob his eyes out," I predict.

"That's why I haven't put on mascara yet," Selene explains with a wry smile. "If he cries, I cry."

"Good strategy," Sasha chimes in.

"Okay, girls, it's your turn now," Selene announces, her voice filled with excitement. "The bridesmaid dresses are behind the folding screen," she explains, nodding towards the wooden piece of furniture in the corner.

I step behind it with a hint of skepticism lingering in my mind. Selene has impeccable taste, but I haven't seen the bridesmaid dress until now. She simply asked me to go into the shop to get my measurements taken, leaving me unsure of what to expect. But all my doubts vanish as soon as I lay eyes on the dress hanging in front of me.

The satin fabric gleams in a rich, deep green that complements my skin tone perfectly. I was worried she might choose a shade that would wash me out or make me look ashy, but Selene never disappoints. When I slip into the dress, I'm instantly enamored. The front is simple yet elegant, accentuating my curves with its strategic draping, but it's the back that truly takes my breath away. The cut cascades down to my lower back, and the sleeves are held in place by delicate golden chains to ensure they won't slip throughout the night. The best thing is the cross hanging in the middle of the chain, a replica of Daniel's tattoo, and I suspect the same one I wore with my golden dress.

Selene is waiting for me. She is holding a gold bracelet with green stones in one hand and a collection of golden hair accessories in the other that remind me of the ones I used to adorn my braids with years ago when we used to live together and I didn't shy away from styling my hair in braids.

"I don't think there's enough time for you to do your braids, but I thought you might like to use these for the hairstyling part," she explains. "You being you, being free and wild, that's one of your best qualities, Miriam. You shouldn't shy away from wearing braids, no matter the occasion."

I try to hold back my tears, but they escape nonetheless.

"I couldn't wish for a better friend." I sob.

"Don't cry or you'll make me cry!" Selene cries and laughs.

"No promises made," I mutter through tears.

Thankfully, Sasha emerges from the cabin, her dress different from mine but perfectly harmonious. Hers is a softer, pastel shade of green, silky like mine but with a different cut. It's off the shoulder with a slit on the leg and adorned with silver accents.

"I don't want to cry," Sasha says, but it's too late, tears are pooling in her eyes.

"Fuck," I say knowing that I won't make it without tissues.

The sun slowly dips behind the mountains, casting a radiant golden hue over Alhambra. The place is bathed in the warm light, making it seem dream-like. I could look at the scenery all day long, but my attention is quickly pulled away as I look at the altar where Philip stands waiting for his bride. His expression is one of pure happiness and joy, and I swear there are tears collecting in his eyes. I want to take a closer look to figure it out, but I feel someone staring at me, and when I look to Philip's right, I am met with Daniel's honey eyes.

His long, brown hair is pulled back, some wild strands making an appearance on his forehead. The impeccably tailored suit hugs his frame in all the right places, leaving little to the imagination. It's enough to make any heart skip a beat. But before I can get lost in the sight of him, Selene's father interrupts me.

"Ladies!" he calls out, his voice filled with emotion. "It's time for you to become a wife, *amor.*"

I tear my gaze away from Daniel to look at Selene and her father. The love and pride in his eyes as he looks at his daughter makes me smile.

"I'll always be your little girl, Dad," Selene reassures him.

"Philip knows his way around cars, but I know my way around guns. If he hurts my little girl, he's gone," her dad jokes, or at least I hope he is joking.

"Papa!" Selene gasps, scandalized.

"I love you," he reminds her.

"Love you too."

The bridal march begins to play, so Selene and her father make their way down the aisle, hand in hand. My heart races with nerves, so I close my eyes for a fraction of a second and take a deep breath. When I open my eyes again, I'm met with Daniel's gaze fixed on me. As soon as we get to the altar, Philip reaches out for Selene's hand.

Eager to get things started, the priest begins his sermon in Spanish, and although I catch bits and pieces, my attention keeps drifting back to Daniel. His intense gaze holds mine, and my mind can't help but wander to thoughts of my own wedding day—the vows he made and I can't seem to fully remember.

Time seems to blur as the ceremony continues. It feels like an hour has passed when the priest finally switches to English so everyone will be able to understand the vows of the couple, even if most of the people present speak Spanish.

"Since it is your intention to enter into the covenant of holy matrimony, join your right hands, and declare your consent before God and His church," he proclaims.

Philip turns to Selene. With a gentle touch, he lifts her veil, so he can lock his eyes on hers while he speaks his vows.

"I, Philip Burton, take you, Selene Soldado, to be my wife." He stops for a second, struggling to keep his voice steady. "From the moment I met you, you became the light of my life, sparks. You ignited a fire within me that has been burning wild since then.

"I promise to cherish you in every moment, to stand by you in good times and bad ones. You are my home, my solace, and my joy. You are the spark that allows me to see in the darkest moments, and I promise to be true to you in good times and in bad, in sickness and in health. I will love you and honor you until my last breath."

Selene gives him a shy smile, struggling to keep her tears at bay. When she has recomposed herself, she grabs the microphone with shaky hands and starts her own vows.

"I, Selene Soldado, take you, Philip Burton, to be my husband. I might be your spark, but you are the gasoline that fuels my fire. Through every joy and challenge, I vow to stand by you, to love and honor you for the rest of our lives. Meeting you, falling in love with you, were the hardest and most beautiful chapters of my life. And now, we enter a new one full of happiness and joy." Selene touches her belly and Philip looks down at it with a coy smile. "This marks the start of the chapter where we build our new family."

"I now pronounce you husband and wife. You might kiss the bride."

The air is filled with cheers and applause. Philip's smile widens as he pulls Selene close and seals their union with a kiss that seems straight out of a movie. White rose petals and rice rain around them, and I catch myself wiping away tears of happiness for my best friend.

CHAPTER THIRTY-SEVEN

The party is in full bloom when the clock strikes midnight. Most of the guests are already half-drunk. Surprisingly, even Philip seems to have indulged a bit too much, which I suppose is to be expected on his wedding night. Jealousy hits me as I take in the scene—it's everything a normal wedding should be, surrounded by loved ones with candlelight casting a warm glow and a historic palace looming in the background. Far away from that shit show that I call my own wedding…

"Thinking about our wedding?" Miriam's voice breaks through my thoughts, her arm slipping around my shoulder as she settles down beside me, a glass of wine resting in her other hand.

"Maybe," I admit, meeting her hazel gaze.

"I was too," she confesses, a hint of sadness in her tone. "I never thought about getting married, always saw myself as the eternal single aunt with cool stories to tell." The laugh that escapes her mouth, vibrates so hard inside my body that even the hairs on the back of my neck rise.

"Well, getting married on a boat as if it was Las Vegas is definitely a cool story," I reply, trying to cheer her up.

For a moment, she ignores my attempt at humor, her eyes scanning my suit until they land on something that catches her attention.

"Why gold?" she asks, pointing to my golden cuffs and the golden pin on my jacket.

"I wanted to match you," I explain, reaching for her back. I gently tug at the golden chain keeping her sleeves in place, forcing Miriam to tilt her head slightly up, her lips parting with the movement.

"You chose the dress?" she asks.

"No, just this," I reply with a grin, touching the chain. "I told you, gold shines next to black."

"Is that a metaphor for us?"

"It's whatever you want it to be, my swan," I reply.

Miriam meets my eyes, and, in that moment, I can see a whirlwind of questions and emotions dancing in the depths of her hazel gaze.

"Dance with me."

"Is that a question?" she asks, playful.

"It's an order."

"So demanding."

"You love it."

She smiles and doesn't deny it, which makes me happier than it should. I take the wine glass from her hand and leave it on one of the tables. Then, I grab her hand and bring us to the dance floor. The music shifts to a slow, melodic tune. My heart starts pounding in anticipation when her body presses against mine and those mesmerizing eyes of hers are looking up at me.

The world around us fades away as we dance. Her warmth envelops me, and, for a moment, it feels like we're the only two people in the room. I know for her this is far from perfect. I know she aches for more, and her sadness is something I will never forgive myself for. I want to give Miriam everything she wants and deserves. My stupid broken heart aches for it too, but how can I give her something that's broken?

I am broken. Aren't I?

Miriam moves impossibly closer to me as the song swells into a crescendo. There's a shift in her gaze, a tension in the air.

Miriam's hand flexes in mine, her nails digging into my shoulder with a mixture of anticipation and longing.

Our eyes lock again, and, in that moment, I can see the silent plea in her gaze. The unspoken desire hangs in the air between us, and we are both begging the other to acknowledge it.

Miriam is more vocal, even without using her voice. Her lips part, and I can feel her nipples growing hard under the soft, silky fabric of her dress, pressing against my chest. With a breathless exhale, I lean in, lowering my head to hers, my heart pounding in my chest.

We both move slowly.

Painfully so.

Until finally, our lips meet in a kiss that's more than just a kiss. We have had others before, raw, passionate, chaotic, desperate kisses. This kiss, however, feels different. This is my soul calling for hers. My heart trying to piece itself back together with band-aids but failing miserably.

Her lips part beneath mine in silent invitation, and I deepen the kiss, pouring all of my pent-up longing and desire from the past month into the moment. The world around us fades away, leaving only the heat of our bodies, the taste of her on my lips. And, in my mind, fireworks of pleasure are exploding.

"Let's get out of here," I tell her, breaking the kiss.

"Why?" she asks.

"I need more of you, and I need it now."

"Oh." Miriam looks confused for a second, but then a mischievous look crosses her face. "What if I don't want that?" she says.

"Who are you trying to lie to? Because if it's yourself, I don't have a problem with it. But I know you want this just as much as I do," I tell her, leaning in so close to her ear that I could bite her earlobe if I wanted to. "I bet you're already wet for me, my swan."

"What about the contract?" she says with a broken voice.

"Fuck the contract," I tell her. "I would give you anything you wanted right now," I tell her, and I am being as serious as I can be.

"I want you," she says.

Three words that make the ground between my feet shake.

As soon as we are back at the villa, it takes Daniel precisely two seconds before he is towering over me, kissing my lips while simultaneously starting to unzip my dress and leading us towards our bedroom. In fact, I trip so much because of the train of the dress and my heels that Daniel ends up picking me up and carrying me to the privacy of our room.

"I could get used to this," I say, slipping my hands around his neck and grazing the skin there with my teeth.

"I will ask you again after I am done fucking you," he says.

"Do you have any ground rules?" I ask, nervous.

I have had sex with both men and women before, but never with a transgender man, and I am feeling nervous about it, uncertain but also eager to explore the million layers of Daniel.

"I don't like my nipples being touched," he explains. "And I don't enjoy any kind of penetrations. Besides that, I would like you to follow my lead."

"Follow your lead?" I ask warily.

"Do you have a save word?"

I shake my head.

"Pick one."

It takes me a minute, but I finally come up with something, right as we make it inside our room, "gold."

I can almost see Daniel smiling under the dimmed lights when he puts me back on the ground.

"Good girl," he praises me and then spanks my ass.

I jump in place, surprised by his sudden movement but also excited to see what else he has in store for me. An eager smile escapes my lips as I look deep into his eyes, and Daniel smiles back at me taking off his usual mask of indifference.

"You are a gorgeous creature," he whispers into my ear leaving a trail of kisses down my neck.

"I want everything," I say leaning into his touch.

"I will give you anything you want," a promise. "But before we start, I need to warn you, I like to have control. Strike that. I need it. I promise I will take care of you, but please use the word if it gets too much."

"I promise," I assure him.

"Good. Now stay still, little swan."

I do as he says, thinking he is about to take a look at me and take me in, but instead, he turns around and grabs his suitcase from the corner, opening it over a wooden desk. A couple of dress shirts fall out of the bag, but Daniel's hands work quickly to put them back in. He fishes a toy out of one side of the bag that leaves my mouth wide open.

"What is that?" I ask, slightly scared.

"Do I really need to explain it to you?" he says, rolling his sleeves up, the tattoos on his arms making an appearance.

I don't answer. Instead, I look closely at his movements and the way he grabs the bench at the end of the bed, placing it in the middle of the room, right in front of one of the armchairs next to the long mirror. Then, he sticks the gigantic dildo to it.

I gulp, fearing the length and thickness of the toy, but I can already feel my core clenching with need.

"Undress," Daniel commands. "But leave the heels on."

"I thought you were going to undress me," I tease him.

"Have I given you permission to speak? Undress."

I take a deep breath, trying to understand my feelings and take in the surprise of Daniel's more dominant side. I was sure he liked more than just vanilla sex, but I didn't think he would be this demanding, this dominant.

Mustering all my courage, I do as he says and pull down the sleeves of my dress, one at a time, and let the silky fabric cascade around my feet, leaving me completely naked in front of Daniel, who has taken a seat in the armchair.

"Look at you, completely naked, not wearing underwear to your best friend's wedding. We have a little slut here, don't we?"

At first, I nod, resisting the urge to speak, but I can't contain myself. "And you love that about me," I say proudly. "Are you dying to know how wet I am?"

"A little slut and a brat too," Daniel points out, fighting back a smile. "Come here." I start walking very slowly towards him, so slow that before I have even finished my first step, he says, "Crawl."

Without hesitation, I drop to my knees and crawl towards him, dragging out every single second and enjoying the way he studies my body. When I am finally in front of the armchair, I raise to my feet and instead of waiting for instructions, I sit on his lap. My bare pussy presses against the fabric of his trousers.

"How drenched are you for me?" he asks.

"You tell me."

"I can feel your wetness soaking my trousers. You are a needy girl."

"Then give me what I need," I almost plea, trying to press myself harder against his leg to get any kind of relief.

Daniel doesn't hesitate. Within a second, his hand flies towards my core, and I can feel my wetness pooling around his finger. Fuck. I need those fingers inside of me. I move my hips, trying to get him to move, but he doesn't. Instead, he teases me, moving his fingers up and down my slit, never inserting them.

"Open your mouth." When I do as he says, he takes his hand from underneath me and pushes the two fingers inside my mouth. "Suck," he orders, and I do exactly that.

I suck his fingers dry, and even if I am not gagging on them, tears still pool in my eyes, and soft moans escape my lips. I am so horny that I don't notice I have started rubbing myself on his leg until I feel his fingers digging into the flesh of my hips, trying to stop me from doing that.

"Have I given you permission to do that, little brat?"

"I do what I want," I protest, "and I want a release."

"You will have it. When I let you."

A wave of pleasure courses through my body at his voice. I want my release now, I need it. God, my body aches, it has been aching for days, and the fantasies I had while pressing my vibrator against my clit are not even half as good as the real thing is.

"Stand up," Daniel orders and I obey. "Go to the bench."

"And then?" I ask, afraid.

"Fuck yourself for me," he explains.

I gulp, not sure how to feel about the dominance in his voice. I have always considered myself kinky, but I feel vanilla compared to him and unsure about everything except one thing. I am into this. I like the effects of his commands.

"Put your legs on both sides of the bench," Daniel tells me, helping me figure out the whole thing. "Squat for me, little swan."

"It's too big," I tell him.

"Relax," he says.

Slowly, very slowly, I start squatting over the dildo, holding it with one hand in place. I am so fucking wet that I can feel my juices sliding down the rubber piece when I insert the tip inside of me. The coldness and size of it make me gasp from a combination of surprise, pain, and pleasure.

"That's a good girl," Daniel praises me when I slowly manage to put the whole thing inside of me. "Now ride it."

Putting the palms of my hands in front of me to have some support, I start riding the dildo. At first, I go slow, but after some thrusts, I feel more comfortable with the size and the situation. My eyes are pierced on Daniel, and I can feel my core clenching as I notice how much he is enjoying this when his hand moves to his crotch.

"Harder," he muses at the same time he takes off his dress shirt, putting his tattooed chest on display. I try to consciously make a mental note to explore it more in-depth later.

I am enjoying myself so much that I close my eyes, feeling Daniel's piercing stare on my body. I don't know how long passes, but at some point, I hear him standing up from the chair, his steps moving towards me. The ride of pleasure that I find myself on is so intense that I can't force myself to open my eyes.

I feel the hotness of his hands coming closer, and eventually, they tug on nipple piercings, so hard that a wave of pain moves through my entire body.

"Open your eyes."

"I don't want to," I protest, riding the dildo even harder.

"Don't you dare come," Daniel says, obviously noticing my hand travelling towards my clit.

"But I need to."

"Open your eyes and remove your hand," he repeats with such a dominating tone that I can't do anything but obey. "You are a little brat, aren't you?" he asks, towering over me and holding my face with two fingers so that I am forced to look up at him.

I nod, and then he leans in, kissing me with such an intensity that I can feel the need inside of him traveling into my body. Daniel stops the kiss, abruptly leaving me with my mouth still open, and before I realize it, he is spitting inside my mouth.

Nobody has ever done something like that to me, and I never thought it would be something I would enjoy, but the way my walls clench around the toy and my heartbeat picks up speed proves me wrong.

"Look at yourself in the mirror."

I do as I'm told, only to be more turned on by the image of myself, my nipples hard with Daniel's marks all over them. I understand why he likes this, I see it too, and the image of myself doing this only makes my ache grow. I need more.

"I will give you more."

"I said that out loud?"

"Mhmm," he murmurs, suddenly tugging on my hair so much that I am forced to stand up. Daniel separates the dildo from the bench and then puts it inside a harness that I had not noticed before.

"On your knees."

"You want me to suck?" I ask.

"I want to fuck you from behind while you look at yourself in the mirror. Now, on your knees."

"Yes, sir," I say with a devilish smile and turn my back to him, only so I can sit on my knees on the bench.

In swift and experienced moves, Daniel puts the harness around himself, making sure that everything is in place. Then, he lowers himself to my slit and licks it before he spits on it.

"Fuck," I moan.

"That's what I am about to do to you. Hold on to the bench, Miriam."

Before I can do that, he thrusts inside of me with so much power and rawness that I gasp, trying to bite back a moan. I close my eyes, enjoying the touch of his hands on my hips, but as soon as I do it, he spanks my ass with so much intensity that I scream, just as the waves of pleasure make my core clench around the dildo.

"Eyes open," he says, furious. "I want you to watch every single moment of this." He grabs my hair and tugs on it, forcing my back against his front.

My eyes are wide open, looking at our reflection and enjoying the view. The wave of pain and pleasure, the way he is fucking me, each thrust more powerful than the last, sending me into a spiral of ectasis.

"Oh God," I moan.

Another spank on my ass. Harder this time.

"Don't talk about God when you are fucking the devil."

I smile, remembering that not so long ago, he was the devil reincarnated for me. Look where life has taken me. Loving the way the same man is fucking my brains out.

In the mirror, I see his hand dropping from my nipple, caressing every inch of skin around my stomach, further and further down, until he finally makes it into the nub of nerves between my legs.

I gasp.

Strike that.

I scream.

I scream like a possessed woman, enjoying the rhythmic circles and the way he is working me while he keeps thrusting harder and harder inside of me.

"I am going to come," I let him know, feeling the orgasm building inside of me.

I watch Daniel in the reflection of the mirror. He is divine, and it's only now I realize how much I needed him all this time. He feels the exact need and want for me that I feel for him. His feelings mirror my own, and I feel like I haven't known sex until now. I haven't known care. No man or woman has ever made me feel like this during sex, so much rawness, intensity, passion, desperation, lust, and need.

I focus on the sensation of his hand on my body again, the intensity of the tug on my hair, the bites on my shoulder, and the way his lips leave a trail of kisses over my neck until he makes it to my ear.

"Come for me, little swan," he orders.

And I do.

I come undone with his name on my lips and the feeling that this is only the beginning. He might not have a heart to give, but I am okay with that if he is willing to give me the rest.

CHAPTER THIRTY-EIGHT

Youngster: So… Philip and Selene weren't the only ones consummating their marriage, were they?

Burton: Mention my wife again and see what happens.

Youngster: Someone woke up feeling possessive.

Me: He wakes up like that every day.

Youngster: Don't ignore my question.

Burton: As much as I hate to say this… Answer him!

Me: Nope.

Youngster: Did he just write "nope?"

Burton: They so did it last night.

Me: I don't know what you're talking about.

Youngster: So, if I come into your room, I won't find Miriam in your bed, naked?

Me: Come into my room and it will be the last time you breathe.

...

I turn off the phone and toss it onto the nightstand, making sure to mute it so Miriam won't wake up from the sound of the notifications. I have been up for hours now. If I'm being honest, I never fell asleep. Last night's a blur. Miriam and I pushed it to four rounds of sex, and when I thought we were done, I went to take a cold shower, only for her to join me and start the game again. After that, we both ended up naked in bed – well almost, I am still wearing my boxers – bodies entwined, skin still flushed and tingling. Miriam fell asleep right after that, her head pressed against my chest, while I stared at the ceiling, coming to terms with the entire night.

Sex has always been my escape, a release, a way to reclaim control when everything else felt chaotic and uncertain. But, this time... this time it's different. It's not just physical pleasure, though there was plenty of that too.

No, it's more than that.

It's the way she looked at me, the way she surrendered herself to me with a trust so profound, it almost took my breath away. Miriam's not like anyone I've been with before, but I didn't need last night to know that.

She's feisty, stubborn, a spitfire.

And yet, last night, she surrendered to me in ways I never thought possible. She could read my every desire and anticipate my needs without me having to utter a single word. And the best part? The way she respected my boundaries, the way she made sure everything was okay with me, without making me feel like less of a man.

Most of my partners take time to understand my needs. But Miriam? Miriam seemed to understand me from the moment our bodies collided. She didn't need a roadmap to navigate the contours of my pleasure. And God, did she make me feel alive. Made me come harder than I care to admit.

This woman is wild. An untamed force of nature, and she's going to be the end of me. Yet, I can't force myself to walk away from this bed. She has laid claim to my body and even a part of my soul, but my heart is still out of reach. She can have everything she wants, but that part of me will remain beyond her reach forever, locked away in a case that requires three different keys to open it.

“Good morning,” Miriam says with a raspy morning voice, dragging me away from my thoughts.

"Morning, swan," I murmur, my voice barely above a whisper as I gaze down at her effortless morning beauty and the after-sex glow.

"Have you been up for long?"

"A while," I reply, the lie slipping effortlessly from my lips. "How are you feeling?" I ask, my fingertips navigating over the soft skin of her arm.

"Happy," she says, exploring my tattoos with her nails, careful not to touch the areas where my scars are. "The dress in Istanbul and the one from last night had a cross. Are they made to match the one tattooed on your back?"

I nod.

"Why?"

"Because I want you to always have a piece of me."

"That is really sweet."

"Look at the engraving on your ring," I tell her.

Miriam takes the black diamond off her finger and looks at it, obviously noticing the same cross engraved in the silver band for the first time.

"What does it say?" she asks, curious.

"It is mine to avenge; I will repay," I cite that passage of the bible that fueled my revenge. "It's from the bible."

"I didn't know you were a religious person."

"I am Catholic, I just don't go to church."

"Why did you choose that passage?"

"Because God is supposed to send sinners to hell once they are dead. But I want to punish them while they are still alive."

I expect Miriam to excuse herself and run away, instead, she presses herself closer to me, and places kisses on my neck, and starts to trail her hand down my stomach.

"Aren't you going to run away?" I ask when it is obvious that she has no plans of fleeing, which makes me question if she has some sense of self-preservation at all.

"You can't scare me away, Conte."

I look down at her, meeting the intensity of her gaze and giving her a soft peck on her lips.

"Can I ask you another question?"

I nod again, noticing how her hand is closer to my boxers.

"Would you like me to go down on you?"

"Do you want to go down on me?" I say, raising a brow. Miriam nods eagerly, making a soft sound with her throat. "Then, by all means, be my guest."

"I will, but is there something you don't like, or something I need to be aware of? I just… I feel so unsure, I want to make you feel good, but what if I fuck up and—"

"Stop." I rush, holding her tightly in my arms. "Nothing you could do would ever make me feel bad, and in case you do something I don't like, I have a mouth and a voice to tell you so. We will learn together what both of us are into, okay? We just need to talk through it."

"Thanks," Miriam whispers.

"What am I going to do with you, my little swan?" I groan, more to myself than to her. She is so perfect for me, it's almost painful.

"How about you start with fucking me?"

I smile and, grabbing her waist, I roll us over so that she is underneath me. Leaning down, I kiss her, enjoying the warmth of lips pressed against mine and her tongue dancing with my own.

"Careful what you wish," I warn.

"You can be careful for both of us. I have already given in to you," she says with a smile, but her words weigh heavily on me.

Somehow, I find it in me to push the thoughts to the back of my head and enjoy the moment.

Miriam

Eventually, and most importantly against my will, Daniel manages to pry me from the confines of the bedroom, though not without going for a few more rounds of sweaty and delicious sex first. The last one left me feeling exhilarated and exhausted.

I always considered myself to be a fairly sexual person, but compared to everything Daniel did to my body, I would say that I am pretty vanilla. Still, I managed to keep up, and I know by the way his body reacted that he liked what I did to him too.

We make our way down the stairs into the dining room, my legs shaking after the past few hours. Our friends are already gathered around the table. Sasha is nursing a cup of her classic black coffee, while João shamelessly pilfers fruit from her plate, much to her mock indignation. Selene and Philip sit together, exchanging loving glances. Philip is trying to feed Selene, while the redhead shakes her head, trying to avoid the piece of waffle on Philip's fork.

"Morning," Daniel greets the group.

"Look who finally decided to grace us with their presence," Sasha quips, shooting him a playful glare.

"You guys had fun?" Selene asks genuinely.

"Are you deaf?" João interjects.

"Watch it." Philip cautions him with a warning glare.

"Come on, we could all hear them last night," João continues, oblivious to my embarrassment.

Oh god, was I really that loud?

Mortification threatens to consume me, but before I can spiral into a full-blown panic attack, Daniel reaches for my hand, squeezing it reassuringly. I hate how safe and grounded his touch makes me feel.

"I've watched you fuck my best friend against a wall. I'm sure you are mature enough to handle a little noise," Daniel retorts, shutting down the conversation. "I'll make sure to leave earplugs in your room next time, João."

"Well, I'm just happy you guys finally got past your differences," Selene says, looking at me with a radiant smile all over her face that warms my heart.

"The friend group thanks you for that," Sasha adds, raising her cup in the air, which earns her a look from Daniel, who remains silent next to me.

"So, what are your plans for today?" I inquire, trying to shift the conversation to something that won't mortify me, then take a seat at the table and pour myself a much-needed cup of coffee.

"We're having lunch with my parents," Selene replies, her expression glowing with excitement. "And then we're off to Mallorca for a week. We were supposed to go to Egypt for our honeymoon, but I figured a relaxing beach getaway would be better until the baby is here."

"Isn't it cold in Marbella this time of year?" I ask, curious.

“Yeah, but I just wanted to unwind, away from the cameras. They have been trailing us for a while between the wedding, the child, my retirement, and then becoming team principal,” Philip explains.

“Remember the simulator test is in two weeks,” Daniel reminds him, ever the responsible one.

“And then it's off to Barcelona for testing!” João adds eagerly.

“Can't wait for the season to begin,” I chime in.

I let my gaze drift around the table while I drink my coffee, soaking in the sight of my friends. There's something so comforting about the easy banter and familiar routines we have set. I have always felt like this with them, but today it hits me differently. It’s the sense of belonging, the one that I've spent so long searching for.

I was a nomad growing up, drifting from place to place with my parents as they chased their dreams. I love my mom and dad, but there's something uniquely special about the family that I've chosen for myself. We may not be bound by blood, but the bonds we have are just as strong.

Setting my coffee to the side, I bask in the warmth of their laughter and the comfort of their company, and, for the first time in a long time, I finally feel like I am at home.

CHAPTER THIRTY-NINE

The Cat lay still in the middle of a desolate field, the scorching sun bearing down on the bare skin of his neck, casting beads of sweat beneath his camouflage attire. His binoculars were fixated on the distant villa where his nemesis, Daniel, was spending the weekend with his wife and the friends of the couple.

The Cat had learned to be a patient man in the last decade, to wait for his moment in the shadows. He wasn't going to lie about it, it had cost him a lot, but that patience had become a very useful trait. After all, if it weren't for said patience, he would probably just have kidnapped his nemesis and made him pay. But this way, he wasn't only going to make Conte pay, no… He was going to make him pay and suffer a fate ten times worse.

A lifetime of obsession had allowed him to come up with the most twisted fantasies of pain. They were originally intended to be inflicted on Daniel, but now Miriam, his new wife, would be his target, and The Cat would let Conte watch as he destroyed the black girl, the same way he had once destroyed Daniela.

The Cat had wanted to kidnap Miriam after the boat party, after all, that is why he had drugged her. But Daniel was far too close, and it had been impossible for him to get his fingers on the girl.

In hindsight, it was so utterly predictable of Conte to buy the Formula One team. Daniel had spent a lifetime trying to destroy it, only to then buy it and cleanse it of all the evil.

The Cat laughed. Daniel did have pure intentions, but he didn't know that The Red Horses were no longer on his team. All of them had fled after the death of Mancini. It was what was best for the organization. Eventually, they would find a new company to corrupt, a new industry to use to their advantage. But that was irrelevant for The Cat. He only wanted his revenge.

And he was getting it.

He knew already that Daniel had received his text, and if that weren't enough, shooting his office window with a bullet might have done the job. It was so romantic seeing the way Conte had thrown himself over the girl to shield and protect her from harm. However, the plan backfired when he decided it was time for Miriam to move in with him. Getting access to her had become more difficult now that Conte was all over her almost all day long.

But The Cat was, in fact, a very patient man and willing to wait for the perfect opportunity.

With a barely perceptible movement, he lit up a cigarette, his fingers trembling with anticipation as he retrieved the disposable phone he purchased for this very moment. His thumb hovered over the screen, ready to send the message he had been thinking about all day long.

"I am coming for her."

He pushed the Send button, and then his eyes drifted back to the binoculars pointing towards Daniel's location inside the villa. It took the CEO a few minutes to check his notifications, but when he finally did, the fear in his body became palpable, etched into every line of his face.

Daniel might have emerged victorious in their initial battle, but The Cat knew one thing for certain:

He was going to win the war.

F1 2026 DRIVER LINE-UP

JOÃO QUERINHO

EMI SAITO

OLIVER MUNGUIA

NANDO FERNAN

LAWSON SROLLER

MARCUS VERSTEEG

ARCHIBALD FITZROY

ALEX SAUD

CHAPTER FORTY

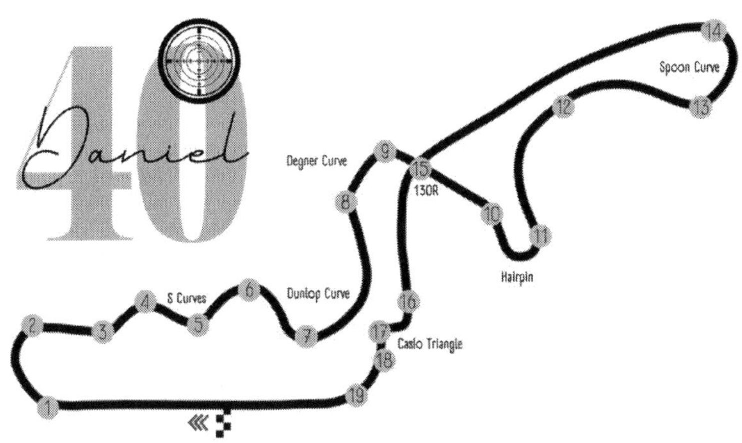

Burton: Punctuality is of the essence.

Me: We are coming.

Burton: Who is 'we'?

Youngster: The wife who is super glued to him, duh!

Burton: I hope she is trustworthy. We are dealing with sensible information today, Conte.

Me: No me jodas!

Youngster: Sasha usually says 'si, joder!'

Me: Shut. Up. Now.

...

We are already in the new year, and it's been two long weeks since that fucking message landed in my inbox, disrupting the equilibrium of my world with the use of five words: "I am coming for her."

Not a single waking moment has passed where I haven't felt the weight of that threat haunting my thoughts and plaguing my nightmares. The ones of the most tragic event of my life have been replaced by the fear of losing her, of losing Miriam. And the worst is the realization of how terrified and helpless I am in the face of this threat.

For someone who's spent a lifetime bending technology to my will, hacking into systems and manipulating outcomes with a flick of my wrist, the fact that I can't uncover the identity of this fucker fills me with rage. It's a bitter pill to swallow, knowing that despite all my skills and resources, I am powerless to protect the woman I—

I stop the line of thought, unable to finish the sentence.

Miriam hasn't noticed my fear—not yet, or at least I don't think so. I've done my best to conceal it, but there have been subtle shifts in the way I treat her, in the way I hover near her like a sentinel, unwilling to let her out of my sight. Since we have been back in London, she has been sleeping in my room rather than going back to hers in the penthouse, which is convenient for more than one reason.

I've also started to include her in my business meetings, insisting that she familiarize herself with every aspect of the company in preparation for when she assumes ownership of her shares at the end of the year. Needless to say, the members of the board are part of an Old Boy's Club, all of them wealthy, white men, who have been working for the company for probably longer than Miriam has been alive. And in like every other Old Boy's Club, they seem to have a particular hate for women and minorities.

Member number 2 has not been too happy about seeing her around, especially now that she has started to work on having more women in our academy program.

Bringing Miriam to the simulator is only partly because of my fear.

"We are here," I announce, as we get head inside.

It takes my eyes a while until they get accustomed to the dimly lit space. Emi, João, and Philip are already waiting for us. Near them, in the center of the room, stands a sleek, imposing car, positioned in front of a massive screen that envelops the vehicle, creating the illusion of a real-life race track.

"You're late," Philip tells me.

"Don't talk to your boss like that," I tease him, earning a glare from the man in return.

Everyone has been working hard on the new car, fine-tuning its performance to perfection in preparation for the upcoming season. With less than a month left for testing, the pressure is on to deliver a car that's worthy of João's championship-winning talent. It's no secret that our engineers have tailored the car to suit João's driving style—he's earned that much after winning the championship at Volpella, twice.

Emi, on the other hand, still has to prove himself in that regard, but he is the only driver besides Philip who has a similar style to João, so hiring him was a conscious decision to ensure that our car would be versatile enough to accommodate both of their strengths. If João wants something done to the car, Emi will have a chance to adapt faster.

"Sorry, I had a meeting that ran longer than expected," Miriam explains, her tone apologetic.

"As thrilled as I am to see my favorite married woman here—though you being married is one of the biggest tragedies in my life," Emi begins, "I need to ask. What brings you to the simulator?"

"I want to learn more about the business so I can make it more cost-efficient," Miriam replies with determination.

"You can start by lowering his salary and raising mine," Emi interjects, pointing a playful finger at João.

"We can talk about it when you beat him on the track," I retort.

"Less talking, more driving," Philip tells the drivers. "Everyone, thanks for being here today," he says to the engineers at the back of the room, who are looking at their screens filled with statistics. Even Aiden Nowey, the brains behind the car, is here today. "We have two weeks to turn this car into perfection, and, as a team, I am sure we will be able to make it happen. We have already tested the car on different tracks over the past few weeks, proving that we can still improve the speed on some. Today, I would like us to try Suzuka Circuit and see where we can improve without damaging the progress made on other tracks."

The engineers nod in synchronization, smiles playing on their faces.

The simulator is a crucial component of the car development process, as it allows drivers to experience realistic racing conditions. It gives them the opportunity to practice and refine their skills without any constraints, and it also gives the rest of the team insights to help fine-tune the car.

The simulator is just as crucial as the wind tunnel, which is absolutely vital in an era where aerodynamics has become so relevant in F1 cars. Unfortunately, since Cavaglio got second place in the championship last year, this season we are not allowed a lot of wind tunnel time in order to keep things fair with teams ranking lower in the Constructor's Championship.

And, as much as I do love the simulator, it also doesn't guarantee you a perfect car. It has happened only a couple of times in this new era of F1, but cars that seemed perfect in the simulator, acted completely differently on the track. Aiden has a million theories about it, after all, he is the expert on how to build a formula car.

"João, you are in first," Philip instructs him.

The Brazilian driver doesn't hesitate and jumps inside the car, already wearing his racing shoes. Someone in the back selects the Suzuka track. He sits behind the wheel, a flicker of determination in his eyes as he prepares to tackle the circuit. The hum of the machinery fills the room as he checks the controls at his disposal, adjusting everything to his needs.

With a gentle press on the accelerator, João unleashes the full might of the simulator, the high-definition screens surrounding him springing to life with the vivid colors of the Japanese circuit. As he guides the virtual car through the first corner, João'ssenses kick in.

He drives through the sweeping curves and tight chicanes of Suzuka, pushing the simulator to its limits, his movements precise and controlled as he seeks to extract every ounce of performance from the machine beneath him.

After a couple of laps, he starts feeling more in tune with the car and gives more feedback to his engineers.

"Entering turn one, the car feels stable under braking, but I'm struggling with a bit of understeer through the exit," he remarks, his voice calm and measured despite the intensity of his focus.

"Copy, we will adjust the front wing to deal with the understeer," the bald man in the back tells him. He used to be

João's racing engineer at Volpella, and, after two championships, he decided to follow him to Cavaglio Nero.

João's comments become more animated when he goes through the Esses section of the track. "The car is flying in this section!" he almost screams, joy in his tone.

Through the hairpin at Spoon Curve, João's voice takes on a note of determination. "Spoon feels good, but I'm losing time on the exit," he observes.

I look at his engineer, who leans forward, his eyes scanning the data for any clues. "Got it. We'll tweak the different settings to give you better traction," he assures him with confidence.

With each passing lap, the feedback becomes more detailed and precise, his intimate knowledge of the track and the car's performance shining with every corner. And though the virtual world of the simulator lacks the thrill of the real thing, there's no denying the passion and intensity with which João drives.

The best lap in the simulator is at 1:27.310, the record is at 1:27.06 in a car that followed the previous regulation. The limit to improve is as high as the sky, but the smile on my face and the one on the faces of everyone working in this room right now tells us that it's a pretty damn good time.

I am so ready to start making history next month.

CHAPTER FORTY-ONE

Me: There is a real snake in my hotel room!

Miriam has sent a picture.

Blonde Dread: Shoot it.

Ginger Bestie: Call reception?

Me: Well, the snake is all over the room phone.

Ginger Bestie: Then there is only one option.

Ginger Bestie: Flea the room.

Blonde Dread: Why isn't Daniel helping you?

Me: He is at the track, preparing for the weekend.

Blonde Dread: No guns?

Me: Not even a butter knife ;)

Ginger Bestie: Run for your life!!!!!

…

The season starts in Melbourne this year, as Ramadan is in full bloom all over the world. Originally, I hadn't planned on attending the Australian race, but after weeks of nonstop grind with the white wigs, trying to push for more opportunities for female drivers in Formula One, I needed a break. So, when Daniel offered to take me with him to Melbourne for a week, I jumped at the chance, no questions asked.

However, I have started to get suspicious of him.

The man hasn't left my side for a single second since Selene's wedding. At this point, I can only go to the toilet by myself. But showers? That's a different topic… I guess, we're saving the environment by showering together now. Not that I'm complaining. I like those moments, like his smell mingling with mine, the touch of his skin on my body, and the perfect rhythm that we have found in the past few weeks. At this point, I feel like he knows me even better than I know myself.

But I'm not naïve. I know that our playing husband and wife charade isn't going to change anything in the long run. In nine months, we'll be back to being strangers, divorce papers in hand, and more money and assets in my account than I had a year ago, but lonelier than before too.

For now, I'm doing my best to bury my feelings and pretend like I don't care. Deep down, though, I know that I'm just fooling myself. Sooner or later, the façade is going to crumble, and when it does, I'll be left picking up the pieces of my shattered heart. But, for now, I'll soak up every moment with Daniel.

"What are you thinking about, little swan?" Daniel's voice pulls me back to the present.

"You haven't called me that for a while," I say, surprised.

We've been holed up in Daniel's office at the Albert Park track all morning, immersed in our respective jobs. While Daniel has been busy sending emails and holding meetings with clients and potential sponsors, I've been strategizing ways to get support for my initiatives with the Old Boy's Club.

I know I should be spending some time enjoying the Aussie sun, and to be fair, normally during race weekends, you'd find me around the paddock with Selene, soaking in the atmosphere. But Selene is only going to the European races because of her pregnancy, and now that I am dating the CEO of an F1 team, I am too afraid to leave the premises alone.

"Sad about it?" he asks with the corner of his lip tilted upwards.

"I couldn't care less." I huff.

"Don't lie to me," he says, leaning across the office table.

"I am not!"

"Miriam." He grunts, but it's playful. "You know what happens when you lie to me."

I bite my bottom lip and press my thighs together under the table, trying to relieve the tension somehow, but I am far too gone, remembering the things that Daniel has done to my body whenever I have talked back, lied, or acted like a brat. He might punish me, but God do I love it when he makes me beg for it.

"I am not," I repeat, playing with fire.

I stand up from my chair and move towards him, then lean over the desk and pretend to look at what he is doing on his laptop, but my vision blurs the second his fingertips come into contact with the back of my naked legs.

Yup, wearing a short dress was the right decision.

"What are you working on?"

"Looking at the new sponsor for the cars. There is a Japanese brand that wants to join us after the summer break, thanks to Emi," he says, his hand raising even more, not stopping until he gives my butt a squeeze.

"How much are they offering?" I ask.

"Seventy million." His hand slowly finds its way to my underwear. When he touches it, I can feel the warm wetness that has pooled there for the past five minutes. I gasp at the coldness of his digits when he pushes the string of my thong to the side and grazes the skin of my slit.

"That's a great offer," I hear myself saying.

"It is." His voice is low, raspy, almost a growl. "Do you think we should go higher? Ask them for more?"

"We are Cavaglio Nero. We can go up to one hundred million."

"Higher it is." He smiles, and then he starts to insert two fingers inside of me. The digits slide effortlessly in, igniting a fire of desire that consumes my senses. At first, his movements are familiar, but then I feel a shift—a subtle change in technique that sends a shiver of anticipation down my spine.

While his fingers explore deeper, I find myself gasping for air, my body responding eagerly to his touch. Then, suddenly, I feel the palm of his hand pressing against my clit, and I bite down so hard on my lip to stifle a moan that I am sure I have drawn blood.

I can feel Daniel's fingers curling inside me, hitting just the right spot to send sparks of pleasure coursing through my veins. His movements grow faster, and the best part is that his palm never moves from my clit, applying pressure that makes the hairs on the back of my neck raise.

"Oh my god," I moan, my voice barely a whisper, as pleasure washes over me in waves.

But then, Daniel stops. Without warning. I open my eyes, thinking that someone has entered the office, but the door is still closed. When the man with his fingers inside of me doesn't say a word and just looks at me with that smug grin of his, I know exactly what he's doing, and it's driving me wild with need.

"More," I plead, arching my back and tilting my neck upwards in silent submission.

A small eternity seems to pass before his fingers start pumping inside of me, repeating the same rhythm, each movement calculated to send me spiraling closer to the edge, but every time I moan or my traitorous body gives away the fact that I am about to come, he slows down, drawing out the exquisite torture until I'm practically begging for a release.

"I need to come," I beg, the words tumbling from my lips.

"Do you?" Daniel's voice is teasing.

"Please, Conte," I can almost hear myself crying.

"Then beg for it," he demands, and I do, my pleas falling from my lips like a prayer.

"Please, please, please, let me cum," I repeat desperately, my voice barely audible over the pounding of my heart, and my body trembling with need.

"Good girl." His praise sends a jolt of electricity through me.

Standing up from his chair, he steps behind me, his fingers still buried deep inside me, while his free hand wraps around my neck in a possessive grip. I gasp at the sudden pressure, feeling a rush of excitement mingled with a hint of fear.

"Make me cum," I beg, as his hand tightens around my neck.

The speed of his fingers increases, driving me closer to the edge with each passing moment. I can feel my climax building.

"Oh my god," I scream so hard, Daniel moves his hand from my neck and slaps it over my mouth to muffle my screams while pleasure gets the best of me. My brain is in a fog, and I am no longer in control of my own actions. "Fuck! Fuck! Fuck!"

Daniel doesn't stop. He pushes me further, driving in harder and faster until suddenly, I feel my own squirt into the palm of his hand.

"Oh my god!" I scream, but this time, it's not from pleasure. It's from mortification. I try to shift my weight and escape Daniel's hold, but he pins me in place with his body.

"Don't you dare move!" he growls. "Show me how hard you can squirt for me."

His words do it for me. I stop holding back. And then I feel it, the release I've been craving, the explosion of pleasure that sends me careening over the edge. My squirt hits his hand, flies all over the desk, and even makes it to the floor. It's a mess, but my orgasm keeps intensifying, and I can't stop myself from rubbing my clit against his palm.

"Fuck!" I cry out, my body shaking with the force of my orgasm as I collapse against him, spent and trembling once the wave of ecstasy and adrenaline is done coursing through my veins.

"Look at what you've done," Daniel says, grabbing my chin with two fingers and forcing me to meet his gaze. "You've made such a mess, little swan." I blush furiously, trying to hide my face from him, but he won't let me. "Don't you dare hide from me." His voice is soft but firm.

"I need to clean that up," I whisper-shout, still feeling mortified.

"Don't worry about it. I will take care of it. You have already worked enough, my swan."

Daniel takes a step back and somehow manages to make me sit in the comfortable leather chair. If I thought we were done, I was far from being right. In a swift move, he opens my legs and grabs me from my hips, pulling me to the edge of the seat.

"Who does this pussy belong to?" he asks, demanding.

"Me," I tease.

Daniel slaps my pussy, forcing me to squirm in the seat.

"Try again!" he growls.

"You!" I almost scream.

"Good girl," he says before giving it a thorough lick. "As much as I would love to stay with you and make you come in seven different ways, I need to go to the garage for the qualifying session," he says, then gives my pussy a soft kiss before standing up and giving me a kiss.

I feel like there must be something wrong with me because when his lips touch mine in a passionate and wet kiss, all I can think of is how much I am enjoying the taste of my own arousal in my partner's mouth. I love it, and I would love to do everything all over again, but time is against us. So, I kiss Daniel with all the passion that I have to give for the brief moment we have left. My hand wanders from his shoulder to his chest, and underneath my palm, I can feel the strong and hectic beat of his heart.

He doesn't have a heart; I remind myself of his words. My hand, however, is telling me a different tale.

And even if he didn't have one, maybe mine could be enough for the both of us.

CHAPTER FORTY-TWO

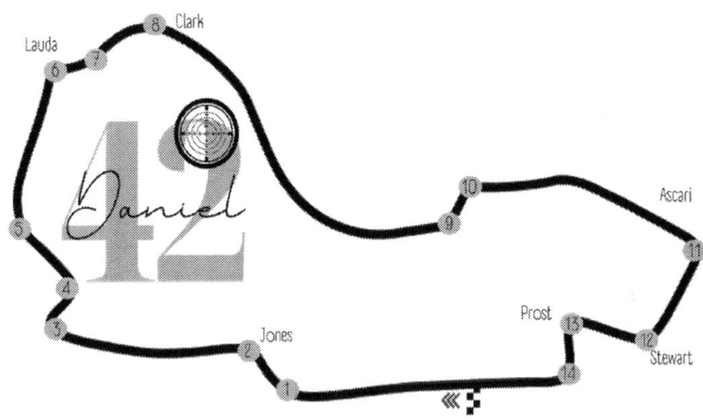

Not a single second has passed when I stopped thinking about the way Miriam's pussy was dripping onto my hands. And, let me tell you, it's been a damn long twenty-four hours with that image replaying in the back of my head. The most agonizing part has been knowing that I need to keep my mind clear today, now that the race is about to kick off.

Thankfully, Miriam hasn't made it to the track yet, giving me a couple of hours to focus on my job instead of her needy pussy, and, let's be honest, all of her. She is a drug, and I am an addict at this point. The first step is admission.

The start line of the track is packed to the brim, the air buzzing with adrenaline. Teams scramble around their cars, drivers perched on the edge of the track, their minds mapping every twist and turn of the circuit in front of them. Our Cavaglio Nero drivers pulled off a one-two yesterday during qualifying, with João leading and Emi right on his tail. Not bad for a team with a brand-new setup that is less than orthodox. I've never been one to play by the rules, and building this team is no different.

I settle into a quiet corner of the garage where I can watch the race with eagle eyes without getting in anyone's way. My attention is fixed on the livestream of the parade when I feel the weight of someone's gaze on me. I don't need to turn around to know it's Miriam.

"Missed me?" Her voice is sultry, teasing, and I can't help but smirk.

"Didn't give me enough time to," I tease her.

"You don't need time or distance to miss me."

She isn't wrong.

"Don't give yourself too much credit," I lie.

"According to our marriage contract, I'm worth a couple of millions," she quips, and I can't help but chuckle. Leave it to Miriam to turn everything into a joke.

When I turn my head, hoping to come up with a snarky comment, I have to force myself to bite my tongue, so my jaw won't fall to the ground at the sight of her.

Saying that I am captivated doesn't even begin to cover it.

Not when she's wearing braids, —pitch-black, waist-long, and adorned with hints of gold in the top and front pieces. Miriam looks good no matter what, but there's something about those braids that exudes confidence. It's like she's wearing her strength and she shows how she doesn't give a fuck about what the world might say, and damn if it isn't the most attractive thing I've ever seen.

"You did your braids," I point out.

"You really are Mr. Obvious," she jokes, rolling her eyes.

"They look great. You look great."

"I know," she says. Then, she gives me a kiss on my chin and takes the seat next to mine, putting the headset on her head in elegant moves that leave me out of breath. This is what I have become. A man who is transfixed by simple hand movements.

The race officially starts after the national anthem is done playing. All drivers make their way into their cars and drive the first formation lap of the season. The air is filled with tension when they finally line up on the grid again in front of lights, which slowly turn on. One by one.

I struggle to keep my commentator's voice silent, but inside my head, I narrate the race as if I was standing next to Sasha in our cabin.

The lights go out.

João gets a great exit, but Emi isn't short of talent and is right behind his rare at the exit. Munguia is right behind the pair, but it's Emi who takes João's recoil.

João is faster. He takes the outside, getting a clean and smooth exit. There are a lot of battles already going on at the end of the group, giving the drivers in the middle the possibility to breathe a little bit and stretch out the group. On the transmission, I can see the fourth driver losing his position to his teammate.

But my eyes are fixed on the cameras following my own drivers. João starts creating a gap, trying to get at least a second between himself and Emi before the DRS is activated, so he can escape his teammate, but the Japanese driver stays there, knowing the importance of that second.

Surprisingly, nobody has crashed, and there are no pieces of carbon fiber flying around the track, which is quite an unusual sight for Melbourne.

Emi is getting closer to João.

Less than a couple of meters, and the drivers will be able to enable the DRS. Emi stays there, only three-tenths behind his teammate. Usually, Philip as team principal, would have to give orders, let them fight, or keep one behind. He has clear instructions from me – well not necessarily. Nobody gives that man any orders. However, we are in agreement.

Let the best man win.

The first few laps pass. Emi is practically glued to João's rear when they cross the finish line lap after lap. He has been trying to find a spot to overtake the Brazilian driver, not finding the right moment yet, but I have a feeling this is going to be an interesting race to watch. Two teammates fighting for P1.

There are four DRS zones, but only two points of detection.

"Oh my god!" Miriam whisper-shouts next to me.

I see it too, Emi going for João. How close he is. Ten laps. It only takes the bastard ten laps before he goes around the outside, right before entering the fifth corner. He overtakes João Querinho.

Emi Saito leads the race.

João is now in second place.

My heart pumps faster, driven by the adrenaline coursing through my bloodstream. The Brazilian driver, however, hasn't given up. He is so close to Emi's rear now that he has DRS, only four-tenths keeping the teammates apart.

I am sitting on the edge of my seat and in the corner of my eye, I can see Miriam doing the same thing. She is even biting her nails.

How will this race end?

Miriam

I am not sure how my heart is still working after the entire race.

Fifty-three laps.

Not a single second of peace.

João and Emi have fought each other every lap of the race. Keeping a clean fight of overtakes that have had the entire team on the edge of their seats, probably the rest of the world too.

The final meters drag out. But it's clear who is going to win the race when the black and yellow car passes Stewart, followed by Prost, and then dances out of corner sixteen on his way to the finish line.

I want to scream.

Fuck, it's so hard to stand still and not jump and make a scene in front of everyone in the room. But when Emi Saito approaches the finish line with João right behind him, only a couple of tenths away from him, I can't contain myself anymore and jump to my feet, almost kicking down the chair behind me.

The Samurai.

The Samurai wins.

The Samurai takes the first position.

Cavaglio Nero has a one-two finish in the first race of the season!

Everyone screams around me. Philip is getting hugs from the crew. The mechanics are long gone, having run to the fence to welcome their drivers to the finish line. It's one thing seeing your favorite team win. But when Cavaglio wins, it's an entirely different thing.

No fan can dislike it. It doesn't matter if you hate their drivers, the car, the people working in the team. It doesn't matter who you follow in this sport. Because when Cavaglio wins, everyone cheers. Nobody is immune to the history and the charm of the team.

"We won!" Daniel says next to me.

"You won!" I echo his words, and without thinking about it, I throw myself all over him and press my lips to his, sealing the first public kiss we have had since our wedding.

Daniel stands up, his hands holding my waist, his lips still pressed to mine. When we finally break out of our little bubble, there is a camera pointed at us.

I want to hide, but Daniel stops me.

"Let the world see who you belong to," he whispers.

"Let the world see who you would die for," I answer. Daniel wets his lips, an intense mix of happiness, adrenaline, excitement, lust and so much more all over his face. When no words emerge from his lips, I say, "Let's go watch your podium finish."

"You are my podium finish, Miriam."

2026 DRIVER STANDINGS

AFTER THE AUSTRALIAN GP

POINTS	DRIVER	Team
25	EMI SAITO	
18	JOÃO QUERINHO	
15	OLIVER MUNGUIA	
12	ALEX SAUD	BLUE CHEETAH
10	NANDO FERNAN	
8	ARCHIBALD FITZROY	BLUE CHEETAH
6	MARCUS VERSTEEG	
4	LAWSON STROLLER	

CHAPTER FORTY-THREE

The season rolls on. Emi's victory down under was a great start, and then João's won in Suzuka, snagging a total of twenty-five points that has left both teammates equal in the championship standings.

Two races down, and I am pretty sure this is going to be one of those seasons that people will remember in twenty years. The Chinese GP is next on the calendar, but there is still a bit over a week before we need to fly there. My attention should be on the team; however, my mind couldn't be further away from that this week.

I've got bigger fish to kill right now.

Just when I was about to give up and take the message I got at Philip and Selene's wedding as a sick and twisted joke, I got another one.

"Ella se esta quedando sin tiempo."

She is running out of time.

Whoever's playing this sick game clearly has a twisted plan, and I am determined to find them, even if I have been unsuccessful until now. Miriam deserves better than this shit show, but I'm struggling to keep my promise to keep her safe. How the hell am I supposed to shield her from someone I can't even find?

I've pissed off my fair share of people in this lifetime, most of them members of The Red Horses. Now, it seems, they're coming back to haunt me. Sasha and I made sure to put out their fires during the 2024 season, but embers have a nasty habit of lasting after the flames are gone.

When I took the reins of this team, I made damn sure to vet every single person in the company who had any sort of attachment to the organization. Most of them checked out clean, but there's always that one rotten apple lurking in the shadows.

Like the white wig yapping away about quarterly reports right now. He has been part of the team for as long as Mancini had been, taking care of the accounts with Varlant. There is nothing pointing towards him having anything to do with the organization. Well, I have not found any evidence yet. But someone in his position and with his power had to know what was going on, even if he didn't actively partake in their twisted games.

I've never found an enemy I couldn't beat, but this... this feels different. Like I'm staring down the barrel of a loaded gun with no idea who's about to pull the trigger. And until I figure out who is behind the curtain, I'm stuck in a game with no rules.

It takes me a while, but, eventually, I am able to focus on the quarterly review of the board meeting again. White Wig Number Two drones on about revenue streams and profit margins, his voice like nails on a chalkboard. The numbers flash on the screen, but all I see are dollar signs swirling in a dizzying haze.

Miriam has been silently sitting next to me, but she has been very focused, taking notes of everything on her laptop. Suddenly, she stops typing. Ever the eagle-eyed accountant, my little swan. "Excuse me," she says, her voice cutting through the monotony. "There seems to be a discrepancy here."

"No there isn't," White Wig Number Two replies.

Miriam ignores him and strides towards the front of the room, her heels clicking. "In that case, you won't mind showing the January figures again."

I smile on the inside, while White Wig rolls his eyes at her, but still does as he is asked and shows her the slide for the month of January.

Miriam looks at the numbers with precision, and, with a flick of her wrist, she points to one of the figures. "Look at the revenue from this sponsor. It's listed as nine million, but according to the monthly report I received, it should be at least twelve."

White Wig's eyes narrow, and I can practically see the smoke coming out of his ears. "That's ridiculous. You must be mistaken."

"I can show you the report, I have it on my laptop. There's definitely a discrepancy here," Miriam says, shaking her head.

"Are you insinuating I am not doing my job right?"

"It's not personal." Miriam's jaw tightens, but she remains composed. "However, it is important to be precise. Those three million are what could make a difference. If you are not counting them at the quarterly report, then what are we doing with the difference?"

White Wig babbles like a fish outside of the water, and I notice how his tie is visibly tightening around his neck. His face turns an alarming shade of red as he tries to untie it.

"I bet this is only a mistake. But look at the bright side, if we had in fact made only nine million, we would still be in green numbers, and passing our goals with flying colors. That money should be used for the female academy project. I talked to a female driver in Melbourne. She's from Thailand, incredibly talented, and has won every single race she has participated in. However, she hasn't found the opportunity to prove herself with the boys of FRECA or F4—"

"ENOUGH!" he screams, losing his temper. "I won't tolerate a woman, and especially not one who intends to tell me how to do my work while she wears those childish braids! "He doesn't say it, but I can see him looking at her skin color, his racism showing from miles away, and his anger building up even more, until he finally explodes again. "It is bad enough that we have a monster and abomination as a CEO, it only makes you worse in my eyes!" he screams, pointing at Miriam, his nostrils flaring. "You're married to a trans man, a monster! And you are the inferior sex! You are only here because you are f..."

"I suggest you don't finish that sentence," I growl, each word dripping with menace as I rise from my chair. With measured steps, I make my way to the front of the room where White Wig is unraveling before our eyes.

"Or what? Are you going to cut my head off?" he taunts.

"Don't tempt him," Miriam interjects, proving us a united front.

White Wig sneers at her, a twisted smirk twisting his lips. "She wouldn't dare," he scoffs, using my pronouns wrong intentionally.

In one swift motion, I close the distance between us, my hand curling into a fist. Before anyone can react, I grab him by the collar, yanking him close until our faces are mere inches apart.

"Listen here, you sorry excuse for a human being," I seethe, my voice low and dangerous. "You mention a single racist, disrespectful comment towards my wife ever again and you won't like what happens next. Your wife will find out all of your little secrets, the women you spend your nights with when you tell her you are staying late at the office. Your children will lose their spot in those IVY League Universities you secured for them. I will make sure that your accounts are cleared and you will watch them be forced to scrub toilets with their bare hands in the shittiest McDonald's the country has. Are. We. Clear?"

White Wig's eyes widen in shock, a flicker of fear dancing behind his gaze. For a moment, he's speechless, rendered powerless by my sudden display of dominance.

Finally, he nods, his voice barely a whisper. "Crystal clear."

"Now tell her you are sorry," I growl.

"I am sorry!" he says, all shaken up.

"On your knees," I say, loosening my grip.

White Wig stumbles onto the ground, his hands laced together as he begs Miriam for forgiveness with tears in his eyes.

"I am sorry," he repeats.

Miriam looks down at him, disdain in her eyes, a dark look I have never seen on her before.

"If I ever catch you being disrespectful towards me, my husband, or any other person, no matter their sex, preferences, background, or color, I will make sure that my husband's threats are child's play compared to what I will do to you."

CHAPTER FORTY-FOUR

The 'quarterly bloodbath,' as I affectionately name the meeting in my mind, turns out to be more of a blessing in disguise than a nightmare. Somehow, I manage to secure a decent chunk of the budget for my project to fund my own Cavaglio Nero Female Academy. It's not the ideal amount, but it's a start. And a promising one at that.

Flushed with optimism, I waste no time in setting up a meeting with Jinghua Liu, a legend in the world of motorsport and an unsung hero of female empowerment. Jinghua comes from a Chinese family who used to spend the summers in England. At some point in her early years, she found herself at Silverstone and instantly fell in love with the sport, like many girls do. She, however, had the guts to get into a kart and fight for her place on the track.

Looking at her as I approach the table on the terrace of the hospitality, I wouldn't even take her for a racing driver. She is a petite woman in her mid-thirties, her full lips curving into a subtle smile as her dark eyes follow the cars on the track. Her silky black hair cascades down in waves, framing her face with messy bangs that exude an air of carefree confidence. She is so small, you wouldn't even dare to say she is the last woman to ever drive a Formula One car in the last decade.

She has never publicly talked about the reasons why she retired, though I suspect it had to do with her not getting a chance to drive for a team even when her free practice test session times were better than some of the men who used to race back then.

Eventually, she did leave F1, but she never left the motorsport world. After she retired, she moved to Japan, where she coached generations of Formula drivers. Those drivers would later make their way to F3, F2, and some like Emi, even to F1. A couple of years ago, she even founded her own karting series in Japan, with the idea of helping girls into motorsport, but she has not been successful yet. There is only one girl who has made it into professional competitions, but the rest couldn't afford it past the hobby that karting was.

"Hi, Jinghua!" I chirp, offering her a warm smile as I approach her at the table. "I hope I'm not butchering your name."

"You're one of the few who've dared to try and say it and even gotten it right on the first try," she quips, rising from her seat to greet me. "It's lovely to meet you in person."

"Likewise!" I reply, shaking her hand firmly.

"Please, have a seat," she says, gesturing to the empty chair in front of her. "You know, I've been in this sport for over two decades, and I think this is the first time I'm conducting business with another woman."

"Then let's make history together," I say with a grin.

"I am very interested in your proposal. Cavaglio finally having female representation might be the domino piece that brings about more change." I know her interest is piqued when she leans forward, and I see the sparkle of curiosity in her eyes.

"Well, I not only want to have representation. I want an entirely female team," I state with ambition. "I want girls in karting, in FRECA, I want them in LeMans and Daytona. There is no lack of talent, there is just a lack of chance, and I have the funds to make those changes happen."

"Sounds like you have thought about this a lot," she answers.

"Just the past two years or so," I joke.

"What do you need me to do?" she asks.

"You were the best in your time," I tell her, admiration coloring my words. "Who better than you to inspire and guide the next generation of female racers?"

She takes a moment to mull it over, sipping her coffee thoughtfully. "Why should I do it? I have a great life in Japan."

"Because you crave a change," I say simply. "No woman should be left behind. You dreamt of winning a championship, but nobody gave you a helping hand. Let us be that hand for the new generation."

"It's easy to speak when you are drowning in money," she says, meaning my marriage and the benefits that it comes with. If only she knew the difficulties it adds to my life too.

"There are a lot of people in this paddock with the same or even more money than me, and none of them are lifting a finger to do what is right. At least I am willing to take a chance. Strike that, I am not taking a chance. I am making it happen."

Her gaze meets mine, and in that moment, I see a spark of something flicker to life behind her eyes – hope, maybe, or perhaps a newfound sense of purpose.

"Let the revolution begin."

Miriam

Jinghua and I dive into the details of our plan, mapping out the next steps. We go over the list of talented young girls currently making waves in the racing world, discussing their potential to break into the Formula series in the coming years. The excitement is palpable as we brainstorm ideas and strategize our approach, fueled by passion.

Eventually, it's time to say goodbye and make my way to the Cavaglio Nero garage where Daniel is waiting for me.

A familiar sting of longing tugs at my heart when I think about him. Daniel, the man who holds my heart in his hands, even if he doesn't realize it. It's a strange realization, knowing that he'll never give me his heart, even when he has mine.

"Shit!" I mutter under my breath, laughing at my own predicament. "He has my heart."

Deep down, I've known it for a while. Even before I dared admit it to myself. Things have been changing, shifting in ways I never thought possible.

I've changed.

I've rediscovered who I am.

What I want and where I belong.

Who I belong to.

In the end, it all comes back to him – the man who shook my world and filled it with color when I was living in a grey blur without purpose or direction.

I love him.

The truth feels strange but also perfect in its own way. I think this is the first time I have ever really been in love. All my previous relationships aren't even a quarter of what this is. I have never felt this way about anyone, only Daniel.

I am lost in my own thoughts as I practically run through the paddock, anticipation to get back to him coursing through my body. Whatever the future holds, I'm ready for it, heart and soul. Even if by the end of the year we have to part ways, I will be happy to have lived this year with him, and I will hold on to the memories like my most precious jewel.

My thoughts are so intense that I barely notice the bustling crowd around me until a sudden collision jolts me back to reality. Before I can react, a man barrels into me with unexpected force, sending me stumbling backward with a yelp of surprise. I am certain I am going to hit the ground, but before my ass meets the asphalt, the man holds me up by my elbow. I struggle to regain my balance, and I can feel my heart pounding in my chest from the unexpected collision.

When I glance up to catch a glimpse of the culprit, I see nothing. Well, not *nothing.* The man is tall and his skin is tanned, but that is pretty much everything I see about him. He is wearing a black cap and dark glasses that cover his face.

"Careful, *menina,*" he whispers too close to my face. "We don't want any harm coming to you." His accent is thick, something Latin American I think, but I can't quite catch it.

"Thanks," I answer, my voice trembling.

There is something about his aura, vibe, energy, call it whatever you want, but it's sinister and dark, and I can feel the hairs on my arms rising, my heart beating faster, and my intuition begging me to run to safety. To Daniel.

"I will see you around," the man says, and then steps away, fading away in the crowd.

CHAPTER FORTY-FIVE

My heart pounds in my chest like a drum, the sound echoing in my ears as I wait for Miriam to slip inside the garage. She's late, far too late, even for her standards. Miriam isn't the most punctual person, but she knows when she needs to be at a place. She knows when things matter.

Perched on the edge of my desk, headset in place, I scan the room with restless eyes, searching for any sign of her. And then, there she is, making her entrance through the garage door. But, as soon as I spot her, I can tell that something's off.

The way she carries herself, so rigid and tense, her features etched with fear—it's enough to send alarm bells ringing in my mind. Without a second thought, I'm on my feet, closing the distance between us in hurried strides.

"Who did this to you?" I demand to know.

Miriam's brow furrows in confusion. “What?”

“Why are you shaking like a leaf?”

“It's... it's cold?” she lies.

“Bullshit.” My patience wears thin. “Tell me the truth.”

“The race is about to start—”

“What are you hiding from me?”

“Nothing,” she insists, but her avoidance only fuels my concern.

“Then tell me!” I press with urgency.

Miriam's breath hitches, her words tumbling out in a rush. “I don't know... someone bumped into me on the way here. I almost fell, but he caught me. He... he was strange, like something was off. I know it sounds crazy, but...”

“Describe him,” I interrupt, my heart sinking at the realization.

“I couldn't see much,” she admits. “He had sunglasses and a cap, and he spoke Spanish. Or at least I think he did.”

Dread coils in the pit of my stomach, a cold realization dawning on me. He's here, the person I've been fearing. He's seen Miriam, touched her, and I wasn't there to protect her. I swallow hard, trying to quell the rising panic threatening to consume me. But even while I am trying to hold my shit together, one thing is clear to me —I'll do whatever it takes to keep Miriam safe, even if it means facing darkness itself.

"Are you okay?" Miriam's hand reaches out to touch me, to offer comfort. But my instincts kick in before rational thought can intervene, and I find myself recoiling, retreating from her touch as if it's a threat, a vulnerability I can't afford to show.

"I'm fine," I force out the words, my tone sharper than intended. "Let's just watch the race."

The air between us changes, and there is that unspoken tension again. Miriam's concern hangs in the air, but I can't even force myself to look in her direction right now. If she sees me, she will know there is something wrong. She will sense the fear that is clawing at my chest.

Fuck, I can't afford to feel any of this.

Can't afford to seem vulnerable.

I can't let my guard down, not now.

Miriam and I take our seats next to each other, in front of one of the screen panels, right when the engines roar to life as rain pours onto the track and drivers. Every muscle in my body tenses from nerves but also in anticipation as the cars speed away from the starting grid, hurtling towards the first turn.

João maintains his lead, protecting his position fiercely. Emi struggles to make progress, his car seeming sluggish compared to his rival's. On the screen, I am able to catch a glimpse of Versteeg right on Fitzroy's tail.

João exits cleanly out of the fourth turn, while Versteeg aggressively gains ground in his Primavert car, trying to climb the ranks and fight for P3. Emi, on the other hand, is fighting to stand his ground under the rain, desperately trying to close the gap to João.

After the first couple of laps, Fitzroy is still maintaining the third place, but Versteeg is giving him a run for his money, fighting the Mexican driver at every turn. Further back, the rest of the pack jostles for positions, but there is not much movement.

The weather conditions of the rain-soaked track ensure that everyone drives as conservatively as they can prioritizing finishing the race over ending up crashing against a wall. Still, the cars hurtle down the straight at speeds nearing 250 kilometers per hour, navigating the slick surface with precision.

The early laps of the Chinese Grand Prix are filled with nerves, the rain only intensifying the challenge. Despite the adverse conditions, João manages to extend the gap between himself and the pursuing Samurai, leaving Saito to grapple with the loss of his DRS.

Attention shifts to Versteeg, whose aggressive driving pays off as he overtakes Fitzroy with ease. As the race approaches its twentieth lap, João streaks past the finish line with a commanding lead of nearly two seconds. Saito may have lost the advantage, but with thirty laps still left, the Japanese driver refuses to accept defeat.

Through the streaming on the screen, I can see João's tires protesting as he breaks into the hairpin, the G-forces threatening to tear him apart. But the Brazilian driver holds his ground. However, the gap between João and Emi becomes shorter, and Emi uses João's mistake to overtake him.

The crowd roars in excitement.

But I am ready to puke my guts out.

Miriam

The final lap of the Chinese Grand Prix unfolds before us. Emi Saito has been keeping his ground for the past few laps, not even a terrible pit stop could stop him from making his way into P1. But he has been locked in a battle with João, and his tires are degrading. I am hoping he will be the one to win, but my heart clenches as João overtakes Emi at corner fourteen to fifteen, and secures himself the first place right before the race is over.

Cheers erupt from the garage, celebrating the team's success, but I can't find it in me to join in the jubilation. Daniel is sitting next to me, his expression unreadable. My stomach twists as I steal a glance at him. His jaw is clenched, but the worst are his eyes —dark, distant, devoid of all the emotions I've grown accustomed to. I have always known he had this side, but I never thought I would be the reason for it.

•

"Are you going to tell me what's wrong?" I muster the courage to ask, my voice trembling.

"We need to talk."

No shit, Sherlock. I want to scream, but I bite my lip.

The words hang heavy in the air, suffocating me with their weight. I swallow hard, my throat tight. My stomach churns with dread as I brace myself for the inevitable conversation, knowing that everything is about to change. I follow Daniel to his office with a sense of impending doom looming over us. The tension hangs thick in the air as he closes the door behind us.

"Sit," he says, and I sink into the chair in front of his. "It's time we set some ground rules," Daniel begins, his voice authoritative and cold.

"I thought we already set those," I say, my voice a whisper.

"Then, it's time you respect them," he retorts.

"Me?" I cry out in disbelief. "What about you?"

"Don't worry about me. I already got what I wanted, and I'm not interested in continuing this thing," he states matter-of-factly, his gaze fixed on some distant point in the room, avoiding my eyes.

"Are you breaking up with me?"

"I am letting you go. Isn't that what you wanted this whole time?" His words are like a dagger to my heart. Yes, it's what I wanted, or at least I thought it was. But not anymore, not after all these months with him. What I want is him in my life —his scent lingering in my bed, the taste of his lips on lazy mornings, the silent moments shared during our drives to the office. The stolen minutes, the angsty glances. His hands on my body. I want him, all of him.

"Why?" I ask, my voice tinged with confusion. "There's something you're not telling me. Why this all of a sudden?"

"I told you, you could never have my heart," he repeats the same thing he told me months ago. But, this time, his voice is tinged with a hint of vulnerability. The change in the tone is minimal, but not to me. I can read him, and he is hiding something from me.

"And I told you I didn't need it," I counter.

"Then this shouldn't be a difficult decision," he replies, his tone final and unyielding.

I rise from my chair, moving closer to him until we're eye to eye. "You know what the good thing about obsessions is?" I ask, completely off-topic, my voice steady. "You can't escape them, not even in your dreams. So put all the space you want between us, Daniel. But I'll be here, waiting until you're ready."

I might not know what is going on with him. I might not be able to solve the problem right now. But I know whatever this is, it's happening because his broken heart suddenly started beating again.

2026 DRIVER STANDINGS

AFTER THE CHINESE GP

POINTS	DRIVER	TEAM
68	JOÃO QUERINHO	Cavallo Vero
61	EMI SAITO	Cavallo Vero
32	ALEX SAUD	BLUE CHEETAH
31	NANDO FERNAN	
29	OLIVER MUNGUIA	
27	MARCUS VERSTEEG	PRIMAVERA RACING
26	ARCHIBALD FITZROY	BLUE CHEETAH
16	LAWSON STROLLER	PRIMAVERA RACING

CHAPTER FORTY-SIX

He watched from the shadows as Miriam stormed out of Daniel's office. A smirk twisted his lips. His eyes gleamed with a calculated malevolence, relishing the sight of the woman running away with tears in her eyes.

He waited for a while, his eyes still locked on the black girl, waiting for Daniel, his lifelong enemy, to run after his wife. But to The Cat's surprise, Daniel never showed up, didn't run after the woman to shield her from the dangers this world had to offer.

The Cat's smirk only grew into a full smile once it was clear the CEO of Cavaglio Nero wasn't coming. This was the opportunity he had been waiting for all this time. He had been trying to get close to the couple for weeks, especially to Miriam, but her husband had been around her like a guard dog the whole time.

This was the first time Daniel committed a mistake of this sort, and The Cat was not willing to let that chance pass, not in a million years.

The Cat started walking behind Mirian, following her with measured steps, not too close that she would notice him, but also not far enough for her to get out of his sight. His mind was dancing with anticipation, the thrill of the hunt electrifying his senses. For weeks, he'd meticulously planned every move, every detail, and now, he finally had a chance to hurt his enemy just as he hurt him.

With a predatory gaze, he started closing the gap between both of them, and the sight of innocent, poor Miriam Lefebvre being oblivious to the monster trailing her, while she loses herself to tears and heartache, was the best sight The Cat had seen in a long while.

The Cat grinned even more when she made it onto the streets of Shanghai, which were full of people, tourists, and locals alike, providing the perfect cover.

Nobody would notice a girl disappearing in a city like this.

Miriam, focused solely on her pain and getting to the hotel as soon as possible, took a wrong turn and entered a side street, slightly darker, away from prying eyes.

It really was his lucky day.

The Cat took the chance eagerly, and with chilling precision, he seized Miriam's arm with a strong grip.

The woman recoiled, fear flickering in her tear-stained eyes, while he only grinned wider, reveling in her terror.

There was something quite lovely about seeing the fear in a woman's eyes when she knew what was about to happen, he thought to himself, remembering his days of pleasure from inflicting terror upon the opposite sex.

"I was looking for you," he purred, his voice dripping with malice.

"Don't touch me!" Miriam yelled, trying to free herself from the man's hold, but nothing could save her now. She was at his mercy.

"Can't do."

"What are you—" Miriam's sentence died on her lips as The Cat pressed a chloroform-soaked cloth against her face.

It took only a couple of seconds for her struggles to grow weaker, consciousness slipping away like sand through her fingers. The Cat's laughter echoed through the deserted alley, a macabre symphony to his twisted triumph.

And then he cradled Miriam's limp form in his arms, his eyes alight with a manic fervor.

She's just the beginning, a pawn in his game of vengeance against his enemy.

CHAPTER FORTY-SEVEN

Sasha: I saw Miriam crying after the race.

Sasha: Trouble in paradise?

Sasha: Okay, I am sorry!!!

Sasha: Is everything all right?

Sasha: Where are you? Answer me!

Sasha: If you don't answer now, I am going to kill you.

Me: We broke up.

Sasha: What?

Sasha: What did you do?

Me: My past found me.

Sasha: I am coming over.

...

I stumble into the hotel room, my heart pounding against my ribs. The empty silence mocks me, a loud reminder of her absence.

Miriam isn't here.

Anguish fills me as flashes of the scene after the race appear in my mind. Her angry face and the tears in her eyes that still haunt me. I caused her the one thing I promised to protect her from: pain. So many times, I promised to keep her from harm and, in the end, she was right. I was the one to harm her by dismissing her when I should have kept her close.

“Fucking hell,” I curse, my voice raw with self-loathing. I reach for the nearest bottle, seeking solace at the bottom of the bottle.

I pour the ember liquid into a tumbler with ice, then chug the first glass down in one large sip, the bourbon burning as it slides down my throat. But even the alcohol can't numb the pain I am feeling right now.

I repeat the motion again. Pour a drink. Chug it down. Shake my head in disgust when the alcohol burns my throat like hellfire.

“Drinking won't solve your damn problems,” Sasha says, walking into the room.

"Who the hell gave you the key?" I bark, my tone laced with venom, before tossing my head back and drowning myself in a third drink, but who is counting?

"I'm resourceful," she retorts sharply. "So, what's with this pity party?"

"It's none of your business," I growl.

"Oh, I see... so you're going to be a complete asshole now?" Sasha snaps.

"I'm not—"

"What the hell happened?"

"It's over," I begin, my voice heavy with defeat. "She's gone."

"What did you do?"

"Why do you assume it was my fault?" I fire back.

"Because you're too damn scared to love," she retorts.

"I don't love. I can't," I protest.

"Then why the hell are you drowning yourself in booze the second Miriam walks out of sight?" Sasha fires back. "Drink if that's what you need. But we're going to have a serious conversation, whcther you like it or not."

I roll my eyes in defiance. "I don't want to hear it."

"Too bad, you are going to listen to me," she counters. "We both had a messed-up start, and it shaped us. It made us who we are today. We had every reason to burn the world down, and yet, we decided to be better than the people who broke us, and we decided to be the light at the end of the tunnel for thousands of victims out there. Don't become a pathetic alcoholic just because you are scared to feel something, Daniel. You deserve to love and to be loved."

"I don't love," I repeat like a broken record.

"Dammit Daniel!" Sasha screams at me. "You love her."

"No, I don't," I protest.

"You loved her since the moment you laid your eyes on her. You loved her the second she opened her mouth. You loved her when you married her. When she moved in with you. And you love her now, even when you are fighting not to! Why don't you just admit it?"

"Because I am scared!" I scream. "Because if I say it out loud, it becomes real. Because if I admit it, then she had the power to hurt me, and I can't take another strike. I can't let someone I love hurt me again, Sasha."

"Daniel," Sasha whispers, pain in her voice. "She isn't going to hurt you. She isn't your parents, or the men who took us away. She is Miriam."

"I know," I admit. "But she has the power to hurt me nevertheless."

"That's the beauty of love. Knowing that the other person holds your heart in their hands and has that power over it. Funny thing is, when we pick the right person, they will make sure to treat it with the care it deserves."

"Well, I don't have a heart, so Miriam is just holding broken pieces in her hands."

"Haven't you realized it yet?" Sasha asks, genuine curiosity in her eyes. "Miriam has pieced all those broken pieces back together in the past few months, Daniel."

I blink at her, confused for a second, but the message strikes a chord. She is right. Slowly and in silence, with small gestures, Miriam has been taking the pieces I was willing to hand her, and she has been piecing them back together one by one. Never has she backed down from trying to meet me halfway. She didn't run the other way when I told her she couldn't have my heart, or when I told her she had to respect our terms.

She stayed. She stayed for me.

Because that's what she does. Stay. Be my anchor. Show me that I can be loved and I can love. I was the one supposed to protect her from all harm, but the truth is, all this time, she has been the one protecting me from myself, my own destruction. Enabling me to be all I am and embracing even the more jaded parts of me.

"I am such an idiot," I say to myself. "I love her."

Realization hits me.

Fuck!

I had to push her away for me to feel the emptiness she leaves behind. For me to realize that she is it for me. I told her she was my podium finish. I just didn't realize everything it meant, not to her, not to me. She is the one who holds my heart. My world. My everything.

The best part? I wouldn't even care if she decided to squeeze it. I am willing to give my life for her. Die for her. And kill for her.

"Now that we are all on the same page, what did you mean by your past found you?"

"I have been getting text messages from an unknown number," I explain.

"Show me," Sasha demands. I take my phone out of my pocket and pass it to her, opening the two texts that have been sent. "Uh-Oh-Oh." Sasha's face goes pale.

"What?"

"Daniel, they just sent another text." Her eyes are glassy, I can see fear in them, and it's a damn rare sight. Sasha isn't afraid. She is the devil. People are afraid of her. Not the other way around.

"Show me," I say, grabbing the phone from her hand.

I am not prepared for what I see next.

A picture of Miriam. Her eyes filled with tears and fear. She is sitting on the floor. Her legs and arms are bound, and duct tape is pressed against her mouth. My world crumbles around me. I want to cry, scream, burn the world down.

And then, another text appears.

'I am waiting for you, menina.'

Menina.

It's Armando! The man who kidnapped me.

The man who killed my sister. He is back.

"I know who the fucker is!"

"*We* are going to kill him," Sasha says.

"No. *I* am going to kill him."

Sasha might have been my partner in crime all these years, we have been a team and a damned good one at that. But this is my demon, one only I can confront, and one I will destroy very soon.

CHAPTER FORTY-EIGHT

Blinking is a struggle; it feels like a monumental effort.

My head throbs relentlessly, a pounding ache that might crack my skull open. Slowly, very slowly, I start regaining consciousness. The memories start hitting me, a blur of images. I try to raise my hand to my head, hoping to massage my temples and help ease the pain, but I can't move them.

They are tied.

Still confused and with heavy eyelids, I look down at myself, trying to work out what is happening, but what I find is terrifying. Gone are my pants, my blazer, and my top. Completely naked, only in my underwear, that's how I find myself, sitting on some sort of carpet with my body on full display.

The memories crash over me.

Someone hit me.

They drugged me.

Someone kidnapped me.

The thought echoes in my mind, refusing to fade.

Memories trickle back in, fragmented and terrifying. Fear fills me, paralyzing me. Panic surges through me, electrifying every nerve in my body. A whimper escapes my lips, but it's muffled by the tape pressed against my mouth.

"Help!" I attempt to scream, but the sound is nothing more than a muffled murmur. Desperation claws at my throat as I cry out again, knowing deep down that my pleas will fall on deaf ears.

The door swings open, and he enters— the man who kidnapped me.

A single tear trails down my cheek. He towers over me, his presence suffocating, his eyes devoid of any shred of humanity. They pierce through me, chilling me to the bone.

"Look who finally woke up," he drawls.

He crouches down to my eye level, his gaze locking onto mine with an intensity that sends shivers down my spine. There's no kindness in those eyes, no mercy—only darkness.

"The things I am going to do to you, menina," he purrs, guiding the tip of his finger across my jaw. I shake my head, trying to escape his touch, but he grabs me by my hair, forcing me to look at him. "The money people will pay for the black bitch who is fucking warming Daniela's bed."

Another tear escapes me, but I refuse to let him see how terrified I truly am. I clench my jaw with so much force that I am afraid I am going to break my teeth, but I don't care that physical pain is better than anything this man is willing to do to me. I hold my head high and try to cling to any flicker of hope I can find inside of myself.

I have a life to fight for—a life filled with dreams, filled with family, friends, and a husband. A husband who was in my position, a husband who survived and who is going to find me. I might be helpless right now, but he is coming for me. I know that. And when he finds me, he is going to burn the entire world down.

He will find me.

"You have spirit," he remarks, a cruel smirk twisting his lips as he notices the glimmer of defiance in my eyes. "But it won't save you. I'm going to break you, just like I did Daniela."

Daniel didn't break, I want to scream at him.

His words ignite a fire within me—a primal urge to fight, to survive. I thrash against my restraints, my limbs uselessly tied in place as I attempt to strike out at him, to inflict even the slightest harm. I have to survive, not just for myself but for Daniel—for all those who have suffered at his hands.

"Shh. *Tranquila, menina. Aun no te voy a hacer* daño." *I am not going to hurt you yet,* he says in Spanish.

Fuck you, I want to spit in his face. *I am going to kill you.*

"I like my girls showered in terror. Their tears dripping down their face. Their screams filled with pain. You still have hope, and I can't fuck you when you still have that. We need you to suffer, so Daniela or Daniel, whatever he prefers these days… can suffer too."

I need to be strong for Daniel.

He will be my salvation. Sometimes it's okay to dream of a knight in shining armor, and I know he is mine. He will come for me. Daniel is my only hope, and he will find me. It's just a matter of time, and I need to buy him some. All I have to do is stay strong so that this sadist will take his time to break me.

I will wait for him.

Finding Miriam is the easy part after seeing that picture.

Fuck.

The photo is etched into my mind—the tears streaking down her face, the raw anguish in her eyes, her nakedness, her vulnerability. My body is filled with horror, but after a second glance, I spot something in the picture that stands out—the ring on her finger.

Her wedding ring.

I notice the ring because I'm the one who put it there, who slipped it onto her finger with trembling hands and whispered promises that I am ready to keep now.

But, most importantly, I notice the ring because I was the one who made a few adjustments to that expensive piece of jewelry. It might seem possessive to some, psychotic to others, but to me, right now, it's a lifeline—a way to keep her safe, to bring her back to me. Installing a tracking device in her wedding ring was the best idea I've had in my entire life.

I waste no time in locating the signal, in tracking them down to Thailand. They are in Bangkok, more accurately, in the fucking Pharaya. I don't waste time booking a flight and loading my guns. Nobody can stop me.

I am coming for my wife.

I know the dangers that await me, but I don't care. Because I won't rest, won't stop fighting, until Miriam is back in my arms where she belongs.

I am ready to face my past so that she can have my future.

Every second is a race against time, every heartbeat a drumbeat urging me forward. I have been such a stoic person for so long, but now I can feel every single emotion inside of me. Fear, desperation, determination—all of them fueling my every step.

I am coming for you, little swan.

CHAPTER FORTY-NINE

Time stretches endlessly in the darkness.

I've lost all sense of time—minutes, hours, days, they blur together into a never-ending nightmare. Each footstep outside sends shivers all over my body, making it tremble uncontrollably, no matter how hard I try to hold still. Silently, I find myself begging for Daniel to find me every second that passes.

The man hasn't returned to the room—at least not yet. But the sole thought of his presence sends me into the worst spiral of thoughts. I know who he is, what he is capable of, and what he is willing to do to me. Alone in the darkness, tears stain my skin, pooling in the hollow of my collarbone, even when I try to stay strong.

I have to survive.

I will survive.

I will see another day.

"Menina." His voice echoes from behind the door like a sinister melody. "I'm coming for you, menina."

I try to cover my ears to block out his voice, to shut him out, but my hands remain bound behind me, leaving me powerless against his threats. Fear pulses through me, and I don't know what to do to protect myself.

I try to regain control of my emotions and my body, but I miserably fail when the man opens the door and comes inside the room, looming over me like a specter of death.

His aura drips with malice. He is so rotten.

How could I ever compare Daniel to the devil when he saw hell first-hand? My husband might have questionable morals sometimes, but the things he does, he does them to help. He always looks out for the greater good. This man in front of me? He is just a twisted sadist.

"Are you ready for me?" he taunts, his voice oozing with cruelty. "I must admit, I love seeing you trapped like this with your hands cuffed. That's what I should have done to Daniela and her sister—bound them so they couldn't escape."

Even if you had, Daniel would have torn you apart, I think bitterly, imagining a young Daniel feeling helpless at the mercy of this sadist.

"I had everything back then when your now husband was nothing but a teenager in the streets of Argentina. People feared me back then. The Red Horses venerated me. So many women taken," he says with pride, full of dreams that are nightmares to others. "So many of them sold to the highest bidder. Presidents, politicians, CEOs… Even kings!" he lists. "Everyone came to me for quality products. *I* made The Red Horses! They became everything thanks to me. *I* was the man in the shadows. Who do you think got Mancini into all of this? *I* did! It was me, and they all turned their heads on me when Daniela escaped! That bitch owes me my life, but it's fine. I am going to take from her what hurts her the most.," he finally finishes, looking at me, desire, anger, and fury written all over his face.

This man speaks of power, of control, of a world built on pain and suffering, and now he wants to end me and all for mere revenge. But I refuse to be a victim. I refuse to let him break me.

It's then that I notice a knife glinting in his hand, a promise of the agony to come. He traces its tip along my skin, a single drop of blood welling up in its wake. I tremble, my breath catching in my throat as he stares down at me, his intentions clear.

"I hope you're not into knife play," he sneers, his words dripping with venom. "Because I want you to suffer when I take you, menina."

The blood pounds in my ears. But as he moves closer, as he unzips his pants with a sickening grin, I cling to a promise, one that I make to myself.

I will survive.

No matter what happens next, I will survive.

The flight to Bangkok stretches on endlessly. Every agonizing second that passes, my mind ends up conjuring up images of her. Miriam. The thought of her is what keeps me going and makes me find strength. I know she is alive, I can feel it, and I'll do whatever it takes to bring her back—to protect her, to keep her safe from harm.

Finally, the wheels touch down in the City of Angels, and I'm ready to leap into action. Adrenaline surges through me.

As soon as I have reception, I take a look at the tracking device, confirming my suspicions—they're still on the boat, floating on the river.

There's no time to waste.

I navigate through the bustling streets of Bangkok with single-minded focus, my senses on high alert. Every shadow, every sound feels like a threat, but I push forward, driven by the need to find my wife.

Finally, I can see the river looming ahead, and my pulse quickens as I approach it, the adrenaline spreading like wildfire in my body. And then I see it—the boat, bobbing on the water like a ghostly apparition. Without hesitation, I make my move, closing the distance with determined strides.

Miriam is in there, somewhere in the darkness, waiting for me.

I take a moment to scan the area hoping to see someone out there guarding the boat. But nobody appears. There are no guards posted outside. It's a reckless oversight—one that plays to my advantage.

"The man of my nightmares sure has a lack of brain cells," I mutter to myself, a grim smirk tugging at the corners of my lips. Either his security team is great at hiding or they are not expecting me here this soon.

It doesn't matter, I don't wait long enough to triple-check. I won't be stopped until Miriam is back in my arms, safe and sound.

I can hear my own pulse inside my ears as I step onto the luxurious boat. The darkness cloaks me, but I press forward, driven by the need to find my wife.

My little swan.

I shake my head. There's no time for idle thoughts, no room for distractions. Miriam's hangs in the balance.

With a determined stride, I walk into the deck, my gaze sweeping over every shadowed corner. And then, like a specter emerging from the darkness, appears a man dressed in a black suit, his face marred by all sorts of tattoos.

He charges towards me, a primal fury in his eyes, but I refuse to cower. Instinct takes over as I dodge his attack, the adrenaline sharpening my reflexes.

In one fluid motion, I draw the knife strapped to my waist, its cold steel a reassuring weight in my hand. He aims a punch at my face, but I sidestep effortlessly, my movements precise.

With a swift, decisive strike, I bring the handle of the knife crashing down on his nose, the satisfying crunch of bone echoing through the night. And before he has a chance to react, I press the blade against his throat, blood flowing from his neck after I am done slitting it open.

It's over in an instant.

But I won't be so merciful when I find the man behind all of this.

There's no time to savor this victory.

CHAPTER FITFY

My heart pounds as I make my way onto the boat, leaving a trail of fallen adversaries behind me. They will meet their creator today, but it won't be God. They will find Satan at the doors of hell, waiting for them.

The way I react to their screams, their pleas for mercy, makes me question if I am not fated for the same end. It didn't matter how much they begged, or how they told me they had a family back home. It all faded into the background.

I want revenge, and I want my wife.

When I am done killing the last two men on the ship, I can hear her cries piercing through the air. Her terror tears at my soul. I can hear her calling for me in muffled screams. Each scream is a dagger to my heart, a reminder that the damn organ is pieced back together because of her, and today is not the day I lose her.

And then I hear him—the man who haunts my nightmares, whose very name sends me back in time to the terror I felt in his presence and makes me relive the death of my sister. His words are like poison, searing into my consciousness with a sickening familiarity.

"Because I want you to suffer when I take you, menina," he taunts, his voice dripping with such malice that I am forced to remember the worst night of my life.

Not again. It stops here. With me and him, on this boat.

I take a deep breath, forcing myself to focus, to push past the trauma threatening to overwhelm me. Miriam needs me, and I won't let her down—not now, not ever again.

With trembling hands, I grip my gun, making sure that it's loaded and ready for action. My palms are sweaty against the cold metal, but I push aside my fear, my doubts.

I have a job to do, a wife to protect.

With a swift kick, I burst through the door open, my heart hammering in my chest as I take in the scene before me. There he stands, the embodiment of evil, looming over Miriam. He is dressed in a black suit and boots that remind me of the way his steps sounded in that old house. His face hasn't changed much in the last decade, he is just older now, his dark hair now the color of salt and pepper, but his is a face I would recognize even in death.

Before I can react, with a fast move of his hand, he drops the knife he was holding and reaches for the gun on his belt, then presses it to the side of Miriam's head, holding her hostage so that I have to think twice about my actions.

It takes me a second to take in the entire scene before I notice the unmistakable evidence of his depravity, his pants are half-open, a sickening drop of wetness staining his briefs. Miriam's body is naked with the exception of her underwear, making her feel vulnerable, and I notice a single drop of blood falling down her stomach. Armando gets off on pain and this was his first step in a dance I know too well.

Anger boils within me, a primal fury that wants to consume everything in its path. But I force myself to stay calm, to think, to plan. He was ready to harm her, but now it's my turn to hurt him.

"Look who decided to join the party," Armando says.

I breathe in, trying to stay focused, my gun pointed at him even though I know I have no chance to shoot him right now. Not if that would put Miriam's life at risk.

"Let her go," I growl. "And I promise you a quick death."

"I know you too well, menina." He chuckles darkly, his gaze flickering between Miriam and me. "You are like me, you get off on pain too, so it doesn't matter if I hand her to you now or later, you will still inflict levels of pain that not even I know of."

"You don't know me," I spit out.

"I'm a man who loves pleasures. Can't keep my hands off them." Armando's smirk twists into a sneer as he tightens his grip on Miriam, his fingers digging into her waist like talons. The sight of her pain, her desperation, makes my blood boil. I clench my teeth, my fists trembling with the effort to contain my anger. "I have to admit, you came before I planned."

"I'm here to disappoint. Always," I shoot back.

"Don't joke. Not now when I have the person you love the most in my hands. Probably the only person you will ever love," he warns.

"I will end you!" I scream.

"Sure you will," he taunts, "but it will be too late for her. And, without her, you will be nothing."

His words cut me to the core, a brutal reminder of the truth. Without Miriam, I'm nothing. Without her, life loses all meaning. But I am not going to lose her. Not in this life. Not in the next. We are meant for each other, and no matter how much I fuck up, how much it takes me to admit my feelings, I will always want her forever.

"It's too bad you came here so early, Daniel, or should I call you Daniela?" Armando muses. "I wanted to have a taste of the pussy that had you so lost you started to make mistakes along the way. I've been trailing you for years, trying to get my revenge. But you had no weaknesses until you found her. A gift from the Lord for me."

"The Lord doesn't make gifts to people like you."

He shrugs, unfazed by my words. "I don't question what the Lord does. Look at you, Daniela. You're a monster, an abomination. And still, He made you."

A bitter laugh escapes my lips, the sound hollow and devoid of humor. So many people have tried to make fun of me, to call me an abomination, tried to convince me to revert my transition and be a woman.

But that's not who I am.

God didn't make a mistake when he made me.

He knew perfectly fine who I was going to become. And I bet the person up there looking down at us is proud of me. It was only a stupid chromosome that got messed up. But I am perfect the way I am.

"I am a monster, Armando," I say, smirking at him, fully at peace. "Look at me. Look at what I became. I left my family to become who I really was. I left my house with a goal in mind, to bury Daniela in the dirt and leave as Daniel. And then you happened. You raped me. You killed my sister, the person I loved the most. You even almost killed me." I remind him and myself. "But I resurrected. I became who I was always intended to be. God might have created a monster in this room, but it isn't me. It's you." I grip my gun tightly, the weight of it a comforting presence in my hand.

"It doesn't matter who the monster is. The only thing that matters is that she will die," Armando screams, pressing his gun against Miriam's temple. "And you will follow!"

My heart pounds with intensity, fear clawing at my insides as I stare into the abyss of Armando's eyes.

"Little swan," I call out to Miriam. "Remember the butterknife?" I ask, and instantly, a flicker of hope shines in her eyes. I swear I can see a smirk under the duct tape. "You don't need a prince charming to save you. Remember who you are, what you can do," I encourage her.

And, in that moment, I see it—the spark of determination in her eyes. We are a team again, there is no me, no her. There is an us.

Almost imperceptibly, I catch a nod from Miriam's face.

My grip on the gun tightens as I prepare for action.

I can see the tension in her shoulders as she readies herself. With a swift movement, she tilts her head back, slamming it into Armando's face. He staggers, momentarily stunned, and instinctively brings a hand to his injured face, hoping to ease the pain.

"Get down!" I command, my voice cutting through the chaos.

Miriam obeys, breaking free from Armando's grasp and rolling away from him. I seize the opportunity and without hesitation, I take aim and fire at the man who destroyed so many lives, including my sister's.

Two shots ring out.

One bullet goes into his knee.

The other into his groin.

I see Miriam darting to my side, slamming her body into mine. I give myself exactly a minute to look down at her and make sure she is untouched, that no bullets have grazed her skin, and that she will survive.

"You are safe," I reassure her, taking the tape off her mouth with extreme care.

"Just get over with it," Armando begs on the other side of the room, his voice tinged with desperation. I forget about Miriam in that moment, pushing her softly behind me where I know she will be safe.

I refuse to grant the man on the floor a swift death.

"Can't do. I like seeing my victims in pain and terrified," I echo his own words coldly as I approach him while he writhes in agony on the floor, relishing every moment of his suffering. Dropping down to where he is lying, I grab my knife, tainted with the blood of his security guards, and stab him in his leg. "Every centimeter of your body will be scarred by my knife," I say and then stab him again three times in different places of his body. "Your corpse will be so disfigured that nobody will be able to recognize you after I am done with you." Another stab. And another.

His screams echo through the room, a symphony of agony that fuels my rage.

"Please stop," I hear Miriam begging, but I am far too gone.

"Did you ever stop when the girls asked you to?" I say and stab him again, this time in his torso. "Did you stop when Miriam called for help?" Another stab close to his heart.

Blood pours out of him, some drops even making it onto my face.

"I am sorry!" he screams.

I stab him.

"STOP!" Miriam yells when I raise my hand in the air to stab him again. "You are better than this," she says.

"He deserves to die!" I tell her, but I pause, suddenly aware of the bloodlust consuming me. Miriam's voice, freed from the confines of the duct tape, is a stark reminder of what's at stake.

"Yes, he does," she agrees, her voice unwavering. "But you don't deserve to become him. If you keep enjoying every single stab, you won't be any better than him. You will become a sadist, just like him."

I take a deep breath, her words sinking in.

She's right.

I can't let myself become consumed by vengeance. I can't let myself become the monster I have spent my whole life fearing. He marked my life, and I am not willing to become him.

"Fine," I concede, my voice heavy with resignation.

With a final glance at Armando, I raise my gun and, without hesitation, I end his life with a single shot to the head.

His body slumps to the floor, lifeless and still.

My nightmares will die with him.

CHAPTER FIFTY-ONE

336 hours. 20,160 minutes. 1,209,600 seconds.

Fourteen days have slipped through my fingers since Armando kidnapped me in China, and Daniel came to my rescue and killed the man who had been in his nightmares for so long. My knight in shining armor. He would hate it if he heard it, but that's what he has become in a sort of romantic, fucked up way. A beautiful beast who rescued me. But in those fourteen days since he brought me back to London, he has been radio silent and it's that kind of silence that speaks louder than words ever would.

When we made it back to London, he didn't even bring me back to the penthouse with him. Instead, he dropped me at my apartment making sure that Selene was at home and ready to take care of me if needed. I should be the one taking care of the pregnant lady, not the other way around. Besides her, there are also guards at my front door every second of the day, suffocating my liberty but ensuring my safety.

The days blur together, each one a relentless reminder of everything I've lost. On the first day of my return, my mother came over, probably summoned by Daniel, her worry etched into every line on her face.

A couple of days passed, Selene and Sasha taking turns watching over me, their presence a comfort in the darkness that has taken hold of me lately. I am not speaking much. All I want to do is be curled up in a ball under tons of heavy blankets and decide whether I want to cry or be happy because of everything I have gone through and survived.

Regardless of my state, my friends show up every day. They keep me informed on what is going, on how my women's program at Cavaglio Nero is progressing. They tell me how hard João and Emi are fighting after Miami to see who will win the championship this year, and what an amazing job Philip is doing in his new role as a team principal. It seems like he has even gained the love of some news outlets this season, now that he is not breaking records on the track.

Sasha and Selene tell me many things, yes, but they make sure to never mention Daniel, and I don't press them for news, afraid that my heart will break if I hear his name or hear that he's not well.

On the fifth day, a therapist came to my apartment. She asked questions that made me feel unsure and dug into wounds that have not healed yet. She asked me about my vulnerable moments. The image of myself sitting naked on the floor of that boat flooded me to the point that tears ran down my face uncontrollably. She spoke about PTSD, and that made sense. She said that I was lucky that Armando didn't get to touch me and that the worst will pass, that I won't feel helpless and vulnerable forever.

A part of me knows the therapist is right, knows that the worst will eventually pass, but for that to happen, I need time. I'm still piecing myself together, trying to live with the fact that the bad guys my mother warned me about when I was a child do exist and tried to hurt me. I don't want to say I am broken, but I am picking up the fragments of who I was before any of this happened. The woman who walked onto that ship is not the same woman who stumbled out.

To be fair, I haven't been the same woman I once was in a long time. The Miriam of two years ago changed, became a robot fixated on her job, and then was lost when she no longer could find motivation. The Miriam of two years ago would have tried to avoid Daniel every single step of the way, scared of the man he was and is. Afraid of letting him into my life.

The Miriam of the past five months has found a new motivation, a new light, and a new purpose. The Miriam of the past few months has been happy, and that happiness is named Daniel Conte. I've known for weeks that I'm in love, even if I wanted to lie to myself. I knew he was it. I'm his podium finish, but he's my everything.

On the seventh day, I reached out to Daniel with a simple message.

Me: I miss you.

I confessed it to him, even though I knew that he knew. The same way I knew he missed me even if he wouldn't grace me with his presence. Three dots danced on the screen, teasing me with the hope of an answer. My heart beat faster, and a faint smile, the first in days touched my lips. But then the dots disappeared, no answer from him. They appeared again a couple of times, then disappeared again, and I knew whatever he wanted to say would just remain in his head.

On the fifteenth day, I wake to a world that feels empty, devoid of the warmth and laughter that once filled every corner of our home. Miriam's absence is a reminder of everything I've lost.

•

I have been sleeping on her side of the bed, trying to keep her close to me even when she hasn't been here in weeks. But her scent is now gone, even after I spray her perfume over the pillows in a futile attempt to hold onto the ghost of her presence.

For over a decade, Armando plagued my nightmares every single night. The death of my sister haunted me during my restless nights. Now, Ximena's face is replaced by Miriam's eyes filled with terror. The image of her tears slipping down her face and her begging for help. I thought after killing Armando I would finally find peace, but the truth is, I have never felt so worried and scared in my entire life.

For fifteen days, I've drowned my sorrows in the depths of whiskey bottles, seeking solace in its numbing embrace. But Sasha and Grace have decided it is time for me to put an end to my pain.

As if it were that easy…

"Drinking your way into oblivion will only make you feel worse," Grace tells me while I rest my head on the cold marble of the kitchen counter, trying to deal with the never-ending headache.

"It numbs the pain," I confess.

"Pain is necessary, Daniel," Grace whispers. "You've endured more than most could bear, but you're still standing."

"I don't know how much more I can take," I admit.

"You're stronger than you realize," Sasha chimes in. "And that's why you need to experience happiness now, Dani."

"I am not sure I am made for that," I confess.

"You are," Sasha counters fiercely.

"You deserve the entire world, my darling," Grace insists, her tone laced with urgency. "Look at everything you've overcome, the battles you've fought and won. You and Sasha have faced more than most can deal with, but still made it through. You've built a life together, a family, and you've made a difference in this world. You deserve to be happy, both of you. More than anyone." Her voice breaks on the last word, a tremor of emotion betraying her.

"She is my happiness," I hear myself whisper, a confession that I have known for a while, but have been scared to even admit to myself.

"Then tell her," Sasha urges me, her desperation palpable.

But the truth is, I can't. I can't risk her safety, can't bear the thought of losing her again. And so, I cling to the memories we have made in the past few months. They will forever be my happy place.

"I just wish I were another man," I murmur. "In another life, I would do things right. I would be able to protect her and love her the way she deserves to be loved."

"You can do that in this life," Sasha insists, her voice fierce with conviction. "But first, you need to heal."

And maybe she's right. Maybe it's time to let Miriam go, so both of us can heal and find happiness, even if I know I will never find mine without her. It's a bitter pill to swallow, but I know it's what I must do. She was forced into this marriage, she didn't even get a chance to fall in love, get the proposal she dreamt of, the marriage she deserved.

The least I could do is give her back her choice.

"Serve her the divorce papers," Grace tells me, as if reading my mind.

CHAPTER FIFTY-TWO

During the first week of May, someone rings my bell. I stumble to the door, still half-asleep. When I see the courier with a brown envelope in his hand, I know what is about to happen. A shiver runs down my spine before I dare to open it. With trembling hands, I tear open the seal, my heart pounding in my chest. And then I see them.

Divorce papers.

The words blur before my eyes as I sink to my knees, despair crushing me as tears blur my world, making my life officially a living nightmare.

My mother runs towards me when she sees my despair, trying to offer solace. But I push her away, the ache in my heart too raw, too consuming to bear. Still, my mom hugs me, but it's my husband's arms I want. I want Daniel to be the one to hold me, to tell me that this is just a nightmare and that we will fix this together.

But he doesn't come.

Instead, I'm left with the shattered pieces of my broken heart. He didn't have a heart to give and now neither do I.

For two months, I've been hiding—avoiding the office, dodging encounters with my ex-husband like a fugitive on the run. But even as I distance myself from everything that went on between us, I can't bring myself to forget me.

However, I force myself to take steps in the right direction. The first one was the week right after I became a divorced woman, when I sent Daniel back the black diamond ring. I mourned the loss of it, the cold metal no longer wrapped around my finger. Months later, it's a strange feeling, but I know, like everything in this life, it will pass and someday, I will heal, even if I will never be the same.

I find solace in my work, or rather, on the sidelines. Jinghua prowls the race tracks like a predator on the hunt while I take care of the finances and the business development plans. The woman's determination is unwavering as she scouts for potential talent for the women's team for the Cavaglio Nero Academy. The project is alive and both of us are ready to make it happen.

After weeks of scouting, one name stands out among the rest—Valentina Mezzacorona. A rising star in F3, she's earned her points on the track, proving herself as a force to be reckoned with. A couple of weeks ago, one of the F2 drivers had an accident and we pushed for Valentina to get the seat as a reserve driver. She did not disappoint, and after only three races, she has more points than some of the boys who have been racing the entire season in Formula 2. We didn't miss our chance and proposed for a test drive at Silverstone in the Formula One free practice sessions.

So, today, Valentina is going to take Emi's car for a spin during FP1, and I couldn't be more excited for the young lady.

I could have easily watched her drive from the paddock next to Jinghua, but in my attempt to escape Daniel, I decided to sit in the grandstands right in front of the podium. I watch from the shadows, hidden behind oversized shades and a cap pulled low over my brow, hoping that nobody will recognize me. After all, my face was seen in a lot of news outlets next to Daniel's.

I can't help but feel a surge of pride swell within me when I see Valentina driving out of the garage and starting her first laps. From the stands, I observe her, my heart pounding in sync with the roar of the car engine. She navigates the curves with precision after a couple of test laps around Silverstone. In the beginning, she has problems adapting to the car, to the speed and sharpness. But the more she drives, the more in synch she is with the beast, and the more fluid and confident her driving style becomes.

When the session finishes after an hour, Valentina scores an astonishing thirteenth place—not a podium by any means, but a victory in its own right. Someone who just stepped into an F1 car doesn't need to give everything on the track the way she just did, but this shows the talent and determination Valentina possesses. She just finished ahead of drivers who have been racing in F1 for ages, and I can't wait to see her beat them in a real race two years from now.

I linger at the stands, the roar of engines and the blur of cars a welcome distraction from the turmoil that has been raging within me for the past weeks. But as the session draws to a close, and the last car disappears from the track, reality comes crashing back in. Still, I stay there, lost in my thoughts for longer than I intend and I only come back to reality when my phone vibrates in my lap. I check the notification.

Ginger bestie: Meet me at the podium?

I look ahead and spot her on the podium with Philip standing next to her. I don't really understand what they are doing up there, but with my curiosity piqued, I make my way to them.

It takes me a long time to get from where I am to the other side of the track, and to my surprise, when I finally arrive, Selene and Philip are nowhere to be found, leaving me alone with my racing thoughts.

Panic sets in, clawing at my chest as I frantically search for any sign of them. I check my phone, desperate for a message that isn't there.

Then, I hear a voice, practically a whisper in the depths of my mind, screaming the word 'menina' at me. A reminder of the trauma I thought I'd left behind. I take some deep breaths and close my eyes, forcing myself to calm down and remember that Armando is dead and he can no longer hurt me.

"You are safe here."

The words send a shiver down my spine, and I know without looking that he's here, standing before me. With trembling hands, I force myself to face him, to confront the ghost of my past.

There he stands, a shadow of the man I last saw. Daniel—my now ex-husband, the man I haven't stopped loving for a single second since the day I tried to stab him with a butterknife. His face is etched with pain that mirrors my own, and his presence is a punch to the gut that reopens wounds I was trying so hard to let heal.

Still, no matter the pain I have suffered the past few weeks and months, my first instinct is to want to reach out to him, to hold him close and never let him go. But fear of rejection holds me back, after all, he was the one to serve me the divorce papers.

His eyes meet mine, and, for a moment, time stands still. Our eyes lock, and I refuse to blink when I see a glint of hope in his.

Maybe, just maybe, there's a chance for us.

"What are you doing here?" I ask, barely a whisper.

"Doing what I should have done weeks ago," he replies, his words hanging heavy in the air as he takes a tentative step toward me.

"Which is?" My heart lurches at his admission

"Doing what I vowed to do so many months ago," he begins as he draws closer to me. With a gentle touch, he takes my hand, leading me to the top of the podium. "I vowed to love you. To celebrate your successes, your achievements, and your wins. But I also promised to be there for your losses. To stand by your side. And, most importantly, I vowed to protect you."

"Daniel," I whisper, my heart pounding in my chest, while the vows I thought were lost in the depth of my memory come back to me in flashes. I start remembering that night, and the way he spoke his vows to me.

Vows he has worked so hard to keep.

"I made promises, Miriam, but I didn't keep them all. I failed to love you the way you deserved. To celebrate you the way you needed. And, worst of all, I failed to protect you like I promised I would."

"Why now?" I ask, my voice trembling with uncertainty.

"Because I can't live without you," he confesses. "Because you took the broken pieces of my heart and made them whole again. You are my happiness, Miriam, and I can't bear the thought of living without you. Without your laughter, your smile, your compassion, and, most importantly, your love for me. The way you make me feel whole no matter how broken I think I am."

"What do you want?" I breathe.

"You," he replies, his voice steady with determination. And then, in a move that steals my breath away, he drops to one knee, producing a black velvet case from his pocket—the same case that held my ring. With trembling hands, he opens it, revealing the black diamond ring that belongs on my finger. "Marry me," he asks, his voice trembling with emotion.

"But… you served me the divorce papers," I remind him.

"You stepped into our first marriage without having a choice. You loved me, yes. I know you still do. But you didn't have a say in how things went, and I wanted to give that choice back to you. I wanted to give you the power to make decisions, to contradict me. And I wanted to give us the chance to live our lives like normal people. To fall in love, get married, have kids, have it all."

"Daniel." My voice falters.

"Give us another chance," he implores. "Let's stop pretending, Miriam. Because I'm done living without you. Without my happiness. Without my little swan."

And in that moment, as tears of joy mingle with tears of sorrow, this is where I belong—with Daniel. No matter what happens, we belong together.

"Yes! Yes!" I cry, dropping to the ground beside him, my arms wrapping tightly around him as if to anchor us both in this moment of happiness.

I missed how perfectly we fit together, his hand cradling the back of my head as I bury my face in the space between his shoulder and his neck. This is where I belong—with Daniel, in his embrace.

"I love you," he whispers into my hair, his words a soothing balm to my battered soul.

I gaze into his eyes, seeing the depths of his soul laid bare before me. There's a rawness in his gaze, a vulnerability that I haven't seen before, and one that I know is only meant for me to see.

When our lips finally meet, it's as if the weight of the past months melts away. The kiss is made up of longing and regret, a desperate plea for forgiveness and second chances, and it's a kiss to make up for all the ones we've missed, for the promise of eternity together.

"I love you," I tell him, struggling to breathe. "And I will marry you," I say, so close to him that I can feel his breath on my face.

Daniel pulls back, only a little so he can grab the ring, and then, looking right into my eyes, he slides the ring back onto my finger where it belongs. A promise of forever that both of us are ready to keep this time.

"Now and always, my little swan."

"Now and forever, Conte." I smile.

THE END

AKNOWLEDGEMENTS

It was over a year and a half ago when I first sat down in front of my computer and started writing what I like to call my daydreams on cocaine, you know that book under the title of Hammer Time.

To be honest, I wasn't sure that I would want to publish that book back then, but I knew that if I did it would be to fill a gap for all those readers out there set to find the best F1 romance. I have always wanted to bring the joy of watching the races from the edge of your seat into the pages of my books, and I am always happy to hear about the joy that my readers get when reading my books, in fact I was determined for this series to be only a trilogy, but thanks to the support of every single one of you out there, I am happy to say that there will be one more book.

I am happy to explore this couple, which has been living in my mind rent free since the day I wrote the first book, and finally it is time to write their story, write about their goals and motivations, their fears and worries. And once again to dig into the diversity that the real world is.

Not going to lie, when I was mid-way through writing Podium Finish, I was terrified. So much that at one point I thought about quitting and not publishing the book. But I am happy that my dear friend Edi (who reads every single chapter over WhatsApp as soon as I am done writing it) pushed me to continue and encouraged me to write this story which she and I knew, was so dear to my heart.

Writing this series, and in particular this book— has been a transformative experience that has touched every corner of my life, and in a way, it has even become therapy for all those thoughts that fill me and I never know what to do with. This is my little grain of salt to change the world and hopefully one day make it a better place.

A special mention goes to all my ARC and Beta reader: to Vic, to Hawke, to Liv, to Kacey, to Caroline, to Destiny and to Sara I am extremely thankful, for all your comments and tips. Navigating the complex themes explored in Podium Finish, particularly those concerning the transgender and POC community, was a humbling experience, and I am extremely thankful to all of you for helping my ideas get shaped. Thanks for sharing your experiences with me, your insight and thoughts on the book. Most important, thanks for educating me and helping me ensure that Daniel's story was treated with the respect and authenticity it deserved.

This book would not be here without you!

And to my editor, Bridget, thank you for always having a million eyes everywhere and pointing out the things I miss. You are one of the reasons why this entire series is alive today, and for that, I will always be grateful to you.

Thank you all for being a part of this incredible journey. Let's see where the road takes us next!

NEXT IN THE CHEQUERED FLAG SERIES

Her Serene Highness Princess Amalia Grimaldi

Invites you to Le Palais Princier for her Annual Party.

Coming later this year

F1 VOCABULARY

UNDERCUT: refers to a pit stop strategy in which a driver comes into the pits earlier than their competitors in order to gain an advantage on track.

OVERCUT: he overcut is the opposite of the undercut. It refers to a pit stop strategy in which a driver stays out on track longer than their competitors in order to gain an advantage when they make their pit stop. The idea is that the driver on fresh tires will be able to set faster lap times than the driver on worn tires and will be able to jump ahead of them when they eventually make their pit stop.

DRS: Drag Reduction System. It is a device that can be activated by drivers on designated areas of the track during a race, allowing them to open a flap on the rear wing of their car to reduce drag and increase their speed. DRS can only be used when a driver is within one second of the car in front of them and is intended to facilitate overtaking and make races more exciting.

DIRTY AIR: When a Formula One car is travelling at high speeds, it creates a wake of turbulent air behind it. This turbulent air can make it more difficult for the car following behind to maintain grip and cornering speed, as they experience less downforce on their own car. This effect is known as "dirty air" and is a significant factor in the difficulty of overtaking in Formula One.

VIRTUAL SAFETY CAR: The Virtual Safety Car is a system that can be used during a race to slow down the pace of the cars on track in response to a safety-related incident, such as a crash or debris on the track. When the VSC is activated, drivers are required to maintain a specific speed and follow a specified delta time, rather than racing at full speed. This is intended to make the track safer for marshals and other personnel who may need to attend to the incident, and to avoid dangerous racing incidents during the slowdown.

RED FLAG: A red flag is used to signal a stoppage of a race due to unsafe conditions, such as severe weather or a major crash. When a red flag is shown, drivers must immediately stop their cars on track and wait for further instructions from race officials.

YELLOW FLAG: **A** yellow flag is used to signal caution on the track. When a yellow flag is shown, drivers must slow down and be prepared to stop if necessary. Yellow flags are typically used in response to incidents on track, such as a crash or debris on the circuit, and are intended to alert drivers to potential hazards.

SPLITSREAM: Phenomenon where the air flow from a leading vehicle can help to reduce air resistance for a trailing vehicle, allowing it to move more quickly.

BALACLAVA: Type of headgear that is worn by drivers under their helmet. It covers the head, neck, and part of the face, providing additional protection for the driver.

UNDERSTEER: Understeer occurs when a vehicle's front tires lose traction, and it doesn't turn as sharply as the driver intends.

Made in the USA
Columbia, SC
13 March 2025